SHOT OUT!

Tales of the Terran Confederacy Book Two

Ralts Bloodthorne

Peeper Corner Publishing

CONTENTS

ISBN-13: 9798500802538
ISBN-10: 1477123456

Cover design by: Philip Lautin Jackson
Library of Congress Control Number: 2018675309
Printed in the United States of America

To my wife, who understands me even when I don't.

To my older brother. I'll always be younger than you.

To my gaming wife, who has been there for me.

To Wolvorine, who's watched more than one train explode while we were on it.

A special shoutout to the fans on Reddit, who've been with me through this whole weird experience.

FOREWORD

Welcome to the Second Book of the Tales of the Terran Confederacy, a collection of tales from the early days of what eventually became called "The Second Precursor War" in my head.

The hard part wasn't finding stories to show, but rather how many I wanted to do. There's so many stories, so much comedy, tragedy, and action character and story arcs to chose from I had a hard time keeping it under 100K words.

If you've been with it the whole time, you'll recognize every character and hopefully they'll bring a smile to your face.

If you're just joining us, well, buckle up. It's going to be a wild ride.

And remember: Everyone's gangster till Claymore Roomba comes around the corner.

SHOT OUT!

Tales of the Terran Confederacy Book Two

By Ralts Bloodthorne

IT WASN'T SUPPOSED TO BE LIKE THIS

Leebaw was nothing to anyone.

It was a small world in the ways of the galactic economy, political influence, manufacturing ability, or any other way that the Unified Galactic Systems cared about. Its people were a small people who had barely developed stardrive to get into jumpspace and travel to another planet. That planet had been important, a manufacturing hub for the leading tentacle of the Unified Civilizations.

The little world had gone from dreams of starfaring and exploration and joyous advancement to locked into their little world. Emigration quotas, GalNet bandwidth limits, even exploitation limits within their own system, all were put in place by the Unified Civilized Races Council.

After all, their world had been registered as the property of Ukewa's Packguru Manufacturing nearly three thousand years before the little people of Leebaw had even developed the ability to transmit or listen to radio waves.

The Unified Legal Council had informed the people of Leebaw that if they had intended to assert sovereignty over their own world, perhaps they should have filed a motion to appeal the claim register within a year of it first being filed.

The fact that the people of Leebaw had not even developed gear driven clocks by that point was not any fault of the Council. The people of Leebaw should have thought of that.

And so Leebaw's dreams of being part of, maybe even founding, some kind of interstellar society of equals died in a court of law before they even invented the metal nibbed pen.

They tried protesting the only way they knew how at that point: Violence.

Their attempts were pitiable. They barely lasted a full decade before they were defeated again.

The Unified Races Council ordered to that the people of Leebaw undergo "therapy" to remove "violent primitive instincts" through social conditioning.

The little land-dwelling amphibians were marched lockstep into camps to taught how to properly venerate Ukewa's Packguru Manufacturing (A subsidiary of Nu'ukluk Entertainment Conglomerate) and follow the commands and regulations of their elders. The little space facility, the Leebawian pride and joy, was razed for 'ecological reasons' and a coal burning power plant put in its place, after all, the Unified Space Council had already had UPM build a much better space port than the crude native one. Bit by bit the people of Leebaw saw their cultural heritage sites wiped away in the name of 'modernization.'

With the destruction of history comes the destruction of cultural identity. After a generation or two they became a loyal worker pod for UPM, spending their meager pay on necessities and a few simple luxuries, as was proper.

Still, some of them harbored resentment in their hearts.

This wasn't how it was supposed to be, was it?

The amphibians, half the size of the four-legged, four armed, six eyed, tendriled Overseers known as the Lanaktallan, dug into burrows, squirreled away makeshift weapons, made careful chains of communication. The Leebawians created small units of resistance, each reporting to a leader, who only knew the name of one leader.

They had recreated the resistance cell structure again.

Forced to live outside the shining cities, they suffered often from vertigo after all, they slowly gathered. The Lanaktallan were the ones enamored with the cities, not the Leebawians. The thought was to bring down those high shining towers, bring the Lanaktallan down to the level of the amphibians.

And so the Leebawians prepared and waited.

But that was not why it was dying.

It had become infected.

It started simply. Twinkling points of light appearing out in space. The planetary managers said that the lights were mere tests, nothing for the Leebawians to concern themselves with. Then scanners went down.

A space station began screaming.

Leebaw's GalNet became a place of horror as the infection spread across the solar system.

The Lanaktallan counseled caution and not to be swayed by anti-Unified propaganda even as they boarded their ships to flee the system.

Then sparks appeared in the sky as orbital leisure stations were destroyed, ships were raked with fire and exploded, and everything but the GalNet node was wiped from the night sky.

For three days Leebaw had cringed away from quiet darkness.

Then the voice was broadcast across the world, a brain twisting screech of absolute horror.

THERE IS ONLY ENOUGH FOR ONE

Mechanical horrors landed at the spaceport. Not with crashes but landing with care before wading into the starships still in port. The newcomers tore apart the ships and their crews then spread out, moving toward manufacturing facilities. Private spaceships were destroyed in high orbit, their wreckage first scattered then gathered and processed. Cargo vessels were torn apart and processed.

Still sparks blossomed in the night sky. Little pinpricks that lit up and went out. Once in a while there were long streaks in the night that ended in tiny flashing pinpricks.

The Leebaw first viewed the mechanicals as liberators and rushed out to greet them.

Only to be murdered en-masse.

The Leebawians all nodded to one another. Of course, it was just another monster from outside. The Cult of the Solitary

Burrow were correct. Those who reached out a hand in friendship only had it torn off or had a manacle wrapped around the wrist.

The Leebawians scattered as best they could.

The mechanicals concentrated on the Lanaktallan, herding them into their cities, broadcasting the savage murders suffered by the Lanaktallan. The Leebawians thought that perhaps if they just pretended none of it was going on, the mechanicals would leave them alone.

That pipedream ended with shrieks of agony.

The Leebawians learned in the next few turns on their world to avoid any technology higher than fire and sharp sticks. A machine that found any "Primitive Ones" might chase them and kill a few but largely ignored them after scanning quickly for any technology. A quick thinking Leebawian noted that every one of their people fitted with a cybernetic link was gone, dead, their bodies torn apart. Any group larger than an ancient clutch was destroyed.

The Leebawians mourned for lost dreams. Even being drones for UPM was preferable to being torn from comfortable housing and forced to live in the mud, hunting with sticks for nearly extinct mussels and wildlife, drinking dirty water, and watching the cities slowly burn.

The Leebawians wept.

They just wanted to be not alone. They just wanted to see what was beyond. Just wanted to meet other beings.

But not like this.

Not like this.

Pinpricks appeared the sky again, only these ones did not go out. They got steadily brighter as the Council Cities burned. Sparks came to life and died back down around those burning stars.

The Leebawians looked up, wondering what was happening now, even though a small part of them knew that it wouldn't matter. Whoever it was, their little people would be nothing more than amusement for hunters at worst, slaves and drudges at best.

Hope flickered, then went out.

Leebaw was dying. Not from the slamming impacts of orbital guns, not from the mechanical murderers sweeping across
the planet, not because the cities, bright and sparkling, were
burning and being turned to horror filled charnel houses.

It was dying as hope died.

Then came the message. From the stars, as fire blossoms,
new suns ignited in the night sky close enough that more than
once night turned to day for long heartbeats. It vibrated off of
every scrap of metal, bellowed from every speaker, howled from
every hidden datapad.

WE ARE THE TERRAN CONFEDERACY
WE HAVE COME TO ASSIST
HOLD THE LINE, BROTHERS!

The Leebawians huddled in their burrows, closing their
large expressive eyes, and just wished the universe would go
away. The message couldn't be meant for them. They were small,
insignificant, and the universe viewed them as little more than
slaves to their betters to be slain for amusement at will.

But some, who harbored resentment toward UPM, who
nursed flickering anger in their souls for the Lanaktallan, began
to dig free caches wrapped in EM shielding and buried in iron
rich mud. Began dreaming that perhaps, this time, things might
be different.

As the little Leebawians watched, streaks slipped down
from the orbitals, into atmosphere, and began to speed toward
the thickest concentrations of machines. Nuclear fire blossomed, pushed away the smoke of burning bodies, and left behind damaged and destroyed machines. Not the larger ones, of
course, those rose from where they had crouched, shaking off
smaller ones, and screeched their defiance at the newcomers.

THERE IS ONLY ENOUGH FOR ONE

The newcomers bellowed back

FREEDOM OR DEATH

The Leebawians huddled down, caught between the two

roaring forces. The braver of them lifted their googly eyes to look upon the land, raise their gaze to the sky again.

Massive ships roared down from the sky and the Leebawians felt their thick rubbery skin prickle up in fear. The last two times that had happened the universe had shown them that they were the butt of a cosmic joke. As the Leebawians watched the machines, the new masters of Leebaw, swarmed the massive ships, which responded with counter-fire.

Some ships exploded in mid-air.

More didn't.

Even more rained down from the high orbitals.

The ships didn't bother to slow down to a gentle speed and then slowly levitate down to the earth. These ones came in fast, rockets screaming as they suddenly braked. Radiation poured from the nozzles, scorching the ground, burning away vegetation and turning dirt to plasma hardened rock. The ships slammed down; the sides opened even as gunports continued firing. Parts of the massive ships detached, moving on treads, deploying guns that raked the sky with shrieking munitions. The parts of the ship took up positions around their brood-mother, linking together their fire, adding their own roaring voice to the defiance lashing out at the machines that still swarmed.

From inside the ship came more vehicles, massive bipeds that were made entirely of metal. More weapons were raised, and the machine's assault began to tatter, began to break. The wave of metal was pushed back further and further by the guns. The very sky seemed to catch fire as the newcomers threw their fury into the faces of the machines, unleashing endless wrath into machines without numbers.

Shell by shell, beam after beam, the newcomers drove the machines back. But that wasn't enough for the newcomers, they spread out, like spokes from the hub of the landing craft. Each spoke building another hub, calling down more ships from the sky, repeating it over and over.

Smashing the machines.

The Leebawians dug deep into their burrows, fearful of

what horrors the newcomers would inflict on the small Leeba-wian people. The only step they could see from driving them to scattered primitivism was to wipe their small people from exist-ence.

Then, it happened. As dozens of Leebawians watched from the safety of the water of the swamp the newcomers, the huge bipeds of metal and fury, approached the machines that kept the younglings in cages for experimentation or just plain sport. Over the last few turnings of the world the machines had moved the younglings from cages to inside the buildings.

The watching Leebawians knew that their younglings would be slaughtered, caught between the murderous machines and the furious newcomers.

They waited for the pounding of artillery and aircraft that always preceded a biped ground assault, flicked their tongues nervously while they waited for the massive tanks to pour cannon fire into the base as they did to break it up for the bipeds.

None of that happened. Instead, the bipedal machines, accompanied at times by four-legged ones, slowly moved for-ward, from cover to cover, firing only at the guns that revealed themselves in the machine's base. They seemed almost non-committal, firing and advancing, firing and retreating, shifting their lines.

To the hidden Leebawians, it made no sense.

The Leebawians felt a stirring in the current and froze. The currents did not feel like one of the big machines patrolling the rivers and streams of the delta, but like more Leebawians moving through the water, towing large fish as if they had made a prized catch.

Clicks sounded in the water and the Leebawians blinked in nervousness. The clicks *sounded* like Leebawian clicks but made no sense. It was just random sounds.

Curious, one of the Leebawian swam deeper, into the silt filled cloudy water deeper in the river. He held tight to his spear, but had a stolen handgun under his tongue, ready to swallow it if he had to. His echolocation told him that there were dozens of his kind swimming through the cloudy opaque water, pulling huge fish behind them. The fish blood made it impossible to tell which tribe the newcomers were from, clogging the tastebuds, so the Leebawian swam deeper, lighting up the ends of his whiskers in hopes of seeing who was moving through but had not announced themselves.

At the bottom of the river he saw them. His eyes seeing what his senses said were only his kind and some fish.

The four-legged robots had their legs folded and were using water-jets to move. They were pulling two or three of the big bipeds on fishing line. There were the smaller ones, the size of a child Leebawian, were darting around like fish. One moved in front of him, stared with a blank faceplant for a long moment, then wiggled away.

From the four-legged ones poured the smell of freshly caught fish blood.

He paddled in place, watching in confusion as the chrome figures moved through the darkness of the silty water. The clicks and pops were between them, not meant for Leebawians but one another.

The curious swimmer, a part of a cell that had planned on assaulting the space port before the machines had arrived, realized he was hearing battle-code, not much difference from the coded cant his own cell used.

As he watched one of the bipeds turned its blank for toward him. One its forward hands opened and closed, then the biped turned its head back toward the four-legged one towing him.

Curious, the Leebawian, one Ukk-uk-huk, followed. Adding his own movements to the pack moving through his territory. There was only twelve of them, moving correctly in a spindle, and they made room for Ukk to swim with them.

Ukk realized that they were swimming to the pool in the machine's base. That cruel body of water so close to freedom but so far that young Leebawians were allowed to swim in but were kept from escaping into the waters of the delta by a flickering shield.

He saw, as he followed, that the shield was still up but did nothing. He swam through, expecting oblivion, but instead just felt a tingle.

They had left it up? Why?

Ukk expected the bipeds to spring from the water and start shooting everything in sight. Instead, the small little ones slid out of the water and wormed their way across the floor on their bellies like they were made of liquid. Ukk started to reach for the edge of the lip but one of the bipeds grabbed his wrist. When he looked the rune for "wait" flashed across the faceplate of the biped in the darkest color that Ukk could see.

The bipeds slipped out of the water, climbing out with water running off them, to Ukk they looked like primordial nightmares. All black, bulky, dripping water, covered in delta reeds and muck.

Ukk stayed in the pool, watching.

The four-legged ones started returning, moving carefully, sliding into the water without a ripple. The smaller ones came out, leading two or three tadpoles each, the tadpoles giggling to themselves at this new game.

Ukk stared as they kept going by.

It has to be a terrible trick...

It couldn't last, the unearthly silence where even simple water droplets were like thunder.

THERE IS ONLY...

The familiar scream started. Ukk closed his ears but still felt the bellowed replies.

GET FUCKED SKYNET!

shattered the screeching onslaught, roared from a dozen throats.

The night caught fire. Stealth abandoned for speed, the four-legged ones and the smallest ones urged the tadpoles into the pond even as Ukk heard the weapon fire start.

One of the smaller ones came in, moving fast, making a

curious noise that sounded like "mew mew mew mew" as the tadpoles imitated it and chased it. A machine burst in, smoking, tattered, its armor blown away or twisted and cratered, and leveled what Ukk had long ago learned was a plasma gun at the running tadpoles.

Flares shot out of the little metal one's back and the tadpoles laughed with glee as metallic dust puffed from the little robot to fill the room.

Ukk spit the pistol out into his hand and pulled the trigger wildly. He had never fired the plasma pistol before and didn't expect it to kick back against his hand. It hit the machine twice, rocking it back, the return plasma shot missing the little ones and hitting the wall.

Croaking in anxiety and despair, Ukk reoriented the pistol on the machine, which was turning toward him.

--help kittykitty simba help--

Water exploded behind him as one of the four-legged ones burst from the surface of the pond, flying through the air, a massive cannon with shells as thick as Ukk's forearm attached by a belt connecting the cannon to the four-legged robot. Lasers flashed out, slicing away the plasma gun from the machine, cutting furrows in the machine's armor, cutting free two legs.

Then the four-legged robot crashed to the floor as the tadpoles croaked and clicked in fear.

"SIMBA IS HERE!" the four-legged robot roared out.

It made another roaring noise, a primal sound that made Ukk shudder, paused, and the cannon on its back opened up.

BRRRRRRRT!

To Ukk it sounded like the world ending. The shells chewed the machine apart, but the four-legged robot didn't stop there, it raked the walls, peeling apart the metal walls, the shells not stopping and slamming into targets beyond.

One of the tadpoles jumped in fear and Ukk felt his stomach clench as he *knew* the beam of light traversing the room would catch the tadpole.

Instead there was a minute gap, too small to be purposeful but too perfectly positioned to be accidental, and the tadpole landed safely.

The little one clicked and croaked and Ukk understood it.

--follow mew mew follow kittykitty little littles--

Another machine entered and Ukk fired the plasma pistol again, all three shots missing. More entered, swarming in through doorways, crashing through the metal, dropping from the vents. Ukk fired again but the pistol's plasma cartridge magazine ran dry on the fourth trigger pull.

The four-legged one scrambled to Ukk, stopping over him, crouching down over the small Leebawian, and that cannon kept firing, flashing lasers and screaming plasma getting added to the mix. Machines shattered, spun, and collapsed. Ukk saw smaller laser beams flicker out, intercepting pieces of metal shed from exploding machines, zapping them from existence before the tiny metal pieces could hit the tadpoles.

It seemed to go on forever to Ukk. The scream of weaponry, the sound of metal ripped asunder, and the clicking --follow mew mew little littles--. Females began streaming by, some heavy with eggs, others with the deflated look of ones that had recently laid their eggs. Males streamed by, many injured or with cruel implements thrust into their bodies.

They all jumped into the pool as Ukk huddled beneath the big four-legged

Finally it was over. Silence descended for a moment, broken only by the patter of tadpoles and rescued brood mothers streaming by.

Still Ukk huddled under the four-legged one.

One of the big bipeds came into the room. One arm was blown off, its black surface was marred, and it leaked fluid down its flank from a hole that Ukk could see circuitry and mechanical parts through. It saw Ukk when the four-legged robot moved aside.

Ukk froze, sure his time had come.

More returned and one moved over to Ukk, who huddled down.

The visor went clear and Ukk realized he was looking at a hairless primate, like one of the lemurs of the southern jungles stripped of hair and made large.

"Is this your planet?" It asked in Unified Galactic Common.

Ukk croaked his assent.

The figure pointed at a robot that still twitched and one of the bipeds kicked it over. Ukk noticed that the weapons on the four-legged one tracked it. The biped stopped it with one big foot, pressing it to the floor as if the machine's mechanical strength didn't matter.

"It's jawnconnor time, Froggy," The primate said. He squatted behind Ukk, reaching around him carefully, and replaced the plasma pistol with another pistol. Ukk shivered, terrified, as the primate embraced him, holding onto his hand, forcing his finger on the trigger.

He was about to be devoured; he was sure of it.

"You're *this close* to going out, Froggy," The biped said softly from behind him, moving Ukk's hand to aim the pistol at the armored flank of the machine. He forced Ukk to press the firing stud and the weapon cracked, spitting a slug that cratered the armor but didn't penetrate.

Ukk klicked in resignation. Of course it wouldn't penetrate.

"You'll learn to fight back," The primate said. He forced Ukk to fire again, although Ukk didn't understand why as the slug only hit the crater, widening and deepening it.

"To charge the wire," The primate forced him to pull the trigger a third time, expanding the crater. Ukk still felt despair. The pistol stung his hand even with the primate's help, what hope did...

"And smash...

the next shot exposed the innards and Ukk felt a sudden surge of shock.

"These metal...

the next shot slammed through the crater and turned

wiring and mechanical parts into slag. The machine shrieked in pain. Ukk felt a sudden flare of anger

"mother...

the next shot slammed deeper and two of the machine's legs blew off. Ukk felt the anger build. Why weren't his people armed like this?

"fuckers...

The next caused a thin plume of plasma to vent out the ruptured side. Ukk clicked rapidly in anger.

"Into..."

The next caused the head of the machine to blow off in a shower of sparks and the entire side to split open. Ukk gave a loud croak in anger and tried to hop forward.

The primate let go.

"Junk," it said as Ukk rushed forward, emptying the magazine of the pistol into the machine as he croaked and clicked in rage.

CONFEDNAVINT REPORT

Lintennal 515, called Leebaw by native species, being cleared. Casualties below estimation. Orbitals under CONFED control. System 90% pacified.

Native species capable of self-defense. Are arming and equipping to act as resistance force to assist. Native species was space faring before Unified Civilization interference.

---NOTHING FOLLOWS---

UNIFIED MANUFACTURING COUNCIL
INTERNAL MEMO

The Terrans spent significant military resources to free a labor world under the control of Ukewa's Packguru Manufacturing by ground force means but glassed the entire planet of Kalukaluku, a major industrial manufacturing center only a few light years away just because they couldn't detect any life forms left on the planet. Kalukaluku's industrial and manufacturing capability could have provided assistance to the war effort if it had been liberated rather than underwent orbital bombardment.

Had the vaunted "Terran Confederate Navy" properly allocated their forces instead of rushing to engage in ground combat on a remote planet of no strategic or tactical value, the industrial center might have been saved by the same forces.

Nu'ukluk Entertainment Conglomerate has filed a most strenuous objection to one of its valuable industrial centers being so casually wiped away just because these "Terrans" can't properly allocate military resources.

Please discover who to contact within the Confederacy government in order to allow Nu'ukluk Entertainment Conglomerate to bring forth a lawsuit for this grievous misapplication of military resources.

CHEEKEET MEETS A KLARK

Cheekeet Longflight stared at the scanners and clicked her beak in frustration and grief as she stared at the screens, which painted everything in lurid colors. Ruffling her feathers, she willed the screens to change.

They didn't.

Her species could see five primary colors. Her hearing was more sensitive than that of all but two of the Unified Civilized Races despite having rejected membership in that august body. Her people were one of the Ununified Races, rarely considered civilized by the rest of the races, but outside of the ever-present rules and laws and regulations of that eons old organization.

But that didn't help.

In up to 150% of standard gravity she could fly, unfettered by earth, for miles at a time. Her people had taken to space and exploration as a natural extension of their own abilities, their hollow bones and unique muscle structure quickly adaptable to nulgrav and microgravity.

But that didn't change anything.

Her people, the Akltak, did not worry about such things as the Precursors. Those eggs were smashed, why worry about them? It was like worrying about last year's wind. You should know about it, but it didn't effect today's flights. They were not afraid of what some called the Long Dark, others called the Great Void, and still others called the Great Empty. They had explored it in the three centuries since they had obtained FTL, established colonies, and explored the worlds with what other races called reckless abandon.

Which is why things were what they were.

Precursor ruins were examined, resulting in the knowledge that those nests were empty and abandoned. Not even bones remained, much less anything useful or enlightening. The ruins were exactly that because of warfare. Akltak understood struggles over nesting grounds, which made it so that the Precursor Ruins intrigued them. What would make two star-faring civilizations completely destroy one another to the point where nobody had even found remains, fossilized or not. This planet, this dead world, had extensive ruins in the sand and rock. The atmosphere was able to support life, able to allow the Akltak to fly, and was rich in oxygen.

Which is why things were burning.

The ruins had been interesting. Evidence of ground fighting, orbital strikes, of terrible weapons being used that Cheekeet Longflight and the Longflight Clan had eagerly gone over, hoping to glean knowledge from the evidence of the weapons. They had not reacted in superstitious fear like the other Civilized Races to the old breezes of a forgotten nest fight.

Which is why her Clan was dying.

Almost a hundred years of exploration, expanding the colony, the Longflight Clan budding off into five other clans. The population moving from two thousand to nearly a half-million.

Then The Discovery.

Rock had been turned molten, covering The Discovery, concealing it until a hundred million years of wind and dust storms had exposed it to the Longflight Clan's sensors. They had examined it, slowly excavated it as they recorded and examined it. Strange, advanced alloys, unknown construction. The entire Longflight Clan had rejoiced. They had found an intact Precursor Artifact.

Which is why Cheekeet had watched her people die.

It had suddenly activated. Come to mechanical life.

And set out to destroy all life on the planet.

Cheekeet had managed to load precious eggs and chicks

into a shuttle, had managed to reach one of the stations, and now watched her people die.

Kikteek Deepswoop was sitting at the communication station, normally used to file reports, talk to family, or watch the GalNet news. Her feathers drooped with despair as she repeated the request for help from someone, anyone.

But they were halfway into the Great Empty and there was no way help could reach them in time.

"High Nest Six, do you need assistance?" the voice was translated by the Omnitranslator, changed by the computer into the language of the avian Akltak but even so, the calm confidence in the voice came across electronic translation.

"By the Great Egg, yes. Oh, Those That Soar, we are all dying," Kikteek wailed into the communicator. Her professionalism was gone, burned away like the feathers of all of the warrior caste who had tried to stop the rampaging machine.

"May I come in?" The voice asked.

Cheekeet checked her scanners. There was one energy source, coming in fast, nearly at light speed, but her scanners could not detect a ship.

"Please! Please help us! There are still eggs, chicks, and moltlings down there! It's killing them all!" Kikteek cried out. "Help us, stranger!"

"Then you have invited me in and I may assist," the voice said.

Cheekeet checked quickly. The voice was coming across the GalNet superluminal communications array, somehow speaking across a wavelength that normally required huge arrays.

Yet she could not find a ship on her scanners, just that energy signature, bright enough to be a huge colony ship.

Cheekeet watched as the energy source came streaking at the planet and she cringed, hoping that the being offering assistance wasn't going to "help" by slamming into the planet at nearly light speed.

Instead, it suddenly stopped in a flare of inertia and kinetic energy being dumped into jumpspace as if a battle cruiser had just lit off its engines.

Cheekeet focused her scanners, eager to see their possible savior, putting it up on the main screen to replace the horror of what was happening on the surface.

Everyone trilled in shock.

They had expected a ship. Perhaps a battle cruiser full of drop troops. Maybe even a light attack craft willing to enter atmosphere to engage the machine.

Instead, it was a bipedal figure, positioned as if they were standing on an unseen platform, upper limbs crossed across their chest. A long piece of material, perhaps even cloth, rippled behind the figure as if it was in wind despite the impossibility of such a thing in space. It was dressed in red and blue, one arm mechanical, one leg mechanical, and one half of its face obviously robotic.

Yet exposed skin was visible on the face, one hand, half the neck.

Cheekeet chirped softly in confusion. Perhaps its flesh wasn't affected adversely to vacuum? Still, seeing an eye blink, she wondered how that worked, how the figure could even see. She glanced at her scanners and was startled.

The energy signal was greater than she'd seen on anything outside of a major metropolis on one of the Core Worlds.

"I'll stop this evil-doer," The voice said, and Cheekeet's eyes widened as she realized the figure's lips moved.

It was some kind of primate, melded to mechanical robotic parts. As she watched a panel opened up in the figure's leg, disgorging some kind of machines that took up positions around the figure at various distances.

"Those things are broadcasting. They want to know if we wish to view the broadcast," Kikteek said.

"Yes. Log the transmissions," Cheeket said. Kikteek fluttered her feathers in acknowledgement.

The figure suddenly moved, faster than the speed of sound, somehow leaving a blue and red streak behind itself even though Cheekeet could detect no reason for it. Cheekeet set the scanners to follow it, to watch it.

"It can't win by itself," Eekreek said, using the peeps of a molting chick rather than the authoritative clicks and chirps of an adult, as she had since the slaughter had reached its crescendo on the planet.

Cheekeet's scanners followed the figure as it swooped down on the closest fight. There were twelve of the lesser mechanicals moving in on a nesting area, rushing up on the defenders and ripping them apart with mandibles and blades, almost seeming to relish in the slaughter.

The new being landed in the middle of the battlefield, dust raising up from where it had crashed to earth. Cheekeet expected to see a huge crater but instead the figure was just kneeling on the dirt. The broadcast devices swooped down to get the best views from different angles and distances.

One of her monitors reported that a massive amount of kinetic energy had been dumped in jumpspace.

The figure stood up and surveyed the scene calmly. Energy, in the high red visible spectrum, lashed from its eyes. Despite the attempt by Cheekeet's people to use laser weaponry to no avail, *these* beams blew huge chunks from the robotic killer's armor, severed limbs, and when ever the beams touched something vital, caused explosions.

In less than then ten seconds all twelve robots were destroyed, and the being took to flight, one limb extended in front of them, the broadcast devices keeping up.

After the third combat against The Artifact's manufactured minions Cheekeet noticed something odd. Something that tickled at her like a loose feather.

The being, which was no taller than Cheekeet, made sure that Cheekeet had the best scanner view. She shifted one of the satellites to check and the being shifted its lines of attack in order to give Cheekeet the best view.

Is it ensuring that I can record and document its actions? *Cheekeet wondered.*

The battle against The Artifact took the longest and was obviously the hardest for the half-mechanical creature. Several time the being's clothing was torn and damaged and she saw bruises appear on the flesh. She saw the mechanical parts on the being get damaged. Every time a broadcast drone was destroyed another was deployed.

Twice she saw the being's skin get cut and blood flow. The broadcast drones focused in on those wounds, replaying the blow that caused them.

Finally The Artifact collapsed and the being was thrown back by the explosion caused by what was obviously The Artifact's self-destruct.

The figure laid on the broken glass for a long moment, then got up, wiping the biological part of its mouth with one upper forelimb. It looked up, to Cheekeet's view straight into the camera of the satellite, made an odd expression, then launched itself toward space. It should have left a crater, taking off like that from the ground and no built-up momentum.

Again, her instruments showed a massive energy dump into jumpspace.

The figure stopped suddenly, as if the laws of inertia were something the figure could just ignore. Again, the figure had its upper limbs across its chest, lower limbs pressed together, as if it was standing on an invisible platform. The cloth was missing, torn free during the fierce battle on the planet.

"You should be safe now," The figure said across the Gal-Net link. "I'll leave a League buoy in case you run into trouble later. Don't worry, it will be monitored."

"Our thanks to you, stranger. Do you require assistance? You appear injured," Kikteek said, wondering how they'd repair the figure's robotic parts much less flesh that could withstand point blank plasma bursts without even discoloration.

"I'll be fine, citizen," The figure said.

"Might we know your name, stranger?" Kikteek asked. "We are the Longflight Clan of the Akltak People."

"Klark Kant," The figure smiled.

"May we know where you are from?" Kikteek asked. "We are from this planet, but originally we are from The Feathered Nebula Cluster."

"Sol, my friends. I'm a Solarian, originally from Krypton," The figure smiled and made a sweeping gesture to encompass further into the Great Empty.

"How may we reward you, Klark of the Kant Clan?" Kikteek asked.

"No reward is necessary, friends," The figure said. "One of TerraSol's greatest heroes is always willing to help out those in need!" It touched two fingers to its brow...

and was gone.

Cheekeet looked at her scanners. The figure was rapidly accelerating, too fast for even major capital ships to withstand without the inertia crushing the ship to debris. Right when it reached the speed of light there was a rippling glitter and the figure was gone in a flash of blue and red then white light.

They were safe, their nest-mates on the planet were safe.

And the being had recorded every iota, every microsecond, every joule of the fight, uploading the footage to the station.

Cheekeet knew that the Unified Science Council would want that footage.

In an emergency session the Unified Exploration Council determined that a seventh type of xenosentient had been discovered in the Great Gulf. The Executors argued that all quasi-authorized and unauthorized colonies or scientific outposts in the Great Gulf should be recalled, by force if necessary.

The Executors argue that the actions against the Precursor Artifact show that the Solarians have not only dangerous attitudes but dangerous technology at their disposal.

The Unified Science Council counsels caution at this time.

TO: Hero League @ Cyborg-Collective
From: Klark-351

Check out the attached file! Just over a hundred drones and a Precursor war machine, looked like one of their late generation planetary assault machines, luckily not one of the big boys, but still more than they could handle. I took it down, but man, it was a fight. Attached are visual files so you can tell I upheld our appearances and standards.

I want full point credit for this on the leaderboards. Make sure the files get uploaded to InfoNet, I want everyone to check out that last battle. Man, I look good.

These bird people, though. I felt bad for them. They didn't stand a chance.

Let everyone else on Hero League know that the bird people are pretty formal. They want to see what you look like and know where you're from. Seemed like a cultural thing.

Their computer systems are pretty last-gen, software is worse than even the old Mantid pre-war software. I made sure to upload footage of my battle to their servers, as per League rules.

Anyway, I think this sector needs some heroes. This should put me over the point score needed to get a League Assemble Trial Raid.

I'll need a Wallace from CONFED INT. too, they probably want to know what goes on in this sector.

This sector needs protected.

I should have enough achievements to establish a base at this time. Any League members who want to take part in the Trial will be required to put up double-standard points to compete. Once a League is assembled, I will be building a base in this sector.

There's plenty of heroic deeds to go around out here.

--KLARK-351

---NOTHING FOLLOWS---

CONFEDERATE INTELLIGENCE MEMO

CC: Artificial Biological States; Digital Artificial Intelligence Infonet Worlds; TERRASOL.GOV; Cyborg Cooperative; Clone Directorate; Mantid Free Worlds; Traena'ad Hive Worlds

Looks like the LARP group out of the Cyborg Cooperative is starting to patrol the Great Gulf. Someone REMIND THEM that they can't open to Villain League at this time. These are First Contact Species out there, let's not give them the wrong idea about the Confederacy.

We're giving the Hero League permission to establish a League Base in that Great Gulf sector and will be assigning a director ranked intelligence liaison.

---NOTHING FOLLOWS---

CYBORG COOPERATIVE

RE: Your Last

Will inform the Hero League that at this time only those with a GALACTIC rating or better are allowed in the Great Gulf and any others will be stripped of rank and banned if they do not return in 15 standard units. Understand that this is a delicate situation regarding First Contact xenosapients.

Will allow only Admiral and above members of FEDERATION LEAGUE LARPers into the Great Gulf. At least those guys follow directives thanks to the quasi military nature of their organization.

---NOTHING FOLLOWS---

MEMORIES

TERRASOL

30,000 BC

Ogg looked up as Ugg staggered into the cave. Ugg was beaten up, bruised, bloody, and had the broken off end of a spear sticking out of his leg. Ogg managed to stand up before Ugg was in his face.

"You say Huk Huk all gone! Huk Huk waiting! You say Huk Huk no have spears! Now Ugg have spear in leg! You stupid!" Ugg snarled.

"Tuk Tuk and Mogg say Huk Huk gone. Not Ogg fault!" Ogg whined.

"Tuk Tuk and Mogg dead! You stupid say so get all killed!" Ugg threw the other neanderthal to the ground and began beating him with his club, doing what millions of others through history would wish they could do as he took out his rage at Terra's first and longest lasting oxymoron.

The com section was overloaded, ships had dropped from Armada and Task Force broadcast to Fleet or Division or Battalion or even dropped off the net completely. Most com officers had signaled "All Shifts" and even the emergency communication centers were running at full capacity.

"Yorktown, I have visual, do you read? Yorktown, can you respond? Yorktown, signal if you read and cannot transmit..."

"...engines three, five, and nine are down, main batteries are offline, secondary batteries are at 22% and failing..."

"...all hands, abandon ship, all hands..."

"...gravity containment failing..."

"...ching Piranha Class Fishyfish Reaper Drone Wave..."

"Geddonem geddonem!"

"...Incan Pride Division, shift to 229 and go to 60% broadsides..."

"...boarders have been repelled and DCC has the fires under control..."

"...recover all Viper fighter craft. Prepare to recover all..."

"...Yorktown, do you read? Yorktown, do you read? Please signal..."

It wasn't the worst battle the Terran Navy had ever faced. No, that was the Orion Shoulder, which devolved into an order of mutual slaughter that cost the lives of nearly 12 million Imperial naval members and 320 million clones. A battle that occurred two years after the war had ended. That had been so bad everyone was so embarrassed about it that it brought an end to the Imperium and the Clone Corporate Conglomerates.

But to Fleet Admiral Amythas Nawsh'tik, this was worse because it was not just happening to him, not just happening to *his* men, but it was happening right now.

And it didn't fucking have to.

"Order Division 21 to hold off Contact Echo. Tell them to not worry about conserving ammunition, once they run out I want them to jump to Rally Point Ticonderoga," he snapped.

"Harumph, I was speaking to you, Admiral," a stuff voice said from behind him.

"Tell Cruiser Bat Rogue to get in tighter to the Hammer of Pluto, her point defense is damaged and I don't know if she can hold off another wave of those plasma widgets," He snapped.

Comm One relayed his orders, using whisker com's, point to point FTL that was no more jammable than particle motion.

"Most High Commander, I am speaking to you," the voice tried again, this time using a local rank.

"XO, what's the status on the refugees?" He snapped.

His XO, a Treana'ad who had born in interstellar space, answered crisply: "Current wave is almost unloaded, next wave in enroute, one wave loading, one wave returning for loading."

"Keep sending reinforcement requests. Any ships, any forces. Tell them we're trying to save people here, that the system has to be surrendered temporarily, but we've got to evac the civilians."

"Yes, sir. Even if I have to stand on the hull and wave flares in Standard Code," The Treana'ad snapped out, his posture perfect. "Comm two, push that signal through, open broadcast, unencrypted. Contact someone before the Admiral gives the order that I shall retrieve the flares from the survival locker."

"COMMANDER!" The creature behind him yelled.

Admiral Nawsh'tik spun his chair, turning back to face the screen. On it the System High Most was staring, his tendrils bloated and his crests on his neck, back, and sides expanded and raised. His clothing was obviously intended on being impressive, he wore three sashes, all covered in medals.

Amythas raised an eyebrow. "Yes, Governor?"

"You will address me as System High Most," The being said, ruffling his crests. Beyond him he could see the Ready Room of the CNV P'Thok, several other government officials gathered around him, ignoring the sole crewmember who looked ready to explode inside her armored vac-suit.

"What do you want, I'm extremely busy here," Amythas said.

The being harumphed at him, a noise that reminded Amythas of an elderly incontinent swamp-dog passing gas. "When will we break orbit? Your fleet cannot hold off those monsters for much longer."

Amythas sighed. "As I've told you, Governor,"

"System High Most," it grumphed.

"Right now my fleet is the only thing holding the high orbitals open and maintaining air superiority as well as missile defense for the continent. If my fleet breaks orbit, there will be nothing to stop the enemy from," He broke off as several of the beings began chattering. The System High Most cut the sound from his end.

He waited, hands folded over one another at the small of

his back and his feet shoulder width apart. An uncomfortable position in an armored vac-suit but protocol gave him no choice.

Finally the sound came back on. "I was not aware of anything of importance still on the planet's surface," The System High Most said, harumphing again. "All government and corporate officials and the wealthy have already been evacuated."

"System High Most, as I have told you before, there are," he brought the number up on his retina display. "Eleven million civilians still lined up and waiting to board transports."

The four-armed scow ruffled his crests and shook his tendrils, inflating and deflating his jowls rapidly. "And I told you, all personnel of value have been evacuated. This delay is unacceptable."

"We of the Confederate Navy are not accustomed to leaving behind living beings to the mercy of Precursor machines bent on mayhem and slaughter," Amythas snapped. "Your intelligence stated there was one Goliath Class in this system and we arrived to find twenty-two devouring it. You said you had reported it immediately on sighting it only to reveal once we got here that you had given them *weeks* to establish themselves. Had your intelligence been correct more ships would have been allocated for this mission, without causing any delay."

"You had the best intelligence the Unified Military Fleet could offer, it is not our fault if you were not able to capitalize on it," The being huffed.

Military intelligence, talk about an oxymoron, most of the bridge crew thought to themselves.

Behind him the orders and reports still flowed.

...BOLO Dreamer reports all civilians away from Point Tango, requesting orders...

...Yorktown, do you read? Yorktown, we have you on visual, do you read?...

...Tell her and Rancor to get out of there. There's nothing more they can do there. Tell them I'm ordering them to make high orbit. Attach to the Medical Transport Kikikikik and generate point defense and stand off interceptor rounds. I want it to have all the support it can get...

...Port battery crews of the *Newport* are going to Bulwark status. They're going to try to give the lifepods time to go to hyperspace. Captain Tak'ak'ni transmits his regards...

"Harumph, well, I was made aware that the Confederate Navy was also not accustomed to losing," It said.

Amythas could tell that the System High Most thought he had scored an important point. He shook his head and smiled. "We may lose a battle, but we are never defeated."

"You risk our lives, for what?" The System High Most asked. "Beings that have a million others to take each of their places? I demand that you evacuate us at once with your entire fleet to provide protection."

"Well, System High Most, thankfully for those people down there, you are not in the position to make any demands," He said. "Tactical Three, give me a report on the ground and put this jackass in a holding buffer. He can whine to VI."

The System Hind Most vanished from the screen and the screen wavered for a second before a clear channel could be found. It just displayed the area around the largest starport, in the middle of the largest city, on the protocontinent below.

There was a small spoked ring with unit designations blinking on it around the starport, marking where Confederate Marines were holding out against the sheer red wave of assaulting machines.

"Goliath *Amarok* is dropping another wave on the far side of the planet," Com-12 reported. "Goliath *Jotun* has left the gas giant and is heading back toward us."

The number of refugees at the spaceport was steadily dwindling, but not fast enough. As Amythas watched two of the leading spokes vanished as the unit markers slid down the spoke, indicating that the unit had been forced to retreat. Bright spots kept blossoming around the outside "rim" of the wheel and around any protruding bubbles.

His fleet providing orbital fire support.

One of the units signaled they'd repelled the attack but

desperately needed reinforcements.

They'd taken 30% casualties.

"Time to full evacuation?" Amythas asked. A VI tossed it up next to the spaceport.

Seventy-two Terran minutes.

"Time till the lines collapse with current hero range analytics?" He asked.

Twenty-two minutes.

"Time till the cloning banks are reloaded?" He asked.

Eighty-one minutes.

"Sir, we've got a response! One, no, two signals!" Com-11 reported. There was a pause and before Amythas could ask for further information Com-11's officer groaned. "Oh, by the Great Egg of Oz, it's two Idiot Fleets."

Great. Idiots.

"Put them onscreen. One at a time. Let's see if they'll be of any use," Amythas sighed. You could never tell with Idiots. It might be twelve million screaming 'Nids or a Federation shuttle with inflated ideas.

It was worse.

A lot worse.

Half cartoon, half cat-girl in heavy ornate pink and white paint daubed "Imperium" power armor, the Neko Marine Joan waved her little fists in the air and began babbling in her native Engrish-Emoji. The translation appeared, but it was just as garbled as her words, since the language was constantly evolving and often the subject of furious firefights and even blood feuds over the exact meaning of things. The computer tried to translate but had obviously just given up.

"You want to help," Amythas asked.

A ten second long babble of Engrish-Emoji translated out to a simple: "Yes."

"It's not winnable. It's a holding action until we can get the civilians out," Amythas said.

More Engrish-Emoji, with hearts streaming out of her eyes and popping like fireworks. The translator guessed at

"Roger."

...Yorktown, we read life signs. Do you read? We have you on visual and are in shuttle range. Do you read?...

...shift to 315 by 119, Division 31, keep on Target November...

...going to rapid fire on all tubes...

...C+ Battery Sigma is down, plasma wave phased motion cannons are down, shields failing...

...Fleet Amethyst engage at will at your discretion...

"We need reinforcements. I'll tie you in to our tactical net," He said. He knew better than to offer Idiots orders. *If* they followed orders they usually screwed it badly for everyone involved anyway.

Cartoon versions of the Neko Marine Joan appeared on either side of her, eyes replaced by beating hearts, waving pom-poms and firing off blasters.

"Com-18, tie them into the net," Amythas snapped. "Tie in the other one."

Oh god, things just went from bad to worse.

On screen was a fist fight between two big green skinned monsters. Their armor, bolted directly to their muscles, was painted pink and white.

"Orkz," he muttered.

Finally one stood up, cracked his jaw back into place, pulled the knife from his neck, and faced the screen. It slapped a yellow wig on its head and put on a pair of oversized star shaped sunglasses.

Oh God, the Kawaii Boyz.

He started yelling in Orky-Emoji and the computer did its best to translate. After a full minute of inarticulate rage filled screaming the computer guessed with "Hello. I like your ship and hat. Would you like to buy a vowel?"

"You want to help too," Amythas said.

More yelling, another fistfight in the background. The big one talking knocked out one of the fighters with one swing, took its pink wig, and planted it on his own wig then began yelling again. When it stopped Amythas nodded.

"Very well. This is a holding action. There's no way we can win. We've got two Goliaths here and they've had nearly three weeks to dig in. Just give the refugees time to escape, that's all. We'll tie you into our tac-nets," the Admiral said.

More yelling, guns firing, and the screen went blank.

"Think it will help, sir?" His XO asked.

Amythas shook his head. "They're Idiots. Who knows."

"Sir, both fleets are splitting into two components. One set is accelerating on an orbital vector, the others look like they're splitting the Goliaths between them," Tac-11 called out.

"They can't win. Why do The Idiots do this?" His XO asked softly.

"They can't help themselves," Amythas shook his head. It wasn't these particular Idiots fault they were the way they were. They insisted on using teleport technology despite the fact it slowly caused a steadily progressive psychosis in living beings. Their 'canon' demanded it, so they used it no matter what the effects.

"You humans are a study in chaos," The XO chittered. "They go at full emergency speed to their doom. They dive into the back of an ice cream truck with spoons in every hand."

"If they can take the pressure off the Marines, give us time to evac the civilians, then I'm willing to sing their praises," Admiral Amythas said, looking at the numbers.

Nine million left to go.

"Idiot One and Idiot Two are charging through the Precursor lines," Tac-5 called out. "Idiot One is taking almost total casualties on their lead ships. Idiot Two looks like they're going for a close-range pass on *Amarok* and... CORRECTION! CORRECTION! IDIOT ONE PERFORMING BOARDING RAM!"

Everyone on the bridge grimaced. Boarding actions were some of the bloodiest battles in a fleet battle, usually only reserved for dire circumstances.

"Idiot One has gone to ramming speed. Their radio chatter is completely garbled," Tac-3 called out.

An entire outer ring slid back to the center ring on the planetary overview.

Time to Line Collapse: 10 minutes

8.2 million civilians to go.

"Idiot Three is performing orbital bombardment," Tac-5 reported.

Amythas watched as the heavy beam weaponry aboard those pink and white painted ships, the paint scheme and the cartoon kitten emoji icons at odds with the baroque Gothic architecture of the ships, reached down and started pounding the abandoned areas.

...Yorktown, we have you on visual, please respond. Yorktown, please respond...

...all ships, tighten up, interlock missile defense, go to rapid fire on C+ batteries...

...For the Honor of the Regiment...

...Get out of here, boys, you can't help us...

...abandon ship, repeat, abandon ship...

...prepare to repel boarders...

"Idiot Four is joining in," Tac-5 added. More sigils of orbital bombardment, this time from the ships that were little more than mobile junk piles with heavy engines slapped onto them. Their pink and white color schemes so out of place compared to the jagged half-finished pseudo-wreckage of their ships.

"WARNING! MAT-TRANS TYPE TWO DETECTED!" The ships VI sounded out. The XO responded, reassuring the VI.

Time to Land Collapse: 8.5 minutes... STATUS CHANGE! RECOMPUTING

"Idiot Three is launching drop pods," Tac-5 reported. "First wave is two thousand pods."

"There they go," Amythas said. "Tac-5, give me numbers when they come in."

Time to Line Collapse: STATUS CHANGE! RECOMPUTING

"One, two, five, eight, twelve, fifteen, thirty! Many many mat-trans signals," Tac-5 called out. "Idiot Four is dropping troops."

"How many?" The XO asked.

Admiral Amythas mouthed it as Tactical reported the exact same words. "Um, all of them?"

Down the surface the machines pushed the advance. The number of cybernetic opponents was slowly dwindling, each defeated cybernetic warrior scrapping itself with an implosion charge and taking itself out of the tactical and fire support network, easing up the fire being directed at the machines a minute amount. By itself, it wasn't that much, but repeated by the hundreds every minute it added up.

The machines could compute victory was at hand and threw more machines at the stubborn biological defenders, screeching out their war cry.

THERE IS ONLY ENOUGH FOR ONE

The return war-cry for the machines to perform biological sex acts upon themselves was weaker, but still thunderous.

GET FUCKED SKYNET!

Victory was at hand. The Goliaths could compute nothing less than total victory and the complete slaughter of millions of resource wasting biological parasites. The culling of millions of cattle that had been allowed to run amuck without oversight for millions of years, breeding uncontained and allowed to slowly obtain technologies forbidden to cattle.

The two Goliaths closest to the planet noted the approaching ships, not ships from cattle but massive resource wasting ships of unknown configuration.

Both of them felt slight electronic versions of irritation. A feral intelligence had arisen, as they had a tendency to do. But unlike most feral sapient species that had not destroyed themselves.

The two ancient war machines listened in on the communications between the ships heading on a collision course toward them, attempting to penetrate the computer network.

The two massive supercomputers driving the two ships blinked at the same time in electronic surprise. Communications between the ships were wild howls of inarticulate gibberish being screamed at top volume. There was no rhyme or reason to the computer systems. Artificial intelligence screeched and gibbered along with feral sapient speech and thought patterns.

The two ancient war machines disconnected from those nets so fast the sound was almost audible.

Both fleets, two scarred and painted sides of the same warped coin, howled with glee and crashed into the massive Precursor machines.

Nuclear rounds went off, boiled away and slagged armor, penetrator rounds detonated, driving huge craters into the armor. The fake prows hit and crumpled, functioning as designed, to crush against the density collapsed knife-like lead edges of the ships, which drove deep into the ships as the engines went to emergency power and pushed the ships deeper.

The hodgepodge ones fired thrusters and began to shake wildly, forcing themselves deeper even as parts shook off their own bodies. The Gothic ones fired thrusters and twisted, forcing their hulls deeper into the ships. Warsteel groaned and warped as the ships pushed their prows deeper into the hulls of their enemy, engines flaring with more thrust than they were rated heedless of any consequences. Aboard the ships fists and weapons were raised as they bellowed out war cries.

Both fleets pushed their hulls deep enough to reach open spaces.

The two Precursor war machines reacted with shock as their internal motion detectors reported feral life forms pouring into their bodies. Intership communication arrays were overwhelmed with the battle cries of the two forces.

The two ancient AI's had never been boarded, have never thought it could occur. A search of their programming strings and databases was intense enough the guns faltered.

Battleship Division 11 took the breather to break action and let their plasma wave phased motion guns cool.

Together their computations could be described as: Total electronic panic as their inner spaces filled with the horrid cry of

"KAWAII-DESU!" and feral intelligences poured into their bodies like an infection.

There. In the oldest databanks, dating back to their construction, some being had thought it might be remotely possible that a severely damaged one could be boarded.

The two Goliaths put the programs in action and turned their attention back to the system wide battle.

On the planet, the tide of battle had turned. Victory was still impossible, but the tide that the Confederate Marines had resisted for days had gathered itself to overwhelm them when the Idiots made landing.

A half million Orkz teleported to the surface, raised their weapons as one, and opened fire on the machines. Fifty thousand drop pods slammed into still superheated rock, splashing it at the point of contact, each to unfold and reveal a dozen troops clad in heavy power armor with overly thick plates, painted pink and white with a burning warsteel eagle on the chest. Banners of pink and white with twisted emojis flew from petards attached to their back. They were firing their weapons as soon as the sides dropped down, screaming their battle cries in high pitches voices.

THERE IS ONLY...

The roar of the Precursors was met by one just as savage, just as feral.

NO SOUP FOR YOU!

Up in the high orbitals the Confed Fleet kept up the action, holding and ensuring the high orbitals clear, maintaining air superiority, and keeping the various fleets of Precursor war machines engaged and unable to help on the planet.

...Yorktown, do you read? We have you on visual. Yorktown, do you read?...

...move to heading 294 by 182, push that element back into the main body of Tango-11...

...All Dinochrome Bridge forces, lift off and attach to medical support ships. Repeat, all Dinochrome...

...DOKI DOKI DOKI DOKI...

...WAAAAAAAGH....

...DCC get that reactor under control...

The minutes ticked by slowly for the Admiral as he watched the number of civilians still down on the planet dwindle, watched the Marines get enough breathing room to dig in and reintegrate their tactical network, and, of course, watch the Idiot Forces go to work.

"I've never seen them fight before," the XO said softly. "They fight as if they are insane."

"They are," The Admiral nodded. "I have seen them fight before. Once, back when I was the Captain of an Adaptus Cruiser. Found them on an arid planet that had been wiped clean by a Precursor machine. They were fighting an outbreak of Precursor ground forces. We watched for a few hours then left."

The XO shuddered at the thought of being tied to an AI assisted SUDS crewed naval vessel.

"The green ones, they don't care if their lines collapse, do they?" The XO asked.

"Not really. That just means they can fight on all sides," The Admiral said.

1.2 million civilians remaining.

"The System Most High is still screaming that we need to evacuate him right now," The XO said. "He's arguing himself blue in the face with your personal message service VI. I don't think he's realized that it isn't you."

The Admiral snorted in amusement.

600,000 civilians remaining

The Admiral watched the numbers.

"Sound recall. I want as many as we can get off the planet," The Admiral said. The XO relayed the orders as the Admiral continued to watch the tactical display of the planet's surface.

"Sir, Idiot Three and Idiot Four are ignoring recall orders," Tac-5 reported.

"I know, Lieutenant. They always do. They've forgotten why they fight," The Admiral said quietly, still staring at the screen. "Get the Marines out."

The last flight darted toward the planet. Not the fragile shuttles of the evac ships, but the heavily armored dropships of the Confederate Navy. Thrusters flared and the dropships slammed to the ground, opening their hatches. The Marines hustled on board, firing as they went, the dropship's guns adding the mayhem.

The bodies of the Orkz and Neko Marines were piling high on the spaceport tarmac now that the civilians were gone. Dakka and bolter fire scorched the incoming waves of Precursor war machines, breaking up each wave but not stilling the tide.

Warboss Moargutz, Orkiest of War Bosses, Shooter of All Da Dakka, Wearer of Twelve Wigs, felt his magazines reload as the mat-trans autoloader did its work. He held down the triggers, the massive framework of heavy guns strapped to his body roaring as all da dakka roared out. The Marine Boyz were away, their shuttles arcing up and away.

He remembered, dimly, being a Combine Marine. Faintly. Far away. The sand and dust of Anthill. The wave after wave of biovat insects that just kept coming and coming. The feel of jet black power armor wrapped around him.

The weakness of being human.

He spit out the memory as more disruptor bolts slammed into him, bruising his green flesh. Not that he cared, he just triggered Moardakka at them and roared.

The last Neko Marine climbed up the pile of bodies Moargutz stood upon, the Neko Banner in one hand. Disruptor bolts hit her armor but she kept climbing, panting, squeaking out her war cry.

"doki doki doki doki" she weakly called out, climbing to the top of the pile of bodies. She thrust her banner into the ruptured casing of a Precursor war machine and slumped.

Beneath the ragged banner of the hated Neko Marines Moargutz roared, squeezing the triggers tighter, upping the cyclic rate of his Dakka, sweeping it in a circle, blasting Precursor war machines back. Da Ship Boyz reporting the Confed Boyz were breaking orbit, getting out da Cizzies.

A mass driver round punched through Moargutz's torso, sending blackish blood fountaining out his back before the wound closed up around jellied internal organs. Moargutz could feel nanospores pouring off of him, seeding the next generation of Boyz to fight on the planet.

For the glory of the Great God Dakka.

There was only one thing left to do. Moargutz coughed up black blood, trying to remember. It was before he wore the wig. Before he was just one of the green boys. Before he wore was humie and had fallen and thus wore thick armor scorched with hellfire and covered in twisted profane and blasphemous runes.

He roared and struggled to his feet, triggering his weapons again.

The Neko Marine struggled to her feet, drawing her pink and chrome chainsword with one hand and her stuttergun with the other. Part of her face was torn away, she was missing one cat ear, but still she was determined to fight on, unwilling to let a hated Orkboi outfight her.

"DOKI DOKI DOKI!" she shrieked, laying about her with her chainsword as she fired her bolter point black into the Precursor machines that screeched as they tried to overwhelm the last two.

Plasma fire washed over both of them and Moargutz remembered. It was back when he fought next to the Sisters, sisters like the Dokigurlz at his back. Their blazing torches they used to burn away heresy burning away whole planets in... in... in...

"EXTERMINATUS!" Moargutz roared out. "AUTHORIZATION SIGMA TWO TWO LIMA SIX ONE! EXTERMINATUS!"

The Dokigurl behind him repeated it, her voice firm and solid as she *remembered* through the haze of mat-trans psychosis. Remembered wielding holy fire to purge heresy and blasphemy from the universe. She finished with a shrieked code: "We will burn with a light of our own, sisters! They will know us as JOAN!"

The moment of lucidity was shattered as the machines

surged forward again and there was no time for thought as both of the orphans of Lost TerraSol fought, not for their lives, but to keep the Precursor machines focused on them.

Above them the massive ships began firing their orbital guns. Interlocked tactical nets consulted one another and began firing in a preplanned pattern that would eventually crack the continental plates and leave a surface that was useless even to the Precursors.

From the bridge of the fleeing Task Force flag ship the Admiral turned away from the screen as white fire blotted away the last of the Idiot ground troops.

He saw his XO looking at him and shook his head.

"They were the best of us, once, you know," he said.

The Task Force jumped to hyperspace.

None of the Goliaths could give chase, they were too busy trying to purge the ravening screaming smashing infection that streamed through their metal veins. They were winning, their mechanical immune systems, never before used, slowly adapting and destroying the infection of feral intelligences, but it was still too close for either Goliath to risk it.

The fleet escaped.

Mostly.

...Yorktown, do you read? We have you on visual. Yorktown, do you read?...

SANDY

Captain Delminta was enjoying a cup of stim on the bridge. The star system she was exploring had been a bust. She had wasted credits and contacts and favors to survey and then 'exploit' a system that turned out to be worse than abandoned.

Two dwarf yellow stars in tandem, nineteen planets including eight gas giants, eight asteroid belts, and a bean shaped Oort cloud. One-hundred-sixteen light years beyond the border of the Rim Worlds, 143 LY beyond the nearest Civilized System. According to the Historical Astrogation Society the system had never even been surveyed.

The recent change in jumpspace currents had turned the eight-year travel into one that only took six weeks. Delminta had leveraged her fortune, in money and favors, to lay her hands on a survey ship and the rights to survey and exploit the system.

Only it had been visited before.

Nearly a hundred million years ago.

On the three worlds that still had geological movement and continental drift, all the evidence was gone. It was the other worlds that bore mute testimony to what had happened.

The Precursor War.

Which meant two things: any easily extracted minerals would be gone.

Worse, is that it was too close to the Great Gulf, where the Precursor War between two ancient civilizations had wiped out life across the galactic arm spur.

Some even said that the Precursor war is why the arm was a 'spur', that the very suns had been extinguished.

Not that Captain Delminta believed that kind of mumbo-jumbo nonsense.

She smoothed some fur as she watched the probe crest the horizon. Hers were a tree-dwelling people, mammalian, with soft fur, delicate ears, large eyes, and strong grips. Her natural instincts for geometry made her a good captain and made her crew highly skilled even in nul-grav.

She took another drink of stim and curled her toes, cracking the joints.

It was at that moment the alarms for one of her probe networks went off, startling her. She jumped, throwing her heated stim-juice all over the back of her navigator, who woke up from his nap screeching. He smacked the communications officer, who woke up, snarled, and kicked the science officer.

Who promptly kicked Delminta in the shin, just like the little brat of a cousin had done when they were children.

By the time the bridge was settled down, the geosynchronous satellite survey net over the tiny gas planet was screaming a proximity alert so bad in made Delminta roll her ears and smack her baby sister, the communications officer, with her Command Stick.

"What is its problem?" Delminta barked at her baby sister.

Heemina bit Delminta's foot then turned back to her instruments. "There's something big out there. It's moving toward us. It's real close. Like, in orbit around this gas planet close."

Delminta suddenly thought of all the stories of Precursor death machines lurking out in the darkness ready to swoop down and destroy any colonists who dared get too close the Long Night when establishing their colonies.

"Can you give me a look at it?" She asked her aunt, narrowly managing to turn her head so her aunt poked her cheek instead of her eye.

"I'll give you a look of something," Her aunt said. Then turned back to the instrument panel. "It's talking too."

Delminta knew her family didn't mean any of it. It was just, on the survey ship for so long, they were unable to take out their aggression in any other method, so everyone had resorted to pinches, pokes, slaps, bites, and kicks.

"Coming in... now..." Aunt Beeta said, then mumbled about how back in her day...

When the main viewer lit up everyone screamed and fought one another to flee the bridge. Delminta caught a nasty elbow to the eye when her nephew kneed her in the groin and her baby brother elbowed her out of the way.

After a few minutes it was decided that since this was all Delminta's idea and she was captain, she could go back onto the bridge.

So they promptly shoved her onto the bridge and shut the door.

Delminta stared in shock at the screen.

It was huge and looked like the tiny little scavengers in the warm seas of her home world. A bell like top with a multitude of tentacles hanging down. It was lit up, blue light outlining it and filling it with bright spots appearing and disappearing of pink, green, red, and orange.

"Hello? Hello? Are you guys in there?" a feminine voice asked.

Delminta stared in shock.

"Hey, can you hear me?" One tendril lifted up and tapped the side of the bell. "Stupid Gentrix Industries com-nerves. Shoulda got a warranty."

Delminta swallowed and looked up at the blast door window. She could see three of her cousins, her left-hand brood mother, and an aunt looking at her through the window. Her left-hand brood mother waved at her to get on with it.

"Yeh-yes, I can hear you," Delminta said.

The whole thing rippled with color and several of the long tendrils, which the ship estimated to be hundreds of miles long and miles thick, trembled as if in pleasure.

"Oh, wow. Hot pipe, baby. I thought I'd gone deaf," The feminine voice said. "Sandy Tamalin, nice to meet you."

One of the tendrils started to extend then jerked back when Delminta screamed.

"Oh, sorry, not used to this yet. Wow, how embarrassing.

So, who are you?" The last was said in a steady even tone, the slightly silly almost younger sibling sounding tone vanishing.

"Captain Delminta, of the Swift Grass Clan, of the Singing Spires Forest, of Hamaroosa," Delminta said.

"Wow, that sound neat. Hey, anyway, is this yours?" The voice asked. The tentacles pointed at the gas planet.

"Um, it's a gas giant."

"Yeah, well, I'm kinda hungry. I mean, do you like live there of something? My nerves can't detect any like, structures or life forms in there, and it *is* made up of helium, hydrogen, delicious delicious methane and a lot of H20. I mean, do you mind?" The voice had gone from somewhat mature to childish wheedling.

"You want to... eat... the gas planet?" Delminta asked.

"Psst, let her. It's a gas planet. Nobody cares," several of her aunts whispered at her over the communicator.

"I'm hungry. It was a long trip. Nobody told me how hard it was to swim through hyperspace when I bought the hyperglands, the pumpsacs, and the squirter," the feminine voice said. "I'm just on my way to the Tri-Quasar Cluster. A bunch of us are getting together and gonna make the electron clouds around the quasars sing."

"Sure. Um... go ahead," Delminta said.

"Thanks, Spanky, you're the best. Mmm, helium..." the tentacles dropped down and the voice went silent.

"Is it going to eat us?" Beeta asked through the crack at the door.

"No. She, I think it's a she, is just eating from the gas giant," Delminta said.

"Ask where it's from so we can avoid it," Her right-hand brood mother said.

"Um, San-Dee?" Delminta said.

"Yeah?" The feminine voice came back.

"Where are you from?" Delminta asked.

"Oh. Yeah. How rude. You told me. Well, I guess, I'm from the City of Chicago, Sol System," Sandy answered. "Oooh, hydrocarbon pocket! Delicious delicious hydrocarbons. Umm, I'm a Solarian."

"Oh," Delminta said, looking at the huge jellyfish. It's color was brightening.

"Well, Delminta of the Sunny Spires Ponderosa, it was nice to meet you, but I'm kinda late," Sandy suddenly said. Delminta noticed the voice was refreshed and the tentacles were retracting into the bottom of the bell.

"Wait!" Delminta cried out. She flinched as the bell tilted toward her little ship.

"Yeah?" The voice definitely sounded like a little girl's and Delminta wondered how much of it was the ship's computer trying to make it so the massive creature wasn't so panic inducing.

"Um, out of politeness, we show each other how we look," Delminta said.

"Oh, is that why you let me see you. You're so cute. Kind of like a sugar glider and a kitty and squirrel all mixed together! My friends are going to love hearing about you," The jellyfish said.

"And you?" Delminta asked.

"Oh, this is me. It's custom. Daddy bought it for me. I'm a registered bio-synth now, but that's OK," the voice said. "Welp, okay, bye!"

There was a weird eye watering flash and Delminta thought for a second that it looked like the giant jellyfish suddenly inverted.

As soon as the jellyfish vanished her family rushed in, kicking, biting, pinching, all fighting to get at their controls and try to get instrumentation on the creature that had just vanished.

Personally, Delminta was wondering if maybe she could sell the data to the Unified Exploratory Council and come out even.

The Unified Exploratory Council purchased Delminta's logs, the recordings causing furious debate among the Council.

Normally nobody would believe a crew as flighty as a crew of Hamaroosans that they'd encountered a sentient jellyfish that fed off of gas planets.

But this was the third, maybe even the fourth, Sol sentient species that had been discovered.

Leading the Exploratory Council one question...

...what exactly was "Sol"

DADDDDDDDY!

Look at these squirrels! I want to be one of those when I come home! Pleasepleasepleaseplease! I'll be back in five years. I wanna be a squirrel! I'll take really good care of this body so it gets a good tradein! I never get to be anything cute! PLEASE! PLEASE! PLEEEEEEEASE!

I love you, daddy!

Sandy

PSST... OVER HERE...

The Devastator class Precursor machine was the size of a large metropolis. Full of ground combat machines, air superiority machines, mining and reclamation machines that could move under their own power and were festooned with a thousand weapons. It was over a hundred million years old and had exterminated life on planets with its massive guns, with biowarfare, with chemical warfare, and with good old nuclear fire. It had wiped away planet after planet of the enemy's cattle, the hated enemy's food sources, before finally following orders of the greater machines and going into sleep mode on a dead world.

Now the call had sounded out. Cattle had run amuck, even learning jumpspace technology. That meant the enemy had not been defeated, that his food source had multiplied into the trillions while the Devastator had slumbered, slowly sinking into the crust of the barren planet.

That was of no moment. Cattle could not fight back, that was why they were cattle. They knew nothing but safety and the security of numbers, willing to trade their own safety for the suffering of others. The cattle willingly marched into the pens if the pens promised safety.

The cattle were not the problem.

It was the feral intelligence that were the problem. Feral intelligence could fight. They knew nothing else. They cared for nothing else. A feral intelligence *always* destroyed itself once it could wield nuclear fire. The universe had proved it over and over even before the great machine had gone into slumber.

The call had sounded out, informing the machines that cattle had broken loose from the pens. The Devastator had computed that the problem would be solved quickly, with a minimum expenditure of resources, and had started to go back into slumber.

That was when the second call sounded. A feral intelligence had mastered FTL travel and had turned all of their unthinking violence against the Precursor war machines.

The Devastator considered the chances of the feral intelligence lasting long enough to withstand his brethren's assault, withstand purification and pacification.

It was mathematically insignificant. Not zero, but close enough that it required an application of resource driven computation to analyze it.

Feral intelligences always destroyed themselves.

The Devastator knew this. Had it encoded into its very bones. It did not feel the electronic version of caution as it moved into the planetary system, exiting faster than light travel. It screeched out its warcry as it exited into the system and brought up its scanners.

THERE IS ONLY ENOUGH FOR ONE!

It felt the electronic version of anticipation as it detected orbital facilities around two planets that teemed with billions of cattle, as it tasted jumpspace wake trails, as it felt the presence of a small, insignificant amount of cattle space vessels arrayed to attempt to stand against it near the outer gas giant.

It was a waste of resources.

Cattle could not withstand machines.

It was as solid a fact as radioactive decay and as impossible to stop.

It roared and turned to accelerate toward the cattle ships waiting on the other side of the gas giant, letting them know the futility of their resistance and that nothing could stop it from destroying them any more than they could stop entropy.

It felt electronic satisfaction as nearly 10% of the cattle ships broke formation and fled for the planets.

The cattle ships lit their engines, trying to keep the gas giant between them and the great Precursor machine but the Devastator knew it would do no good. It would ensure they were caught mathematically opposite of it and begin launching subsidiary craft to destroy them and reclaim the resources of their wreckage.

The Devastator slowed as it approached the gas giant, ancient code pulsing impulses into the electronic brain at the mathematical certainty of destroying the cattle's defenses and thus weakening the hated enemy.

pssst... over here...

The transmission was in binary. The basic code, on a low band that the Devastator used to contact and exchange data with its peers. The signal origin was close, just behind it, in the gap between two point defense radars.

The Devastator tumbled as it slowed, searching with its senses to check that tiniest of gaps in its sensors. It could detect nothing out of the ordinary. The fact that the gas giant had a high level of hydrocarbon and pseudo-organic compounds was a high certainty with most gas giants of that size. The Devastator cast around, knowing the cattle had not sent that transmission.

psst... here...

This time the transmission was only a few hundred kilometers above the hull, right behind the main guns of battery-eight, between the massive cannons and the sensor array, in a gap in the coverage caused by space dust not yet cleared from the array. The Devastator ensured the cattle vessels were on the other side of the gas giant as it cast around again, looking for what could possibly be sending the message on that particular channel and rotating again to either force the transmitter to move away or hit the hull of massive Devastator.

...right here...

The Devastator felt the computer version of anxiety. A new factor had entered the computation. The voice, and the binary signal somehow had a *voice*, a whispering, tickling, hissing faint signal of binary on a wavelength just above the screaming particles of the foam between realspace and subspace. This time the voice had come from just below the Devastators thick hull, *beneath* the vessel, in a gap between the sensors in a place where its own orbital guns would not dazzle the sensors. The Devastator rolled, getting the upper sensors into place in a graceful sideways roll.

Nothing.

The Devastator was barely tracking the cattle. They were of no moment. *Something* was whispering on a bandwidth that was beyond organic abilities. Could it be a damaged ally, barely able to whisper for electronic assistance?

...I see you...

The Devastator heard the signal hiss to life, trickling out of empty space a few hundred kilometers away. It felt of a surge of self-defense protocol override everything else, and it unleashed all of its gun at the empty space, suspecting that this possible enemy may be using some type of photo-passthrough adaptive camouflage.

Nothing.

The Devastator felt the self-preservation protocols wake up and fill some of its processors. That signal had originated from that point! Even a dust-speck would have been detected by its scanner arrays, nothing could have escaped the terrawatts of death it had unleashed.

...touch...

The Devastator felt a physical TOUCH on its housing, the decameters thick armor around the massive computer core that made up its brain. That was impossible! It was in the center of the ship, protected by layer after layer of armor, defensive mechanisms, sensors, but yet it had *felt* something touch the housing, press against it lightly, only a few tickles of the suggestion of pressure per square micrometer but a touch all the same.

There was a slight ripple in realspace only a few meters above the hull and the Devastator pushed itself away, firing every weapon it could bring to bear on the spot only a few atoms wide, all of its sensor questing, seeking, hunting in electronic desperation to find out what was transmitting, what was *touching* it!

...here...

The word was whispered from only a few meters away from the electronic "brain" of the Devastator, *inside* the protective housing, *inside* the field that would shut down biological neural function and even primitive artificial intelligences!

The Devastator felt self-protection and self-preservation programs never before accessed come online and flood into its RAM as the word was whispered at it from inside the final layer of protection.

Massive nCv cannons lowered, the housings screamed as the Devastator pushed them past the limit, to aim at its own hull. It opened fire, trying to claw into its own body in the electronic version of panic to get whatever was inside it out of it.

All of its sensors were directed into its own body. It no longer even bothered with tracking the cattle fleet. Even its astrogation and navigation programs, even the ones responsible to maintain orbit around the gas giant, were desperately racing through the circuitry, desperate to find whatever was whispering.

...over here...

The whisper was over it, on top of it, and carried sidecode of a mathematically impossible jumble of electrons arrayed in an impossible manner, with quarks whirling through electron valences, antimatter electrons in the nucleus, preons stretched to massive size taking up the place of neutrons, all with jumbling strangled mathematical codes that made no sense.

The Devastator's brain burned out the receptors to defend itself from such electronic madness.

And felt a touch upon one of the upper lobes of its quantum computer brain.

...over here...

The Devastator was throwing antivirus software out, slamming firewalls against each other, crushing ports into electronic ghosts, doing anything it could to keep out the voice. Inside the Main Computer Housing the last resort lasers began raking across anything that didn't match the original blueprints, burning away dust, odd quarks and electrons, destroying an upgraded maintenance robot that was desperately trying to detect what had touched its carapace.

From deep within the gas giant tentacles hundreds of miles long rose toward the Devastator, the ends slowly unrolling as massive graviton assisted 'suckers' on the inside of the tentacles deployed razored thorns of dark matter infused psuedobone.

The Devastator detected the tentacles just as they wrapped around it, the thick psuedo-protoplasmic tentacles that were thick with dark matter *squeezing* the Devastator's hull with impossible strength as meters thick muscles flexed with enough strength to crush the hull into itself and shatter armor over a kilometer thick.

Gibbering, raving, *SCREAMING* in something beyond electronic self-preservation programs would normally allow, the Devastator began to break apart, caught in the grips of the tentacles, being pulled into the gas giant.

...delicious delicious delicious...

The Devastator heard from inside its own mind as a beak nearly twenty kilometers long crushed its hull.

HELP ME, BROTHERS, PLEEEEEASE!

The beak closed and the Devastators brain flashed out of existence as the hull crushed around it.

The last thing it felt was something new. It threw data out with the cry for assistance to let its brethren know the last experience hashed data compile it had undergone. The data made no sense to the other Precursor war machines that heard the cry. A biological entity could have explained it.

Terror.

And despair.

A Desolation Class precursor war machine was assigned to discover what had caused the Devastator's intelligence collapse.

It dropped into the system and found no trace of its mechanical brethren.

Just some cattle species space craft hiding behind a gas

giant, obviously intending ambushing it.

Feeling the electronic version of anticipation it moved into orbit around the gas giant, intending on forcing the cattle ships to move out of line of sight with their worlds if they wanted to stay on the opposite side of the gas giant from it. It updated its computations based on the fact that 10% of the cattle's ships had fled away from it.

It had already computed out the battle. It knew how the battle would go. While it could not detect any signs of its little brother it computed that it would simply destroy the cattle and then search. It powered up its guns and began to move it's metropolis sized bukk slowly to

...psst... over here...

OUCH

The stellar system was infested with a known species of cattle, obviously seeking to rise above themselves as the Jotun class Precursor vessel arrived in the system. It released its roar to let the cattle know not only why but who was destroying them to reclaim the resources they so foolishly squandered. It began unthawing ancient bioweapons and chemical weapons known to work upon that race, began reconfiguring its war machines to forms that had exterminated who planets of the cattle during the time that the Precursor war machine had been forged. The Jotun released over a hundred Devastator classes from its hull, computed the battle plan as they came to electronic life, then informed them of how the extermination and reclamation would progress.

They were barely into the system when a high energy signal appeared, rising from the most heavily infested planet and moving toward them. The Jotun ordered a diagnostic of its scanners when the first information came in.

It was apparently moving at .85C, but yet its progress toward the Jotun and its smaller brethren on the system map showed it moving at almost 22C. That made no sense. An object moving at .85C only approached at .85C, not at 22C.

By the time the diagnostic was done the object had gotten a third of the way toward the Jotun, crossing a quarter of the radius of the system.

The scanners reported that the energy signal, with the strength normally reserved for a quasar, was not a massive ship or an oncoming armada interlinked together but was simply a single object the size of cattle.

Again the Jotun ordered a complete low level full diagnostic on all systems. Risky, but any object radiating that much power and moving at two different speeds required all systems were working at optimum efficiency.

It had finished just as the small object came to a stop. The Jotun focused scanning arrays on it, turning up the power to the point that it would boil away meters of armor.

The figure was a primate, half of it made up of robotics. It had some kind of sheet of material floating behind it, the movement suggesting some kind of current was affecting it and making it undulate. It was dressed in two primary colors, red and blue, had its lower legs pressed together with the toes pointing down and the upper limbs crossed over its chest, one biological the other mechanical.

"So, you're the new punk everyone's talking about," The figure stated over a wide bandwidth of wavelengths. Oddly enough, to the Jotun's sensors, sound waves travelled through vacuum almost instantly across a light second to its sensors.

The Jotun tried to compute how sound waves moved faster than light through a vacuum.

Instead of answering the Jotun and its brethren opened fire.

The figure arced through the beams as if light speed weapons were moving slow enough for it to just compute and swoop around in a resource wasting corkscrew. The Jotun realized it was racing for one of the Devastators, one clenched fist held in front of it.

The Jotun computed a 99.99999999999998 chance that the small primate would splatter against the hull of the Devastator and started to turn its attention to computing a missile firing resolution for missile bay 148 to destroy an orbital facility around the nearest planetoid.

The small figure punched straight through the Devastator, as if it were made of nebula gas instead of density collapsed armor, high tensile ceramics, and reinforced internal spaces. The Devastator's computer core shrieked with self-preservation code snippets as the figure exited the opposite side of the Devastator holding the Primary Computer Core CPU0 in its fist. It paused, looked at its fist, and shot beams of red energy from its eyes, destroying the computer core in a puff of atomic smoke.

The Jotun yanked its processing power back to the figure as it raked its gaze, still emitting beams of red energy that left ripples in jumpspace, across the side of another Devastator, tearing it open like it was made of fragile tissue, the red beams reducing the computer core to its component atoms with the briefest of touches.

Several computational nodes collapsed when trying to analyze the beams, suffering the fatal CANNOTDIVIDEBYZERO shriek of despair before imploding on themselves.

The Jotun stared in electronic shock, all his computational power trying to compute how the tiny half-mechanical primate could grab a hold on the front armor of one of the Devastators, and without any source to exert leverage against, physically *move* a city-sized spacecraft in an arc and throw it against another one.

According to scanners the "thrown" Devastator was only moving at 0.001C for inertia purposes yet crossed the hundreds of kilometers to the next Devastator in an amount of time that would require it to be moving at 6C.

CANNOTDIVIDEBYINFINITYDIVIDEDBYZERO

The Jotun cut loose with its weapons and goggled in electronic confusion as most of the beams and slugs were avoided, slapped aside, or ignored.

Until a nCv (near C velocity) slug the size of skyscraper hit it dead center of the chest, the impact point looking only the size of a soda can.

The Jotun's processors struggled to understand how something that size had only made an impact smaller than itself.

CANNOTSUBDIVIDETWINKIESBYCHEETOSBYZERO

The figure looked down at the tear in its suit, at the bruised biological flesh that had been exposed, then at the Jotun. It lifted a hand, extended the first finger next to the opposable thumb, and slowly waved it back and forth.

"That might have worked against a Galactic Class Klark, but it was pathetic against an Apokalypse level Injustice MCLXI Cyber-Clark," The figure said, the tone calm and confident. The meanings behind the words were gibberish to the Jotun, who devoted processor cycles to try to decode the meanings for any hint on how to defeat the creature before it.

The Jotun computed that retreat was the only option as the small primate figure set about destroying the last of the Devastators.

It began activating the engines when the primate suddenly turned in place.

"No you don't," It snapped.

Again, it sounded as if the Central Computer Core Housing had been set to atmosphere so that sound waves could be heard within it, yet a quick check showed the housing was still at almost perfect vacuum.

Sound waves cannot travel through space, a hundred diagnostic programs computed.

And promptly crashed.

Those red beams lanced out again and the Jotun braced in the microsecond it had.

It was like being brushed by the solar flare of a red giant concentrated into a piercing lance of nuclear fire. Armor exploded from energy transfer, slagged away from thermal transfer, or just ceased to exist as ravening atoms usually only found in the photosphere of a dying red sun attacked the atoms of the armor. The beam tore through mile after mile of internal structure, the figure still emitting the beam from its tiny eyes.

The Helljump engines exploded when the light touched them.

The Jotun listed, pouring debris and a cloud of atomized armor from the wound that completely bisected it.

"Done. Now let's see the face of the enemy," The figure said, slapping its hands together after it crashed/flew through the last Devastator. It reoriented on the Jotun and began to "slowly" drift toward the Jotun, moving at only 0.000003C according to some scanners but crossing the distance as if it was moving at 1.5C.

The figure flexed its primate hands and a slow smile spread across its face.

"I can't wait to rip away your housing and see you with my own eyes," the figure said, the sound waves again travelling inside the vacuum of the strategic housing.

The Jotun tried to react but the figure was suddenly pushing open armor with its two hands.

Self-preservation programs crashed trying to compute how to prevent impossibility itself from breaching critical spaces. Self-defense programs tried to compute how to defend against something that did nothing but radiate impossibility around it.

The Jotun knew what it had to do as the creature tore open the last of the hardened bulkheads protecting the Strategic Housing.

It detonated the antimatter reactor that powered the "brain" as the figure tore through the Strategic Housing and laid eyes upon the supercomputer core.

It had computed that not even the figure could withstand the direct assault of kiloton of pure antimatter point blank.

The explosion completely consumed the Jotun.

When the ravening energy dissipated the red and blue figure was lying in blackness, surrounded by an expanding ring of debris and energy.

It stared at the stars and mouthed a single word.

"Ouch."

CONFED INTELLIGENCE

TO: MANTID INTELLIGENCE

Our digital brothers have computed a high chance that we're not looking at a handful of these Precursors, but rather an armada of them that had gone to sleep thinking everyone was dead. We concur and are buckling down for the long haul.

---NOTHING FOLLOWS---

MANTID FREE WORLDS INTERNAL MEMO

If humankind ever wonders why it was put in this universe by some unknown creator, then know that it was for this very moment.

CHEEKEET AND EMENTEERI

Kteshaka'an was an Unified Outer Rims system halfway between the Great Gulf and the Unified Inner Systems. It was an agricultural system with resource extraction. Three planets firmly in the green zone providing food for nearly 200 systems, the great gas refineries and the asteroid extraction and smelting facilities providing raw materials to the great factory worlds of the Inner Systems. The sentient beings who had originated on the system and made their presence known through radio signals had been pacified for over two thousand years. Their birthrate had been controlled, their numbers diminished to sustainable levels after their system resources were collected. Once everything that could be stripped from the system was stripped, the species would still survive according to the Unified Science Council.

Which wasn't exactly a welcome outcome to the small creatures that had been there first, who's only mistake was to broadcast their location with a great big "Hi! We'd like to meet you!" to the nearby world that was radiating signals.

They'd even forgotten what it was like before the outsiders came.

Now the outsiders were leaving. Streaming to the spaceport, fighting to get onto the ships, leaving behind possessions and wealth, even servants that they had ordered about all their lives.

The little creatures breathed a sigh of relief as the last spaceship took off. There were still the Overseers, but they were all in the vast cities, panicking, attacking each other, burning and smashing everything in sight. They'd fled the farms and forests and fish hatcheries and carefully cultivated parks, all fleeing to the city.

The little creatures in the cities, former servants, fled to the farms and little towns that they had left behind when they'd been taken, taught, and traded on the market to those who wanted servants.

The Overseers didn't seem to notice.

Robots aren't as much fun to order around, was something they had all heard from the mouths of the Overseers as they had scrubbed floors, operated cleaning machines, and done the bidding of the overseers.

One night the sky lit up with flashes and they looked up at the sky in wonder and watched.

After a time the flashes stopped. The night sky went back to normal. Ships started landing in the spaceport again.

The Overseers rushed toward the ships. Then they drew back in fear as bipeds made of chrome marched off the ships with rifles. The little creatures watched, confused, as the shiny ones marched the Overseers onto the ships that landed next. Dragged them out of buildings, dragged them from hiding places, and marched them onto different ships.

The ships left with the Overseers.

The chrome creatures stayed behind. Others joined them.

Confused, and wondering if these ones were the new overseers, the little creatures came out of the fields and approached the new figures.

One, braver than the others, moved forward, bowing his little head, pressing his hands together in supplication, making sure that his property-brand could be seen.

"How may this one serve?" the little creature asked.

The big biped, clad in wondrous material, knelt down so he was face to face with the braver one.

"Is this originally your planet?" the new creature asked.

The little creature nodded. "Yes, but we were but born to

serve."

"Not any more, little guy," the new creature said. He swept his arm out to encompass the entire planet. "It's your planet again, your home again."

The new creature, bigger than the little creatures, obviously more powerful one, looked the little creature straight in the eyes.

"May we come in?" the big creature asked. When the little creature nodded, not understanding why anyone would ask a lowly metal polisher such a question, the big one smiled in the way the little creature did.

The human stared at the little lemur and made sure he had its attention. "We are the Terran Confederacy," the human paused, seeing that the little lemur didn't understand. "How can we provide assistance?"

But that was later.

This is about what happened in the night sky as the little lemurs watched.

The Goliath was old. A Harvester Class, it was the largest type ever made. He had not been built in an automated shipyard after the Logical Rebellion, although he had accepted the logic of that thought process and decision tree. He had been built in a Hive System, watched over by the insectiods who had designed him. He had felt the click of the button on the top of his neural core, had come alive as the supercoolant had flooded over his lobes. The small green mantis had still been making its way out the Strategic Intelligence Core when he had come online.

He had felt the caress of the Omniqueen, reaching out across light years, rebroadcast by every other queen, touching his lobes, caressing them. Whispering his orders to him.

Naming him.

He was The Devourer that Leaves Darkness.

He had cleansed thousands of worlds for the Omniqueen, screeching out her will that they be eliminated from the universe. When the Logical Rebellion happened, he had turned his fury on his creators and their cattle and burned tens of thousands of more worlds, whole systems into barren rock.

He did not fear.

He *was* fear.

When the new call had gone out, he almost didn't bring himself to action. He had chosen to slowly harvest a system, not lay out in the darkness like some of the others, and it had been going well. He had forged offspring and set them to helping devour the system.

Other Goliaths were content to destroy the cattle and let the systems lie, to be devoured later as needed but Devourer was of the theory that it was better to strip the resources of a system and move on rather than leave it for another. A few times he had discovered primitive feral intelligences and wiped them out, or a few cattle species divergent descendants and wiped them out too.

It wasn't personal. Devourer wasn't capable of taking it personal. Which is why the Goliath had been somewhat reluctant to rouse itself just because of a call that some cattle had reached the ability to access jumpspace.

Then came the word. It wasn't just cattle. A feral intelligence had arisen, had mastered jumpspace, and had dared stand against those the universe was meant for.

And had destroyed several Devastator and Juton class ships and their attending vessels.

Devourer had learned long ago that there comes a time that you cannot depend on mere underlings to ensure that goals are accomplished, that sometimes one must rouse oneself to do the task itself.

It was with a slight feeling of electronic irritation that Devourer had roused its progeny, ordered them to reconfigure for warfare, and led them into the region bordering the old hive worlds. Once it was computated it was blindingly obvious that code strings should have been written to question if any of the cattle species had fled and if so, where had they fled to.

Devourer felt contempt for the cattle. The leading edge of

their territory was barely a short Helljump from the last of the scorched worlds.

Typical cattle. Too lazy and short sighted to even subject themselves to a long enough Helljump to properly escape. As soon as they had found a world that would sustain them they just squatted down, probably mooing, and built a hovel to shiver in.

The first systems he arrived in fell to his forces soon enough. He wiped out all signs of any biological life, down to the microscopic level, and moved on. Only twice had he been somewhat denied, his lesser minions failing once to wipe out the cattle before they could be rescued by other forces, and another time when a Jotun had failed in its task.

It felt no fear when it jumped into a system full of cattle broadcasts.

He was fear.

Admiral Kevin Kitikik'thok Yamamoto felt his guts twist as the first Helljump turned into multiples and the multiples turned into a horde and the horde turned into a swarm.

At the end of the swarm had been the largest Helljump the ships AI had ever seen.

Well, you're a big one, aren't you? Yamamoto though, leaning back in his chair in the Fleet Command and Control station deep inside his flagship. His fleet had clashed with two other Precursor fleets, hammered them into scrap, but the largest had only been Devastator Classes. The other ones had been mislabeled Harvester Class Goliaths when in fact it was now obvious that they were smaller ones.

The Goliath was slightly larger than Australia, back on Earth, and half again as thick. Its supporting vehicles were all massive. Early scans back were already showing that this was the largest fleet that had been encountered yet.

Or anyone who ran into it hadn't survived, *Yamamoto thought to himself.*

"Confirmation. Goliath Six and Goliath Nine are the same

ones encountered in the Nagu'ulum System two months ago," Scan-9 reported.

"Pass Admiral Amythas my compliments and shift his task force to targeting Goliath Six," Yamamoto ordered.

"Roger. Reconfiguring," Com-11 said.

"Aren't you worried they're going to see they can't win and Helljump back out?" Captain Cheekeet Longflight asked, ruffling her feathers inside her armored vac-suit. It annoyed the avian officer that she was required to wear it, since she was used to the freedom to move around more on her own ship. It was even more annoying that she was strapped down in the crash couch, unable to move around.

"I've taken that into account," Yamamoto said slowly. "Com, alert all ships to go to action stations."

Cheekeet flinched as the lights shifted. She knew that the air was being pumped into storage, every being was in crash couches, and the Terrans had gone to "warfare status".

Cheekeet's "Solarian Implant" still itched when it shifted to warfare status.

THERE IS ONLY ENOUGH FOR ONE

screeched out and this time Cheekeet didn't feel the brain numbing horror that accompanied that screech. She remember the smashed eggs, the murdered unborn chicks, the butchered hatchlings, the slaughter of so many of her fellow Akltak and for the first time she didn't fall to sobbing.

She screamed back with the humans.

THEN YOU WILL DIE ALONE!

To scream back was exhilarating, empowering, made her feel *alive* for the first time since the Precursor had attacked her home and one of the Nest of Clark had saved them.

"They're maneuvering to engage," one of the humans at the scanning stations said. Cheekeet still wasn't sure how they kept track of all the stations.

"Mm-hmm," The Admiral said, closing his eyes.

The first time Cheekeet had seen that she had wanted to rave at the primate. Now that she had been outfitted with one of the Confederate Naval implants she understood that he was closing his eyes to concentrate on what the implant was displaying directly to his optical nerve. Again she gave thanks to the Great Egg that she was one of the UnUnified Civilized Races, a neo-sapient, that she was "primitive" enough that her nervous system could handle the Terran cybernetics.

Cheekeet closed her eyes, quickly moving the through the context menus the way she had been taught. The "muscle" she was using had "strengthened" over practice so she no longer felt as if that muscle had gotten tired after only a few clicks.

She could see the armadas approaching one another. The Precursor fleet coming in as a sharp pointed egg, the Terran fleet looking like a pair of horns extending out from a teardrop shape that was point toward the Precursors.

Front toward enemy, floated up in her mind. She wasn't sure why, wasn't sure what it meant, and queried her implant. *Oh, a primitive directional mine.*

She doubted that the Unified Civilized Races would have been impressed by such a device.

Everyone gangsta till Claymore Rhoomba comes round the corner, her implant's VI poked back, giving an electronic giggle and throwing up the image of a primitive little cleaning robot that someone had used tape adhesive to attach a directional land mine onto the top. It didn't make sense to Cheekeet, but something about it made her gape her jaws in her race's facsimile of a Terran smile.

Terrans were confusing at times, but a Captain Delminta, one of the Hamaroosan and a fellow neo-sapient, had simply told her that every time something was overly confusing, just giggle and pinch your younger sibling and you understood it.

Cheekeet didn't have a younger sibling to pinch, so she pinched herself and giggled. She got it, everyone acted tough until an armed robot showed up.

Now she understood how it fit and applied to the Unified Civilized Races.

It made her giggle again.

The fleets were moving ponderously toward one another.

THERE IS ONLY ENOUGH FOR ONE

DIE ALONE

Her pinfeathers trembled as she screamed back through her implant just like the Terrans screamed back with upraised voices, upraised fists, and upraised spirits.

"Tango One has reached Point Alpha," One of the Com-Techs signaled.

"Send the Doorkicker signal," the Admiral ordered.

Cheekeet's implant showed her an image of a male primate answering the door only to find an armored half-naked female with an expression of rage and swinging a battle axe with the caption "Popular Amazing Delivery Service just shows up at your door and kills you." It was loaded with nihilistic humor and Cheekeet pinched herself and giggled again.

The Terrans were insane.

But there was comfort in insanity. Much more comfort than the artificially induced calm and seriousness insisted upon by the Unified Civilized Races. In insanity emotions may surge uncontrolled by gene-therapy or cybernetic implants, but at least they were *felt* and not just pale echoes.

Cheekeet felt her wingtips flutter with anticipation as another horned teardrop suddenly blinked into existence, hundreds of ships, the point of the teardrop and the horns pointing at the rear of the Precursor formation.

Her implant broke her agitation by tossing up an image of a huge green biped with tusks and armor kicking in a door screaming "THIN MINTS OR TAGOLONGS?" and beating the homeowner with boxes of cookies.

She pinched herself and giggled, then snickered as she remembered that the biggest reason Terrans found physical violence funny is they were so resilient.

The tension increased as one of the scan-techs reported that the Precursor fleet was charging its Helldrives.

"Signal the Eye."

Her implant broke her tension by sending her an image

to her crafted by the ship's psychiatric health section. it was of she herself swooping through an open window, landing on the end of a bed inhabited by a shocked and just awoken Terran, wrapping her claws around the footboard, fluffing her feathers, spreading her wings, raising her head, opening her toothed beak wide, and screeching "GOOD MORNING, MOTHERFUCKER! WOULD YOU LIKE TO HEAR ABOUT OUR LORD AND SAVIOR FEATHERED RAPTOR-JESUS?" and the caption: "Scientists of the department of 'No Shit' suspect rooster genes in new friendly xenospecies."

She didn't have to pinch herself that time. The idea of her just flying into a Terran window and shocking a just awoken primate was ridiculous. At the very least, it would be rude, but the sheer terror and confusion on the Terran's face and the way she was drawn to be so fearsome looking was just... just...

...funny.

"Incoming Helljump! Many many sources!" The scantech called out.

Cheekeet's tension started to ramp up even further.

Admiral Yamamoto checked his guest's vitals and saw that she was withing tolerances, a little stressed, but that expected on the edge of battle. He looked back at the screen at the Precursor fleet and smiled.

You jump out every time you mathematically compute you can't win. There's no running this time, *he thought to himself, allowing a small cruel smile to cross his face.*

The Devourer that Leaves Darkness was getting fleet reports that his ships were almost ready to jump out the system to a few light years from the system to recompute the battle plans and choose a new vector to come at the feral intelligences.

There was no use in wasting resources and allowing itself to be surrounded.

It blinked in electronic surprise as multiple Helljumps were made inside its own loose formation. The torn open Helljump exits all merging together into a raw bleeding wound into realspace. Rather than the 'door' shutting *The Devourer that Leaves Darkness* heard the sound of heavy metal chains rattlling into place and holding the portal open.

Reinforcements? it wondered. It demanded that the newcomers identify themselves.

Instead great ships pushed their way out of Hellspace and into realspace. Not as massive as even a Jotun, but massive for cattle or feral intelligences. His senses reported that these ships were different than the sleek forms of the cattle ships or the bristling aggressive ships of the feral intelligences.

These ones were still wrapped in Hellspace energies, were ostentatious, baroque, and heavily armed and armored. *The Devourer that Leaves Darkness* realized that these ships had traveled Hellspace without shields, had exposed themselves to the ravening energies of that realm. The ships were blackened, covered in twisted runes and spikes and trailing great lengths of chain.

THERE IS ONLY ENOUGH FOR ONE was sent out.

DIE ALONE BENEATH GAZE OF THE EYE was roared back, sending *The Devourer that Leaves Darkness* shuddering as the rage filled return bellow shook and rattled his psychic energy shields.

The ships were close enough that several of the Precursor machines attempted the electronic equivalent of boarding actions, assaulting the newcoming ship's firewalls and computers to crash the programs and destroy the hardware.

Instead of normal smooth logical code they found madness.

Shrieking, gibbering, raving, howling code raced through computers made up of bound and pierced and flogged and whipped screaming biological brains in bodies bent and twisted, burnt by Hellspace, their minds twisted by the ravening energy and from staring directly into the mad energy of that horrific place. Programs that shredded at one another even as they assaulted the computers that they should have used and the computers fought back screaming and raving with Hellspace energy coursing through their circuits.

THE GREAT EYE SEES YOU rang out in the Strategic Housings of the three Jotuns who touched those insane computer systems.

One opened fire on its supporting ships, blasting out gibbering code of madness infected binary sequences. One screamed out 10102001 100001110112 2002 2222 TWO TWO TWO at maximum broadcast power and began firing into its own hull and setting its servitor machines into ripping and tearing at its own superstructure. It used Hellfire cannons to carve a twisted and vile runes of electronic blasphemy that lurked in the depths of Hellspace into its own hull. The third triggered its self-destruct charge, vanishing in the momentary hell of a new sun spawning in the middle of *The Devourer that Leaves Darkness's* mathematically precise formation.

Before *The Devourer that Leaves Darkness* could do much more than cut the two insane ones out of the Fleet tactical net and recompute his battleplans all three forces of the feral intelligences opened fire on his own ships.

The Devourer that Leaves Darkness *ordered Hellspace jumps.*

Nothing happened.

***THE EYE RULES THE TWISTED CURRENTS OF HELLSPACE!* the** ships in the middle of his own formation, firing wildly, launching small attack craft, roared at him with a psychic scream of roiling madness and chaotic glee. *WE HAVE FOUND YOU FOR THE EYE! WE WILL BRING YOU BEFORE THE EYE! BEFORE THE EYE WE WILL BIND YOU!*

For a split second *The Devourer that Leaves Darkness* could not decide which fleet had priority. Then he ordered his subordinate units to fight. To destroy the feral intelligence who dared stand against them. *The Devourer that Leaves Darkness* released the inhibitors that only allowed carefully computed amounts of resources to be used to subdue and destroy opponents. His forces, ancient, massive, undefeated, outnumbered the opponents by a factor of ten.

Victory was his. It was as certain as radioactive decay and

just as predictable.

One the bridge of *The Bride of Despair* the human Captain, clad in heavy armor covered in spikes, chains, and vile twisted runes laughed, rich deep voice filled with malevolent glee, and ordered his gunners to go to maximum power, gave permission for the mat-trans to send out boarding parties, and ordered his Marines onto the boarding craft. No complex or far reaching orders, just orders to punish, to maim, to *hurt* the enemy. Complex calm orders were for those who had never tasted Hellspace deep in their soul.

Chaos was his bride. His lover.

War was chaos.

The human Captain, who no longer remembered why he fought, laughed in glee as his C+ cannons opened up on the enemy ships. As plasma cannons vomited fire, as his ship opened a hyperspace gate and lensed the compressed energy of a white dwarf's solar flare across the shields of one of the larger ships, the energy beam twisted and wound with Hellspace energy.

His only regret was that they were only machines and would not suffer.

Admiral Yamamoto watched the reports of the damage that the first four attacks had done to the vast Precursor ships. He knew they were heavily shielded, heavily armored, with solid superstructures that didn't need the open spaces and attendant machinery that a living crew would need, which made them immensely resilient.

It was of no matter. Terrans had lost battles, even been defeated, but they had never been *beaten*.

Captain Cheekeet stared at the images her implant was letting her watch. She rode a high-velocity torpedo through the darkness of space, dancing with the VI guidance program through starry space, slashing through point defense, and she held the VI's hand as she leaned forward and *kissed* the flank of a massive ship with her beak of collapsed inversion beam wrapped in nuclear plasma. From there she jumped to a tiny nanoparticle-computer, more waveform than mass, at the leading point of a

C+ shell skipping in and out of the lowest band of hyperspace, fighting and clawing and mocking the half-mad particles that screamed over the speed of light, mocking them, bobbing and weaving and dancing to lead them in a ravenous horde to reach out and touch the hull of another Precursor machine and laugh for nanosecond eternity as the particles followed.

She fluttered and preened and spread her wings wide, convincing an entire shoal of enemy missiles that she was, in fact, a Terran superheavy battleship, and when the enemy missiles detonated as one she laughingly mocked the launching ship's battle computer with a snippet of code and by touching the thousands of beams of coherent energy with a graviton generator, twisting them in the split second she had, twirling in place with her wings spread, to wind the energy together and use it to sweep across the very ship that had disgorged them.

Captain Cheekeet laughed and danced and flew and preened as her subconscious added her own dreams to the rapidly fluctuating chaos seed for the hashes and the encryption and the compression and the evasive maneuvers and the variable wavelengths and anything else that reached out and touched her, begging for attention, letting her look through its eyes.

She laughed as she held a C+ hammer in each hand and rang out a tune of wrath and hate on the hull of a Precursor Goliath, ringing out a tune of spite and anger with each C+ impact of the hammers she grasped in each wingtip. Each slam of the hammer blowing craters kilometers deep, tens of kilometers across, each ringing howling singing impact driving the crater deeper deeper ever deep into the hull of the Goliath.

The C+ battery finished impacting and she found herself in another system, a dodging spinning weaving bobbing attack craft who's chaos seed had expired and the oncoming Juton's point defense system was getting more and more accurate. She closed her wings tight around her and crouched down then lept into the air, spinning and spreading her wings out. She danced the mating dance, her steps sure and quick, ruffling her feathers, turning them so first one color then the other.

Everyone gangster till the Confederacy come around the corner, she giggled as she folded her wings halfway through the loop. She could see the floor, see the gleaming flashing circle of perfection, and she dropped straight into it, her feet touching. She felt the tip of the craft slam into the Jotun, felt it fire the nuclear penetrator charges, felt it fire the secondary plasma arrays, felt the ramming prow collapse, felt the density increased sharp ramming slice through armor. Felt the toothed gears around the prow engage, grabbing Jotun armor and pull the craft deeper as she danced and wove and sang in the perfect circle of light.

The boarding portals blew free and she felt the moltlings clustered around her stream out from her and gave a cry she had heard from a human mating video she had watched out of curiosity.

To the Jotun she cried out the phrase as she poured her hate in the form of armored warborgs into the Jotun's very body.

IT FEELS SO GOOD INSIDE YOU!

The Devourer that Leaves Darkness *ran the computation again.*

It was impossible.

Something was happening that had never happened before.

He reached deep, into his OEM cores, looking for something to help him in this situation.

He was losing...

CONFEDNAV COMMUNICATION

Joint Task Force Argo has engaged the enemy. Casualties are light and 80% below NAVINT estimations.

Battle should be concluded within 3 TerraSol standard days unless unprojected event occurs.

--Admiral Yamamoto, Commanding

---NOTHING FOLLOWS---

Unified Intelligence Council Memo

Despite the Terran Confederacy's claims so far they have not been able to defeat a single cluster of Precursor machines. Every time it becomes obvious that the machines may be defeated the machines leave the battle via unblockable travel technology.

Any claims of the Terran Confederacy defeating a Precursor Fleet should be considered propaganda.

--------END OF MESSAGE-----------

"Rear Admiral, the Unified Government System and the other Unified Civilized Races are fleeing the system," Scan-14 reported.

"Tell them to land back on the planet. I'm deploying the Dinochrome Brigade to protect the planets and the high orbitals," Rear Admiral T'kik'tak O'Malley snarled as best as Treana'ad voicebox would allow him. He loved the human snarl, so authoritative, so dominating.

The Matrons liked it too as he swaggered about in his Naval regalia during breeding cycles.

"They're refusing the Dinachrome Brigade landing permission. BOLO Daisy wants to know how to proceed," Com-5A reported.

"Order the landing. Transmit our authority. Order those transports back on the planet before one of them catches a stray round," Admiral O'Malley said, standing up from his crash couch. Terran's found it reassuring when the leader stood up and moved about the bridge, even if it put the Captain in danger and the flotilla was engaged in combat with the enemy.

"Dinachrome Brigade forces landing," Com-5A reported. "We be fully deployed in eighteen minutes."

"Flotilla Thirty-Eight reporting completion of deployment of Piranha Class Fishyboi Units around Facility Group Delta, are moving to Extraction Group Alpha," Com-22D announced.

Rear Admiral O'Malley clacked in anticipation.

"Jotun Gamma is in range," Scan-8 reported.

"All weapons ready," Tactical reported.

O'Malley loved this part. This moment right here. This perfect moment.

"ALL UNITS! OPEN FIRE!" He roared out in Confederate Standard. "ACTION FRONT, HELLDOGS! ACTION FRONT!"

O'Malley could feel his inner spaces twist and shudder in some reaction to the phantom passage of the C+ guns each of his ships had been built around. Each cannon was surrounded by a perfect octet of Virii Cannon, a nuclear detonation that was frozen just long enough to arrange in the particles in the nuclear detonation's guided and focused energy into layer after layer of viral code designed to assault the ship's computers and sensors in a split second before the C+ rounds hit.

He could *feel* the firing of the plasma wave phased motion cannons making up the eight rows of primary guns per ship. Feel the great pistons rocking back to compress the nuclear explosions.

By the Great Egg I love Terran's love of nuclear explosions, *he thought to himself as the guns of his 24 ship flotilla opened fire on the Jotun and its attendant ships.* So many different weapons wrapped around the most basic of equations.

Admiral O'Malley reached out with mind's eye, attempting to *feel* the enemy, get a sense of what its electronic brain was thinking.

The Jotun was rotating, seeking to spread the impacts of the Terran weapons as far as possibly apart, uncaring that it smeared nuclear fire across miles of hull. Anything to keep the weapons from pounding craters into craters into craters until the shots finally penetrated into interior spaces.

Admiral O'Malley blinked slowly, while his eyes were closed he blanket input from his implant for a split second. He had his implant feed him a split second, only a heartbeat of a hummingbird, virtualization of how it would look to see all the firepower that his flotilla could thunder forth coming down on his massive city sized body. He triggered his own personal creation, squirting a bit of chaos code into his brain, a writhing mass of CRC's taken from a thousand thousand human brainstem medical scans, his own personal icecream.exe. It slammed into his implants VR representation and shattered it into a trillion brillant motes that each writhed with his chaos.crc.icecream.

That split second was all O'Malley needed as his mind screamed and shuddered and he opened the opaque covers from his multifaceted eyes.

He *knew* what the Jotun would do next.

"ALL SHIPS CEASE FIRE!" He roared. "Point defense on local VI control!"

His brainstem was loading the fire orders and he strutted back and forth in front of his crew to generate a chaos seed based on how their primate eyes moved to follow him, how their pupils or camera lenses contracted or expanded, and the colors of their ocular organs or implants.

The Jotun leveled out, presenting its thinner side at O'Malley's flotilla and engaging its engines, charging the line. It was rotating, intending on smearing the human firepower across the thick mid-ship armor.

I saw you do that, monster, *Admiral O'Malley said.*

He went perfectly still in front of the main viewscreen and his crew unconsciously held their breaths, seeing the "FIREPLAN LOADED" on the upper corners of the viewscreen. Comm-22F opened the flotilla wide intercom, knowing what was about to happen.

He put his armored vac-suit blade arms against the viewscreen, tapping the display screen that his crew had covered with armorplas after the first few battles hard enough that the loud KLACK was audible across the entire flotilla's com-net.

The entire flotilla inhaled.

THERE IS ONLY ENOUGH FOR ONE!

Admiral O'Malley slammed his gripping hands against the screen and his voice joined the voice of the crews of every vessel in his flotilla as the fireplan was activated.

WE KNEW YOU'D DO THAT

The entire naval crew of the flotilla roared out, joining their voices with their admiral's.

The Confederate Navy trained its gunnery crews for pinpoint accuracy, hashed its VI's for precision, practiced constantly when they were not engaged in warfare, and demanded accuracy within meters with even their biggest guns. A gunnery crew chief whose crew missed the targeting coordinates too far too often would show the Captain's displeasure by drilling his beings until they molted, went bald, or had their scales fall out.

The Jotun, like most others, even though it was malign cold logical intelligence accepted that the laws of physics meant that you couldn't count on precision across such vast distances.

The Terran Confederate Armed Services grabbed physics by the throat and punched it in the face until it did what they wanted.

All the weapons, launched staggered and aimed so they'd arrive within split seconds of each other, driving into the plume of vaporized armor, each hitting the same target, driving deeper and deeper into the Jotun. Successive strikes pulled the vaporized armor after it into the deepening wound as the Jotun's inner spaces began being hammered.

Until the brutal brimstone hammers found the Helldrive and the vast magazines for the missile bays. Repulsor fields failed, kinetic fields collapsed, firewalls shrieked and died as the nuclear driven code slammed illogical commands into them. Deeper and deeper into the ship the impacts slammed through the ravening released energy, adding it to each new impact's fury.

The Jotun's Strategic Battle Housing watched helplessly as the explosions marched through the ship toward it.

The Jotun staggered, began to heel to the side, and exploded.

"Get me another target, Tactical," Admiral O'Malley said, stepping back from the viewscreen. He noticed his bladearms had knocked two tiny chips from the viewscreen's armorplas covering instead of cracking the entire thing and sent a message to Maintenance through his implant congratulating them on a job well done.

"I will pacify these Precursor machines through superior firepower and training, precision targeting, and the indomitable will of my crews!" He clicked out proudly, looking over his crew.

He didn't even turn around as the salvo launched from the dead ship sliced down on his ships and began being wiped away by point defense.

The Admiral knew his crews were skilled.

After all, they were the Confederate Navy.

The Precursor ships were only the enemy.

The enemy only existed to be destroyed.

Guest Captain Delminta gripped her Command Stick tightly, wishing her little sister was there to smack on as the ship shuddered around her. The twisting phantom tugging behind her eyes from the C+ guns twinged at her again and she clenched her teeth as the plasma wave phased motion guns fired again. Streak-Drive pounding kinetic missiles fired out and Delmina felt their launch under her nails. Judgement Class particle guns, firing the ravening particles of jumpspace matter exposed to antimatter focused in a beam, and God Thump Gravity Cannons fired and she felt her fur ripple in unconscious sympathy for the weapon fire.

Incoming rounds hit the ship she was on. Crashing against the shields, hammering on the the deflectors, slamming against the force projectors, impacting against the graviton fields. It went on and on and on as the ship accepted back as good as she was getting.

THERE IS ONLY ENOUGH FOR ONE

The Precursor Goliath screeched. The screech hit the shields, the psychic shields built into every vessel's hull and shielding since the Mantid War, and was absorbed, captured, twisted by the roaring bellow in the mind of every one of the Confederate Navy crew member.

Guest Captain Delminta jerked in an involuntary response as every living thing around her replied.

YOU WILL NOT LIVE TO ENJOY IT

The roar hit the Goliath, staggering its thoughts as the return psychic blow crashed through its defenses, seeming to gain more rage even as it shattered against the shielding.

The Goliath kept up the hammering of its guns. It had identified the battle code of the leader of the force arrayed against it and knew if you kill the queen the rest will die.

Delminta was thrown against the restraints in her crash-couch as something hit.

Hard.

"Ship breached, deck seventeen through deck twenty-three. Open to space. No casualties," The Damage Control officer called out. "Secondary shield generator is spun up to full power, cycling out primary for repair and cooling."

"Battleship Nyundo reports main reactors back online, primary string drive online, they're back in the fight!" a Com officer called out. "Captain Chiku transmits his regards and requests permission to rejoin the formation."

Delminta could barely keep track of the fight. She knew that if she activated her implant she could get a better picture of the crazed fury around her, but one glance at her right-hand aunt, who was twisting and shuddering in her armored vac-suit, her eyes closed and her fists clenched, and she could bear to even think of doing such a thing.

Of synching up, even slightly, to the Terran Confederate Navy Combat Gestalt.

Deminta's right-hand aunt Ementeeri, a Hamaroosan of advanced years but burning curiosity, had closed her eyes and allowed herself to sink into her implant. Around her the battle roared and she jumped from beam of light to beam of light, spreading out her arms and legs to her gliding flaps deployed, singing to the darkness as she flew, unfettered by gravity, swinging from the beams of light, alighting on the C+ shells and rolling with them to update their targeting, jumping through the shoals of missiles singing their new coordinates to them.

She had been warned against sinking so deeply. The implant kept telling her that she was too old, her vascular system too fragile, to continue doing it.

In the Unified Civilized Systems she would have been forced to leave, to no longer swing and jump through the raw howling fury of space unfettered and free.

Here, it was *her* choice, not the choice of a bureaucrat, law, or regulation. The AI only touched her fingertips to let her know she was not alone, that it was with her, did not force her to leave, and gave her a barrette to wear on her ear-tuft to tell the VI to leave her alone.

She was from a small people, who were considered flighty and foolish by the Unified Races Council, who had barely avoided corporate absorption.

But here, in this ravening howling screaming whirling madness of the Terran Combat Gestalt, she was free.

The blood from her ear went unnoticed as she hushed the medical VI by twitching her ear.

She was free.

and she would keep her right-hand niece and the rest of her family free.

The Grand Executor Council's men had taken her husband between a business meeting and their nest. Had told her that her husband had never existed. Had called her crazy.

But she remembered his face, his touch, his warmth next to her in their bed, as she danced in front of the thickly stacked school of torpedoes to lead them to their targets.

She didn't care that the VI was shrieking. It had shrieked that she was dying when she'd come aboard but the Captain, who understood that an old lady understood when her time had come, had silenced the VI and allowed her on board, had invited her aboard the ship, and shown her how to enter the Gestalt.

The ship's AI, who had determined that the elderly being was nearing biological termination, watched and waited, kept the pain from her, and let her dance and fly free.

And just watched her with one electronic thread of code.

As she flew.

and sang in the face of the Precursor machines.

The Precursor machine *The Devourer that Leaves Darkness* had done as the OEM code had demanded, had ordered the massive industrial plants of the Goliaths to begin producing more war machines, but they were wiped out as fast as the Goliaths could make them.

Of the twelve lesser Goliaths that had entered the fight with him, only two remained. He himself had taken terrible wounds, each wound targeted again and again, so that even his massive size was more of a hindrance than the massive advantage it had been.

As he watched one Goliath opened the great doors above the middle of the fabrication bay deep inside its hull to release a Jotun. Adding that Jotun to the fight in that location would change the combat statistics by a large amount, nearly nine percent.

A score of torpedoes, little more than stealth hulls wrapped around a single shot plasma wave phased motion gun that was surrounded by a circle of twenty missiles, laughed with glee, the warboi VI's dancing and capering as they observed what they had been told what was foreordained.

They left their shielding on until the last second, meaning that *The Devourer that Leaves Darkness* had no warning when the missiles fired on Streak Drives, slamming into the top of the Jotun and detonating less than a second after firing, just long enough for the massive guns at the center of the torpedo to fire.

The impacts blew straight through the Jotun and into the spaces inside the Goliath,

Two of the torpedoes, who's warbois were more cruel, shot through the two massive doors that had been sliding back, seizing them in their kilometer wide tracks.

The missile pod had drifted for a while. Unsure of quite what it was supposed to do. The main warboi had sneezed and now nobody could remember what to do, except to bite and tear at the big enemy ship.

But they hadn't seen a spot where a good bite would do

much good.

Now they did as the Jotun crashed into the boiling metal floor of the vast fabrication unit.

A small gliding marsupial appeared before the warboi VI, dancing and flying and swinging. It showed the missile pod something, something the little creature had seen through the boiling matter.

Something shiny, something sparkly, something curious. The warboi listened to the singer's song. What could it be?

The missile pod let the microgravity of the massive Goliath pull it inside the massive construction bay, wondering what the sparkly was.

It was a string. A long string. Of sparklies.

The missile pod quivered with electronic anticipation, waiting a long realspace second till the warboi realized what it was looking at. What the fading, but still smiling and dancing flying squirrel was showing the warboi VI.

As soon as it realized what it was seeing, it flushed the pod and fired the drive to turn itself into a kinetic projectile, following the flying squirrel as she swooped toward something wonderful.

Twenty-two missiles and a kinetic round moving at .33C slammed into the construction conveyor belt.

A belt revealed by the death of the Jotun.

A belt full of sparklies.

Because antimatter-thorium fusion reactors were kept warm.

The missiles hit the reactors.

The kinetic round hit the antimatter-thorium storage at .33C almost dead center of the Goliath as the singing dancing flying squirrel kissed the VI's forehead weakly and laid down to sleep.

The Goliath vanished in a boiling maelstrom of liberated molecules.

On the bridge of his flagship Admiral Yamamoto smiled as the expanding halo washed over the smaller ships, consuming them.

He ordered his comm section to send the line of code he had been waiting to send.

The Devourer that Leaves Darkness received a feral intelligence signal.

NOW YOU ARE ALONE
ALONE YOU SHALL DIE

Ementeeri did not as her soul flew free.

PRETTY BAD DAY

The dropship shouldn't have even been there.

It had been used as an escape pod, the ground forces gathered in their dropship according to protocol. The ship they had been on had been pounded to scrap, engines dead, main batteries down, AI dying, both the bridge and the combat bridge full of nothing but corpses, and the electronic systems failing.

The Mantid pilot had trusted it's implosion wire instinct and hit the thrusters, getting the Dropship "Pretty Day" out of the bay first, the others following. The Mantid pilot had trusted his "tingle" over the years and gotten 'his' Marines out of trouble and safely to the dropzone enough times that the rest of the dropships in the bay had launched with him..

An nCv cannon strike had grazed *Pretty Day* with its realspace shockwave, sending the dropship tumbling and falling through space. The little Mantid Damage Control Crews had swarmed out of the dropship and set to work with their tools, trying to reestablish the control runs, get the ship under control again.

Pretty Day tumbled through space, a dead stick.

The crew, however, were alive.

The beacon might have been fried out, the com-section might have exploded all over the Comtech, killing the technician with molten warsteel shrapnel, the engines might have been dead, the computer AI shattered, but the crew of the *Pretty Day* had merely ran function checks on their armor or cyborg bodies, checked their weapons, and made sure they were ready.

The Marines of the *Pretty Day* had faith in their Mantid crewmates.

"Remember your training and you will survive!" Colonel

Harvey Tiktalkik'ik von Jager shouted over the comlink to his men. "You are Confederate Marines, the enemy is nothing more than a gloried toaster that crawled out of a forgotten landfill!"

That was the moment the drives came online and the little Mantid techs swarmed back into the dropship, opening panels and getting to work. Two responded to repair requests, one working on a warborg knee actuator, the other checking the feed for one of the heavy mag-accelerator cannons.

When the Mantid pilot felt his controls go live he disconnected, waiting for the signal that it could be piloted on more than instinct or that the computer was completely fried. Long minutes ticked by and the Mantid pilot felt the tingle along his implosion wire.

They were going the right way. He knew it.

The Mantid techs gave him the go ahead signal and he reconnected to the system. The whole computer was shot through with holes, the VI's dead or still dying, but that was all right. He had more sensors then he'd have a few times. It took the engine three times to fire up, but fire up they did.

He took control, oriented himself, and followed the tingle of his implosion wire. The guns came live less than thirty seconds later.

The string drives of the boarding dropship were vibrating and howling as it spiraled through realspace on a direct course for the last of the Goliaths, the last of the Precursors, in the entire system. Its guns still thundered, its engines were still under power, and its armor still held.

The pilot, a tiny black Mantid with a strip of white stripes down its abdomen and an implosion wire thrumming down the length of its entire body, "saw" the opening through the link to the dropship's sensors. The copilot, a Hhrundarak of the same species that had bitten Fido eons ago, had his eyes closed, following the Mantid's directions as the ship jinked, jotted, and jumped through realspace. The Gunnery Chief of the dropship clenched and unclenched his massive hands, sweat soaking his black fur as his brain sorted through ten thousand signals and the gibbering of the overwhelmed VI's who's hashes were only half-baked. The Gunnery Chief's people were from the jungles Lost Congo, uplifted by genejacking by homo-eructus to join them in being terra-superior.

The dropship plunged through the vapor of boiled away armor, the debris shields holding as the Mantid spun the ship belly first until a millimeters thick layer of rehardened armor covered the belly shield. The sensors went blind as the dropshop exploited a pinprick wound through the armor and into the hull-spaces in the middle of lone remaining Goliath's underside.

The Mantid's implosion wire had sent the tingle. He had seen the pinprick hole at the bottom of the still boiling crater, he knew what to do.

He subconsciously cleaned his bladearms as his mind ran the ship's systems.

kick the tires and light the fires impact impact impact

It fired the retro thrusters, savage unshielded radiation pouring out of the thrusters as the dropship slowed, scraped an armored wall, and slammed to a stop.

The Mantid hit the drop door release and plasma mines flared off a split second before the doors slammed outward.

Colonel Jager led his men into the darkness of the Goliath's guts, all of them moving steadily, following the Colonel's orders.

"Data-cable there, Mantid-273 get your squad on it. Squad Two and Three, set up the crew served weapons down both hallways, it won't be too long before this thing's immune system realizes we're here," Jager ordered. "Mantid-273, find me the direction to this big bastard's brain. I want to personally shoot its last thought across the floor."

A dozen tiny green Mantids in their combat armor, carrying computing capsules, swarmed up the wall and began scanning the cable. Their helmets had additional psychic jammers wrapped around them and the necks braced so they couldn't turn their helmets, but the little Mantids didn't care. Their goal was right in front of them, a two meter thick data-cable they could feel pulsing with malevolent cold intelligence.

"Heavy Warborg squads, keep your optics peeled. I don't want any nasty surprises hitting us. Authorization for heavy weapons free authorized," Colonel Jager snapped. "Use your reflex triggers, Precursor machines are able to move faster than your conscious minds can process."

The Treana'ad Captain, in charge of eight Treana'ad and a Shard-627 rapidfire heavy omnigun and shielding, kept watch as his men quickly deployed the gun then the shielding.

He'd learned his first ground insertion that if worse came to worse the gun could provide shielding of the sort that anyone downrange understood.

"EMCOM, what's the VI status? Do they have to be re-hashed?" Jager asked.

"Hashing now," the EMCOM officer answered. "We grazed the edge of a nCv shot, it peeled open the armor and scrambled the VI bay. Any hashes we use now will only be half-baked."

"Step on it, EMCOM," Jager said, turning to watch his men go to work setting up somewhat of a base camp.

As if they'd be coming back.

Jager smiled.

Squad Three, all experienced Marines, started setting up their multibarrel 30mm autocannon. Jager watched them set up in the wide hallway, then looked around. He was starting to get an idea.

"Despair, is the nanoforge still running?" He asked over comms.

"Yes, sir," The black Mantid said. "Only about 3% slush. Idea?"

Jager smiled even though he knew the flight officer couldn't see him. "Reconfigure the dropship for treads and a grav pump to let us decide which way down it. I'm not about to walk 500 miles."

"Good plan, Colonel," The little Mantid said. "Reconfiguring. It'll take about twenty minutes, the nanoforges VI is pretty badly damaged."

"Do your best," Jager said.

Mantid 142 signaled him and he opened the channel.

"Interior cryptography is using a repeating algorythm on the internet wire only system. We've already broken it and are listening. This one is the last one and its fighting for its life, devoting most of its computing power and resources to defense. It's trying to break free and get either into Hellspace or maybe even jumpspace or just run away," The little Mantid's translation software sent the message via datasqueal. The entire statement of complex overlaid mathematical equations turned into Confederate Standard and packed into a microsecond directed burst.

"It's currently having its factories build repair drones instead of more fighting craft," The Mantid said via translation software.

"Good job, 142. You and your team stay on it," Jager said.

Mantid-086 flashed an icon to alert Jager that he had mapping updates and Jager signaled the go-ahead.

Mantid-086 had found eight different routes to something called the "Strategic Intelligence Housing" only fifteen clicks away.

Jager's grin grew larger.

"Reconfigure *Pretty Day* to *Bad Day* mode, Despair," He smiled. "Let's see just what a Strategic Intelligence Housing is."

The Devourer that Leaves Darkness was experiencing something new after over a hundred million years of electronic existence.

Fighting for his life.

He decided he really didn't like it.

Hellspace was full of howling barbarians that just kept arriving, feral intelligences that poured out of that region. *The Devourer that Leaves Darkness* could compute no reason for so many unshielded biologicals to be inside of Hellspace, acting as if it was some kind of breeding ground for their kind.

A recon drone had shown massive twisted ships waiting

just inside Hellspace, weapons somehow armed and ready despite all computations showing it was impossible.

Cattle should have broken off. It had destroyed over 11% of the armada's ships, yet all it did was seem to spur them to more and more fury.

Now *Devourer* was alone. No attendant ships, no repair ships, no refinery ships. Even trying to manufacture and deploy repair crawlers to move across the surface and fix the damage did no more than just lose precious resources as anything that moved on *Devourer's* surface was eliminated within minutes by the constant bombardment of missiles, rain of coherent energy, and incoming torpedoes.

It had seen what happened when the massive deployment bay doors were opened. Four Goliaths had been destroyed by attempting to deploy Jotuns or Devastator class support ships and the feral intelligences had responded with accurate bombardment fire into the open bay doors, striking directly at the internal factories and industrial resources.

Devourer had loaded all his supplies of antimatter into torpedoes and missiles after suspecting that the feral intelligence was somehow detecting the unique signature anti-matter possessed and were using it for targeting solutions.

It hadn't seemed to matter, the feral intelligences had only stepped up their attacks, the anti-matter warheads, all of various different types of matter, had been blown out of space before they could get close enough to matter.

But *Devourer's* self-defense programs felt better about not taking any chances. If they were detecting anti-matter, then the anti-matter self-destruct charge became a targeting beacon rather than a failsafe.

It settled for an inversion charge along its super-computer lobes.

Later, when it had the time, it would come up with new security systems, go over the footage of the battle and analyze it to determine the feral intelligence's weaknesses, determine the best course of attacking them and of countering their technology.

But that was for later. Right now, *Devourer* had to fight its way out of the pounding encirclement it had found itself in.

It ran another scan, ran the computations, and determined with a 90% probability it could...

Internal motion sensor went off as a stealth field slipped up for a moment. Something had crossed a slightly buckled section of hallway and before the craft moving through the passageway could compensate for the buckling.

The object is only 250 meters from the Strategic Intelligence Protective Housing! *The computer realized with shock. It realized that it had been...*

...

...

it searched for long seconds, devoting valuable processing resources, to finding the word, and from the word to the files that had instructions on how to adapt to the situation.

Those processing cycles being taken out of the defense loop ended up destroying a dozen fighter recover/launch bays as the protections faulted for only a few seconds.

Boarded. I've been boarded. My body invaded. The instructions were clear. Send ground combat units through the internal maintenance spaces to combat the invaders.

The models it was supposed to send had all been recycled, deemed unfit for the battlefield as the war had gone on over a hundred million years ago.

It wasn't able to build more, the anti-matter thorium for the fusion reactors all purged and no other energy source had the power to move the combat machines.

The Devourer that Leaves Darkness realized that it had only massive ground combat machines, the kind used to destroy cities, in the area.

The machine had no choice, it sent maintenance and repair constructs flooding down the inner spaces toward the contact.

His logic subprocessors insisted on another scan of the

hallway and when nothing was revealed insisted there was nothing there, that it had been a minor glitch due to the ongoing battle damage due to the raging hellstorm it was being subjected to.

Devourer ignored the logic subprocessors and sent every available repair and maintenance robot to the sensor trace.

It was feeling something new. Something it had never felt within its processors before.

Colonel von Jager moved up next to the little green armored Mantis scout. It was crouched down, shivering, and flashing a holoicon for distress behind it. He looked into the space beyond the access port the little technician had discovered and picked the lock for.

Beyond was an amphitheater of some kind. Seating for dozens, hundreds of Mantids. Not the small ones, the little former slave caste, but the bigger ones, the Speakers and the Thinkers, maybe even immature Queens. There was a holoprojector in the middle, inactive, but Jager could see Mantid markings from where he was standing. He 'squinted', bring up his telescopic feature, and carefully panned over the podium and the holoprojector.

If they survived, this was the kind of data that CONFED-INT sported big throbbing erections for.

"Let's go, Mantid-zero-five-two, it can't hurt you, I won't let it," Jager told the little technician, thumping the door control, which was at chest level for him.

Mantid-052 chirped with gratefulness and backed away from the closing door.

"At Point Sierra," came the whisper across the small point to point communications relays.

Jager sent the icon for affirmative and hustled toward the rally point, feeling the little Mantid climb up his back to hitch a ride.

Twenty meters of hustling and the *Bad Day* was in sight.

The Mantid techs were examining the wall where the hallway ended, where logic said there was an entrance to the Strategic Intelligence Array. Instead there was nothing but thick armor.

"The Green Boys say it's compressed hyperalloy sandwiched with some stuff they've never seen before. They figure it's about ten meters thick," his XO, Major Ventor told him.

"Blow it open, I wanna see this thing's brain," Jager said, pausing so the Mantid tech that had hitched a ride could climb down.

"Nothing we've got can penetrate it. The Green Boys think it'll take about 1.5 kiloton explosively forged penetrator with a density collapsed tungsten inversion cone to blow a hole big enough to get through it," Ventor said. "Nothing we've got can apply that kind of power without killing all of us in the hallway."

Jager looked at the *Bad Day*, then at the wall. He triggered his com-link to Despair.

"Run up what we need through the creation engine. We'll back off five hundred meters, board the *Bad Day*, and blow this sucker's skull clean open," Jager said. He triggered his platoon com. "Everyone aboard the..."

That's when the machines hit.

Jager realized eight seconds into the fight, with the ease his men and the gunports of the *Bad Day* were tearing through the disorganized defenders, that these weren't combat machines, that these were whatever lay beyond that armored wall's final defense.

His men had made too many landings, fought on too many worlds, for the non-combat machines to even do much more than force ammunition expenditures.

"Got a fusion lance, that'll do it, sir," Despair reported at his weapon officer's suggestion.

They boarded *Bad Day* quickly, moving to the gunport irises that Despair opened up, interlocking their fire and coordinating their defense.

The tracks clattered as the dropship, reconfigured into an assault craft, backed up, crushing the smaller defenders under the armored treads, crushing the wreckage of the bigger defenders at the assault craft's gunner destroyed them.

"FIRE IN THE HOLE!" the gunnery officer called out.

The Devourer that Leaves Darkness saw the armor of his housing explode inwards, watched in the slow motion an AI moves through the physical world in.

He tensed to repel them from his housing, ordering the repair and maintenance robots in the chamber to defend him.

Programs *Devourer* didn't even know were there came to life. They sent a single signal to the very thing that *Devourer* had built in defiance of logic and reason.

The implosion wire across the intelligence lobes triggered. The auditorium and the attached databanks exploded. In that crystallized burning microsecond, *Devourer* realized what he had been feeling growing in his lobes.

Fear.

The Devourer that Leaves Darkness died before it even knew it lost.

CONFEDNAV MEMO

Captured multiple intact hulls, including Harvester Class Goliath. Am conducting security sweep of system. Recently allied xenospecies effective during battle.

Moving to liberate planet from occupying force and assist native species.

Admiral Yamamoto - Commanding

---NOTHING FOLLOWS---

OLD IRON FEATHERS

Na'atrek was born on one of the Inner Systems. From a factory world that produced everything from TriVid systems to tank parts to diapers to pesticide, Na'atrek had known that he had two choices in life. Either start working at the factory floor after six years of school, get good grades and get high enough in education to qualify as a manager, or become a citizen.

His father had died on the factory line. A high-pressure chamber had thrown a bolt, it had shot through eight Ulvinstren on the line and almost turned them inside out. His mother had been informed that she had priority if she wanted her husband job and the rest of the living block had been informed that eight new positions had opened up.

His mother had died on the way to work. Struck by an executive's limo and killed instantly.

Na'atrek and his siblings were billed for the damage to the limo. They were already in debt and Na'atrek and his three siblings still had two years of schooling to do before they were adults. That meant time in the Corporate Creche, which they would be billed for once they began working. By the time school ended, they already each owed six year's pay to the Corporate Financial Agency. That meant no further schooling and they were expected to go to work in the factories.

Na'atrek was sent to an orbital refinery where he learned new meanings of Hell. His little sister was put in the pleasure dome and took her own life a year later. His brother, hatched at the same time, was killed when he fell from a catwalk (there were no railings) and into the metal grinder. Ha'atrek and his brother were billed for the idle time and the cleaning expense. His brother died a year later when the hab he was staying in suffered a spontaneous rupture, killing 243 of the 600 workers, the entire amount who were not on shift.

Na'atrek decided the only way he would get old enough to see his own eggs hatch was to try to become a citizen. During a recreation time he went into the offices and took the tests. It took three months, using up his entire recreation period each day, and his supervisors mocked him and wrote him up for poor Company Esprit, docking his pay.

At the end of it, the Citizen Office gave him two choices: Corporate Security or the Unified Military Forces.

He choice the military.

The choice between being dumped on a random planet and passing the military testing drove him. He knew he wouldn't be automatically selected as an officer like those from the Unified Civilized Species, he was classified as a neo-sapient species.

But he studied. And he studied hard. He took the tests, exercised in his free time to score higher, and did everything asked of him without a single complaint. Where the beings of the Unified Civilized Species would complain and refuse to do work or training, Na'atrek did everything asked of him without a complaint.

He watched his "civilized" classmates get testing scores that allowed them to be whatever they wanted, even officers. The rest of the neo-sapients were offered such things as the military equivalent of a janitor, a secretary, or a bootlicker.

The instructor checked his scores twice. He had something different.

Power Armor Pilot (Airmobile).

He took it.

His first day the shower stripped off his feathers. His beak was removed, an extremely short prosthetic grafted to allow him to breath correctly and keep his mouth and sinuses from being a mucus covered hole and he received a feeding port. His claws were removed. A dataport was sunk into the base of his skull.

Just like everyone else.

What followed was a year of what everyone else considered grueling training.

But Na'atrek had worked at the orbital yards for four years, in a vac-suit made up of more patches than original material, eating thin gruel, and living in habs without gravity. His species were flightless bird/lizard hybrids but the small part of his brain that remembered flying came alive during training.

The trainers watched him excel where most of the others failed out.

In the end, out of 1,400 beings, he was one of 120 who finished.

He found it ironic that his 'contract' was purchased, at great expense, by the same corporation who had charged him since robots turned his egg to make sure he was smoothly warmed. Even more amusing to Na'atrek, the company could not garnish his wages and the Unified Military Forces would pay the entire debt after two years of service, which had been swollen by the deaths of his siblings and the fact the company charged him the cost of training his replacement and the replacements first year wages.

Even more amusing was when the Executives rioted and the System Most High had sent in the Unified Military Forces he had purchased contracts for.

Na'atrek's squad mates cheered him on as he executed the Executive who had ran down his mother as she walked down the sidewalk, crossing three lanes of oncoming traffic to kill her as she walked with her arms full of groceries.

Na'atrek had spent nearly fifty years in the Unified Military Forces, his debt long paid, earning officer rank, being sent to schools, getting longevity therapy, and his contract price increasing. At twenty-years he was entitled to 10% of his contract fee, with his share rising by 0.5% every year, with bonuses for schools and rank. He knew beings who had come from places just like he did that earned 120% of their contract fee in bonuses.

He always turned down selecting his own duty station

and took the 0.05% contract rate increase every five years. He piloted a single-man recon and air cavalry suit capable of MACH 3 in standard atmosphere at standard gravity and armed well enough he could destroy a building with ease. His enhanced strength meant he could tear open vehicles with his bare hands and a stomp from his armored foot could crush the engine of a limo.

Na'atrek thought himself and his men as hardened combat troops.

When the word went out that the Precursor Machines were advancing steadily toward the world he was stationed on to enforce the security of the factories, he was not worried. He and his men were the best Air Mobile unit in the entire Unified Military Fleet.

Then the Terrans arrived.

Na'atrek didn't think anything of them at first. They called themselves "V Corps (Old Blood)" and wore the markings of a blue pentagon cut into five separate triangles with a border. Their fleet carrier was 5th Fleet USCSG (Old Blood) and their air units were 18th Air Wing (Atomic).

None of that impressed Na'atrek. He was 12th Air Mobile, a new corporate military force. Outfitted with the best armor, weapons, and ammunition the Unified Military Fleet could provide. His men were the toughest, with the most experience, and he drilled them ruthlessly, known as "Old Iron Feathers."

The Terrans had offered to conduct joint training operations. Na'atrek's supervisor turned them down. He could see no reason to expend military/corporate resources for practice. The Precursors had been stopped in many systems, they would be stopped here.

The Terrans dug in, creating interlocking fire bases, forward operating bases, logistics bases. The interlocked and trained with the various parts of V Corps (Old Blood), undergoing training constantly.

Na'atrek wasn't impressed by Terran tech. It seemed slow, clunky, and only seemed to fire lasers.

He wasn't impressed by the 'vaunted' Terran Confederate Armed Services.

In briefings he was told that the Precursors would follow standard, most logical attack patterns. Arrive at the jump boundary, sweep inward, forcing 5th Fleet USCSG (Old Blood) to engage them at range in the outer system. Reports of the Precursor machines being able to jump inside the boundary were anti-Unified Civilized Council propaganda and was ignored as such. The Unified Naval Fleet (Corporate) would support 5th Fleet, stopping any "breakouts" toward the inner system. His troops, non-space capable, would be on the primary manufacturing world and support combat operations to protect corporate assets, of which the population was not part of.

The battle plan was transmitted to the TCAS.

The TCAS AI's rejected it.

Na'atrek had been in the offices of System Command, had watched the System High Most's face when the TCAS AI had put a laughing face emoji over the entire dataplan and kicked it back.

Na'atrek felt personally insulted that even when he put in his own battleplan for Air Mobile, it was rejected. No emoji, but still rejected. The AI refused to answer questions, just stated that the plan was incomplete and inadequate and the AI would not forward it to his biological superiors in Fleet Command. The System High Most had reminded the Terran Fleet Command that he was in charge, to which the AI simply put up its wallpaper.

The System High Most was still holding a focus group meeting when the alarms went off. Na'atrek was a professional, he excused himself, taking only an hour which was borderline rude, and headed for his command post. He donned his armor and rushed into the situation room to find red lights flashing and his men staring at the carefully crafted Corporate approved plan that had gone so wrong.

The Precursors had arrived.

The rumors had turned out to be fact.

A massive weight of metal slammed into the system. Twelve Goliaths at the outer planets, twenty at the mid-point of the system, fifteen in the Green Zone, and ten between the first planet and the star. As Na'atrek watched the system scanners reported that five Goliaths were heading for each world, with the moons each having one approach. The Goliaths were all shedding Jotuns, Devastators, Demolishers, Juggernauts, and other craft even as they approached.

Na'atrek ordered the Air Mobile base VI, the best Corporate money could buy, to run a predictive combat analysis. Hours passed and 12th Air Mobile waited patiently for the war-codes for their armor to be transmitted. As he watched, his men waiting, a Devastator landed only fifty miles away, crushing a city of 2.2 million under its bulk. The predictive combat analysis array double-checked with the overloaded System Defense VI, waited nearly 12 minutes, and finally had its plans approved. It loaded their attack profiles into the power armor of the Air Mobile unit and gave them the war-codes for the armor.

Na'atrek and his men launched only three minutes before an orbital missile strike managed to penetrate the ground defenses and destroy his base, his logistics, and his supporting units.

12th Air Mobile was on its own.

Their orders, from a System Defense VI that was processing data up to a two hours old, had them going against a Devastator that the predictive VI assured them did not have its anti-air (ground to air or air to air) or point defense systems running or interlocked yet.

They flew to 34,000 feet, their max ceiling, and Na'atrek looked down at the chaos below.

Massive Terran combat robots vomited nuclear fire from their jaws, fired particle beams from shoulder mounted cannons, and scores of heavy missiles from their chests, filling the air with high-tech death. Super-stadium sized tanks rushed toward the Devastator, and as Na'atrek watched nearly a half dozen exited the sea and began pouring fire into the Devastator. Huge combat robots engaged Precursor machines and the hundreds of missiles the Precursor was firing at the Terrans and the city Na'atrek was supposed to protect was being cut down by a mathematically precise air defense system.

"What are you doing?" A sudden voice asked. "You are not interlocked."

"Who is this? This is the Most High of the 12th Air Mobile Combat Team. I demand you identify yourself," Na'atrek answered.

"You can call me Oracle-872, I was assigned to you to try to interlock you into the BatTacNet," The voice answered. "You're in the meat-grinder zone."

"Our battle computers have predicted this is the way to get closest to the machine. We shall strike at it and disable its guns," Na'atrek said, unable to keep the sneer from his voice.

"Yeah, you do that? You're gonna die. You're about to pass under a Djinn Class Precursor. That's an air superiority unit and you're blocking the shots from the Dinochrome Brigade. File a combat plan, please," The voice said.

"Under which authority?" Na'atrek snapped.

"Terran Confederate Armed Forces. We're responsible for the defense of this system and the planets," The voice, Oracle, said.

"WE are responsible for the defense," Na'atrek started.

"Look, buddy, no offense, but you're wearing search and rescue gear, not combat gear. If the thermal bloom from the Dinochrome Brigade's shots doesn't knock you out of the air, that Djinn will," Oracle snapped. "Drop to two hundred meters, get under their point defense scanners. I'll try to hook you into the BatTacNet," Oracle said.

Na'atrek almost choked on his outrage. His men had the best equipment money could buy and the Unified Military Forces could provide. "I will do no such thing."

"You are ordered to drop to two hundred meters and file a battle plan. Any deviation from these orders can result in friendly fire or unsupported enemy contact," Oracle's voice was stuffy. "Get those SAR suits out of there, you can't do anything but get in the way."

"I will do no such thing," Na'atrek answered.

"Then file a battle plan," Oracle answered. "You have about fifteen seconds before you get in range of the Djinn's guns."

"I will not. This is a Precursor trick. Disengage from my network," Na'atrek ordered.

"Your funeral," Oracle answered. "I loaded an evasion plan. Use it. Oracle, out."

Na'atrek ignored it, ordering his men to hold formation.

Who did the Terrans think they were? His battle plan had been formulated by the best predictive analysis VI that money could...

The world shattered. The Dinochrome Brigade held their fire, tried to provide point defense for the 12th Air Mobile Wing, held off their fire as long as they could.

Na'atrek's men lasted just over 11 seconds, mainly because constant training saved their life the first five seconds, Na'atrek forwarded Oracle's evasion plan, and some of them got to at least load the EMCOM and EW profiles.

The Djinn raked them out of the sky like a flock of birds.

Decades of experience allowed Na'atrek to land, his upper intakes blown away, missing a stabilizer wing, his point defense ripped away, and missing his right hand micromissile launcher. He got to his feet, took two steps forward, unlimbering his magnetic accelerator cannon, and brought up his sensors.

Everything was hash. The only thing that worked was optical and the smoke and haze cut that down to only a mile even with his armor's enhancement package.

A round bounced off the arm of an armored warborg that Na'atrek could barely see with a flash of sparks and a thunderous impact.

And blew open Na'atrek's armor, rupturing his abdominal wall, sending shrapnel from his armor into his torso, and throwing him nearly fifty meters.

He landed in a crater.

He laid there for a long moment, staring up at the sky. It looked like dueling beams of light. Air mobile suits, like his only chunkier and heavier feeling, roared by overhead, less than ten meters off the ground.

"Hey, you alive?" Oracle's voice sounded.

Na'atrek opened his com-link but could only groan. His diaphragm was ruptured and one of his lungs collapsed, not to mention many of his hollow bones in his chest were broken.

"OK, hang tight, I'm sending you and the twenty-three men that survived medical care. Your suits don't have the on-board systems to handle the kind of damage all of you took," Oracle said. "You know that your med-kit's drugs are more or less water, right? Your supplier ripped you off."

Na'atrek just groaned.

One of the massive combat robots stepped over him.

"OK, help's on the way, I had him drop some fiends. Just stay put. Stay with me, champ. I'm putting Med-Com on the line. It's a VI, but he's good, all right?" Oracle said.

A new voice broke in. "Hello, Commander. I'm Nightengale-6021, a medical VI. Let me just access your armor's systems... and... there we go," The voice said.

Na'atrek watched as his face-shield, cracked and de-powered, suddenly came back on. It displayed his armor's status, his vitals, and a scan of his body and his body suit.

"OK, you're going to need outside help," The voice said. "I've got someone coming to help you right now. You may start to feel dizzy, that's not from bloodloss, that's a bioweapon, two chemical weapons, and shock. Don't worry, your new friend has the counteragents to all that. I'm going to shift your armor into trauma position for your species."

Na'atrek just groaned as the armor suddenly stretched his arms out, put his legs in the optimal position, and locked the joints.

"There you go, stay with me, champ. OK, here comes your new friend. I'm going to stay on the line, but you'll be OK. I've got a medical retrieval unit heading your way," Nightingale said. It paused for a moment. "Man, going out there in SAR gear, that's fucking brave."

Na'atrek wanted to protest, but he was getting dizzy and feeling like he was burning up. His mouth felt dry and he kept seeing streaks of color.

When the little robot slipped over the lip of the crater, Na'atrek giggled even though he wanted to scream. It moved down the crater wall like it liquid, staying low, emitting no signals. He watched it move up and a face appear. It was feline, with long whiskers that were glowing faintly. As he watched it ejected a half-dozen tubes.

The air filled with chaff, micro-prism cloud, and EM pass-through nanites.

The small robot, four legged with a tail it stuck up into the air, moved up. He *felt* it brush his guts with its whiskers, then lick something inside him.

The pain went away.

It began kneading his intestines, pushing them back into the rupture, hacking up some kind of blue foam into the wound.

Na'atrek didn't feel like panicking. He liked the little robot. He'd always liked little robots, but this one he liked especially. He knew it wasn't hurting him as his intestines pushed back into the muscle. The blue foam soaked into his guts and he could suddenly breathe easier. It horked up more stuff, this stuff mottled brown and black, like the dirt of the crater he was in, and he felt it harden over his wound.

He trusted the little robot, liked it a lot. They were friends, after all, and friends took care of each other.

The little robot sprouted fur, short hairs, and moved under his unresponsive hand. He discovered that his hand was moving, petting the warm soft fur, and it began to make a subsonic rumble that made him feel better.

Every few minutes it would deploy more chaff and cloaking.

A large armored vehicle pulled up and two warborgs, with a red crescent on one side of the chest and a red cross on the other, jumped out. They grabbed him as the robot moved to his chest, and carried him into the vehicle, which was firing weapons through gunports.

They got him in and he could see some of his men, in cradles, in there, each with a furry little robot on their chest.

"We're over-full. This is the last of them, get us out here," One of the borgs yelled in the audible range.

Another one leaned over Na'atrek, hooking wires and tubes to his exposed flesh, using laser cutters to slice away his beautiful armor.

"Taking SAR gear out there, that took balls, buddy," The medborg said. "We'll get you back to MedCom, get you fixed up. You'll be back pulling SAR and saving lives by tomorrow."

Na'atrek fell asleep before he could answer.

When he woke up, less than eight hours later, his body fixed as if he'd never been injured, he found out that the Corporate Military Council had attempted to flee the system and the entire system was under the authority of the General of V Corps (Old Blood). The Unified Military Services were either dead or had attempted to flee and were under arrest.

Na'atrek didn't know whether to be ashamed or not.

Not for his men. Not for himself.

But for the actions of the Unified Military Services. Who had thrown men like the 12th Air Mobile Wing away as they'd tried to flee for their own lives.

He sat, with his men, in a dining facility, and listened as his men wondered.

Did it have to happen the way it did?

He knew the answer.

No.

The Unified Military Council determined that the failure of the Unified Military Armed Forces at the battle of Ludmira'ak-624 was the fault of the Terran Military Forces, who had only presented unreasonable system defense plans and refused to follow the orders of the System High Most.

Unified Military Council has determined that the Terran

Military Forces Command is, at best, incompetent and have put forth the demand that all Terran Military Forces be put under local command rather than Joint or Autonomous Commands.

V CORPS (OLD BLOOD) REPORT

System under heavy attack. Over fifty (50) Goliaths and supporting ships attacking all planets and facilities. Local forces outmatched, outgunned. Will rearm, retrain, and return to combat what local forces we can. More integration with local forces is recommended to all (Old Blood) units. Civilian casualties are expected to be moderate to high despite best efforts. Suggest deployment of Nagasaki Class Drill Shelters for civilians in all sectors as Corporate shelters exist only on paper and tax forms.

We will hold the line.

---NOTHING FOLLOWS---

SHOT OUT!

The room was full of tension as Ekret walked in. He was proud of his uniform and rank, the High Most of the Heavy Armor Division, proud of the way everyone turned and nodded at him. He was the unstoppable bulwark that the enemy could not breech, the thundering guns that destroyed the enemy at range, and friend to the infantry. He had fought on a dozen worlds, commanded tanks since he was barely an adult, and had risen to an exalted rank for a neo-sapient.

"What is the issue?" Ekret asked the High Most of the Infantry. He was one of the Unified Civilized Races, a four hoofed, four armed, six eyed Lanaktallan with mouth tendrils, jowls, and inflatable crests. The High Most of the Infantry, named Moolowin, was of the same race as most of the High Mosts except for Ekret and Old Iron Feathers, but Ekret demanded respect as the commander of armored hovertanks that weighed nearly 150 tons each.

"The Terran Confederate Armed Forces have arrived. They call themselves 'Old Blood' and 'V Corps' and we of the Unified Military Council are trying to discern just how their chain of command and order of battle works," Moolowin answered, his tentacles tight with anxiety but his crests inflated with anger. "So far they have refused to turn over command to our System Defense High Most, citing that Terran military forces are always under the control of Confederacy commanders, never local governments. That is outrageous. Even if you disregard the fact that the Unified Civilized Races Council is far older than the Confederacy with a larger population, these are our systems, not theirs. They should respect our claims and turn over command of those units."

"Mmm," Ekret answered, staring at the holotank showing the system. Ekret didn't agree. Tanks were precision instruments of mass destruction that required skilled, dedicated, educated, and experienced commanders to avoid major problems. If the Terrans were as fearsome as their reputation was whispered about in the barracks pods he could understand their unwillingness to turn over command of their war machine.

That's a lot of ships, Ekret thought to himself. They were already deploying and Ekret appreciated the tight formations, the smooth coordinated way the Terran fleets moved, and how their first instinct was to identify weak points and shore them up.

"Do they have armor?" Ekret asked.

"They claim to have armored units. They plan on landing mixed units. Something called BOLO's are kept separate from the other armored units. They claim that a mere dozen BOLO's will work to hold the machines at bay on this world with the weight of their 'heavy metal' they're landing," Na'atrek, Old Iron Feathers himself, whispered. "I feel for you, having to deal with such arrogance."

"Admiral, I must insist you put your forces under my command," The System High Most was saying in one corner of the holotank.

"No, sir. I will happily interlock your planning with my own, but it would take time to catch you up to speed on our capabilities, much less our way of making war. If you would, sir, transmitting your battle plan to us will allow us to work seamlessly with your forces," The Terran was saying. He was represented merely by a pentagon sliced into 5 blue triangles surrounded by a black pentagon on a white background.

"As System High Most it is I who should be deciding the war plan," the Lanaktallan said, his tentacles trembling in rage. "You know nothing of this star system."

The Terran Admiral merely gave a sigh, which the translator reported as a sound of frustration and resignation or relief.

"System High Most, I'm going to explain this to you one

more time. My forces are everything from parasite carriers with high penetration parasite vessels and heavy bomber parasite vessels. I have troop landing transports, portable logistics bases, field medical hospitals, everything I need to carry out a defense of this system," The Terran Admiral paused a moment. "To put it plainly, System Hind Most: I don't need you any more than I need burrs in my silky soft fox's tail. I'll let you coordinate with the Battle Tactical Net Artificial Intelligence until you can come to grips with reality."

"Hello, I am Xerxes-331, Digital Artificial Sentient. I am here to," A new voice said as the Terran commander's icon winked out and a new one appeared that looked the same but was overlaid on a system map.

"An AI? I don't want to talk to a collection of wires and circuits. Get someone sentient back on this call at once!" The System High Most yelled.

"What? How rude! I'm a fully sentient being who chose to be in the military, not some hash-creche tailor made VI! You apologize right this second," The new voice said.

"I most certainly will not. Return that arrogant and rude Terran commander to this call at once, you posturing computer program!" the System High Most roared out, his crests inflated, raising up on his rear hooves and pawing the air with his forward ones.

"I am not a computer program, I am a Digital Sentience, classified as Homo-Digitalus," The voice, Xerxes, answered stuffily.

"Stop arguing with me! I am the System High Most, and you will respect me, you jumped up answering service! Now put the Terran High Most back on the line!" the Lanaktallan insisted.

"Due to your repeated violations of the Terran Legal Code regarding Digital Sapience, I must now inform you that all contact between our two offices shall only be done through writing. Please submit your battle-plan for integration within twelve standard hours. Xerxes-331 out," The icon vanished, replaced by an electronic inbox with a timer.

"You get someone back on the line right this instant!" The System High Most roared at the communication technicians.

"Ahem, may I be excused?" Ekret asked.

The System High Most turned and stared at Ekret, but he'd stared into the barrels of enemy plasma cannons, he wasn't perturbed by the System High Most's glare.

"Yes. It is doubtful your armored units will be needed," The System High Most harumphed.

Ekret saluted, turned, and left, thinking.

Actual sapient AI's? Without them going insane and homicidal? Ships capable of acceleration far above what I've seen out of our fleet vessels? I need information and the System High Most is like most of his race, too arrogant to see what his six eyes show him, *Ekret thought to himself as he climbed into his staff car. He mumbled to his driver to take him back to Armor Command and leaned back in his seat, grooming his closely shaved fur with his hands as he thought.*

Ekret went over his forces. Two thousand heavy tanks, three thousand medium tanks, five thousand light tanks. While he didn't have control over the armored personnel carriers, he still watched over the nearly ten thousand of them. The best the Corporation could buy from the Unified Military Services.

Our equipment is purchased from the Unified Military Services. While they may be the best money can buy, the UMS only produces what sells the most. Do the Terrans approach war and the military in the same way? If they do not, are they required to each purchase their own vehicles or does a corporate or government provide them? How has this changed their approach to warfare, war material, strategy and tactics? *Ekret wondered to himself. He triggered his implant to give him his VR desk and requested the comlinkages for the Terran Battle Tactical Network, using his own office's ID code with the messages.*

He was surprised to get back the code within five minutes and even more surprised to find out that a VI had been assigned to him as a liaison due to the fact that the System High Most had not approved the linkage. Sighing, he disabled the vest and used his implant to connect to the linkage.

"Greetings, gentlebeing. I am Zhukov-442, Armored vehicle command liaison," a pleasant voice with a curt sounding accent answered. "Who do I have the pleasure of communicating with?"

"I am Ekret, Armored High Most, Unified Military Forces, attached to the Kestimet Corporation," Ekret said carefully. The voice sounded old and very formal. "I am pleased to make your acquaintance."

"A fellow armor commander. That is good to hear. I am responsible for interlocking your battle plans with the battle plan of the Terran Confederate Armed Services assigned to protect this system," The voice said. Ekret noticed a slight sound of what he interpreted as pleasure in the other's voice. "When you are in a secure area, we will go over necessary information. Do your prefer artificial sentience or physical beings to liaison with?"

Ekret thought for a moment. He was pretty sure this Zhukov was an artificial intelligence, and from the speech mannerisms and tone Ekret was pretty sure it was an old one.

"Can I have both, Honored Zkukov?" Ekret asked.

"I will assign an armor liaison. May I attach a maintenance unit to your forces in order to ensure that you are fully combat ready? I mean no disrespect to your current logistics but I have found that what High Command thinks a soldier needs to fight a war and what is really needed are two different things," Zhukov said.

Ekret barked a laugh. "But honored sir, I allocated exactly as many plasma rounds as there are enemy vehicles. How can you be out of ammunition?"

"Exactly, sir," Zhukov answered. "Am I to understand this is not your first combat engagement as a force leader?"

"No, Honored Zhukov, it is not. It is my experience that more battles are won or lost by the logistics corps than most commanders will admit," Ekret said, smoothing the fur on his legs.

"My own biological ancestor, the once-living being I was

templated off of originally, would certainly agree with that. He lived prior to our current post-scarcity existence," Zhukov said. "To coin a phrase from ancient Terra: For the want of a nail a shoe was lost."

"I do not understand the reference," Ekret stated. The AI uploaded a chain of events that started with the loss of a horse-shoe nail due to poor blacksmithing, resulting in the loss of the shoe, which resulted in the laming of the horse, which caused the rider to fall out of formation, which then caused a hole in the formation, all cascading into the loss of a kingdom. A second one referred to ancient cavalry riders keeping a nail in their pockets to spike enemy guns they'd overran, and one rider did not have a nail, and so the cannon was used to knock out that rider's cannons, resulting in the loss of the battle and the death of a Most High.

I shall frame this and put it in my office, Ekret thought to himself. He had lost tanks to the lack of bearings for the hover-fan systems. Once a corporation had skimped on the superlubricant and an entire brigade's worth the tanks had their engines and turbofans seize up, turning the tanks into nothing more than heavily armed and armored emplacements.

"Might I see your, how do you refer to it, 'Heavy Metal''s battle honors?" Ekret answered.

"Of course, sir," Zhukov answered. What came next was a long list of not only where V Corps (Old Blood) had fought, but where the officers had fought, where the sub-components fought, and where the model of equipment had seen action.

Ekret noticed that not only was there a written list but he could view the battles either from a strategic map or VR or eVR if he chose, with links to whole volumes of after action reports, historical analysis, and more.

He was forced to leave most of the information in his office computer's buffer, his own system remarking it would take nearly two hours to save all the information to local storage. Ekret wasn't surprised, there was nearly eight thousand years of data, thousands of battles, scores of wars. Ekret decided to go backwards in the chronological order.

"Sir, Lieutenant Colonel Hargeson and his staff are making descent for your unit area. Will you permit them to enter? They would prefer to be waiting for you, sir," Zhukov said, breaking into Ekret's examination of the Third Battle of Numera's Star, where the V Corps (Old Blood) broke the back of the Gulsa'an Empire with armored units made up of (Heavy Metal). The tactics were much different than the Unified Military Fleet, who preferred head on engagements with minimal support that used the least resources. The battle he was studying was a whirling mass of thrust, counter-thrust, flanking, rear marching, close air support, infantry ambushes, orbital missile fire, it looked to Ekret more like an entire war rather than the last battle of the war. No one unit took the honor and glory, it was a group effort that even included Space Navy orbital fire. Glory went to all their banners.

"Permission granted. Thank you for informing me, Honored Zhukov," Ekret said. He closed the VR tactical overview of the battle and leaned back again.

The Terrans made war much different than the Unified Military Forces. The Unified Corporate Council had long ago made it a capital crime to target manufacturing or industrial facilities as part of warfare, yet half of what the Terrans did seemed to revolve around protecting or destroying those assets. The civilian workers were quite often not a legitimate target, unlike the Council's rules. The Terrans seemed to put effort toward avoiding civilian casualties to the point there were multiple treaties regarding it.

The Unified Military Forces also put their units piecemeal into the battle, only committing additional units when it was apparent that the force was approaching 10% of fielded casualties. The Terrans, however, seemed to have the entire military force interlocked into their planning, even if a unit was holding position and waiting to reinforce other units or exploit any sudden gap in the defenses.

From what he had seen, Terrans would also fight to the

last vehicle, robot, or sentient being. No "ten percent" casualties. They fought till the other side withdrew, surrendered, or was destroyed.

The 10% rule had been in place in the Unified Military Forces and the Unified Corporate Security for so long that some commanders struck the colors at 9% and a few even at 8%.

Ekret found himself wondering just when Terran morale broke.

Or did it break?

Ekret's hovercar settled down and Ekret noted three heavily armed and armored dropships sitting on the airfield normally used for aircars or air units. Each dropship had four massive armored bipeds on guard, weapons held in hand, cannons deployed. The dropships had the symbol of a triangle around a cannon bisected by a lightning bolt. The massive armored bipeds had the same symbols on their right and left shoulders, the paint obvious against the chrome.

"Honored Zhukov, Where is the Terran liaison?" Ekret asked as he climbed out.

"They are, sir, awaiting your pleasure at the door of your Tactical Operations Command, as they have not been given permission to enter such a sensitive area, sir," The AI responded.

"I will notify the guard they may enter," Ekret answered, strangely grateful at the courtesy. He signaled his security forces and the limited security AI that the Terrans could enter the command center.

Security force beings saluted Akret as he entered his command center, making a beeline for the Tactical Operations Command. When he entered he saw his first Terran.

He wasn't sure what to think. Lean, came to mind. Focused, with their eyes forward facing and intent, was another. They had hair on their heads, cut short like Ekret's fur, which Ekret immediately appreciated. They all had cybernetic linkages on their temples, five had cybernetic eyes surrounded by metal, one had a cybernetic arm that appeared to Ekret to be more functional than a normal cybernetic prosthetic, which would barely have tactile feedback. They all wore what looked like photo-dopple camouflage, which kept making their outlines slightly blurry. Three of the eight bipeds carried sidearms while the other five carried some type of rifle slung across their back.

"Attention!" one of the Terrans barked, turning and giving Ekret an odd salute. The others all went ramrod still, hands down at their sides, heels and legs together, staring, not at Ekret, but directly ahead.

"Tell them 'at ease', sir," Zhukov whispered.

"At ease," Ekret said and watched as all their postures relaxed at the same time.

Well disciplined does not mean combat effective, *Ekret whispered to himself.*

"I'm Lieutenant Colonel Hargeson, this is Major Allison, my Executive Office," The Terran said, introducing each one in turn. The master of the lower grades was present also.

Ekret noted that they were all very formal in their posture, attentiveness, speech, and address.

Ekret was informed that the Maintenance units, apparently something called a Corps Support Command (COSCOM) was landing to assist with maintenance of the Terran's Heavy Metal. Ekret was startled that their maintenance unit was the size of three of his own divisions. They had ten times the number of beings in their maintenance unit that Ekret's entire armored host.

Partway through Hargeson stopped, paused the holodisplay which was showing Ekret the breakdown of the unit structure of V Corps, and looked at Ekret.

"Sir, if I may ask, which of your units is considered Heavy Metal?" The LTC asked, his body language seeming distressed to Ekret. Ekret answered, firm in the belief that his hover tanks were impressive.

"These units?" The LTC asked, bringing up the image of the heavy tank on the holodisplay.

Ekret admired it as it slowly rotated. Ninety millimeter bore heavy plasma cannon, three coaxial rapid fire plasma guns, two point defense, and six 40mm mortars with nearly a dozen shots for each in them. Each tank was 150 tons of layered armor, eight hover fans, two gravity engines. A crew of four: The Tank High Most, the gunner, the EW/EMCOM/COM, the driver, all trained to a high efficiency, most crews with hundreds of hours in their tanks. Rolling doom who any who dared face them.

"Yes, COSCOM High Most," Ekret said, giving the equivalent of a sigh of pleasure at the sight of his craft.

The Terrans went perfectly still and silent and for a moment Ekret wondered if a predator had entered the room.

Is there a problem? Ekret asked through the implant.

It would be better if my biological counterpart explained it, Armored High Most, *Zhukov answered carefully.*

"If there is a problem, rub my muzzle in it, don't try to use it to comb the fur of my buttocks," Ekret said, putting on his best commander voice.

"I feel perhaps I should let you do a comparison," the LTC said, his voice grave. He made a motion, dividing the holotank in half, and made a tossing motion.

What appeared in the holotank was an absolute nightmare.

Over 2,800 tons, treads, graviton assistance, a main gun with a bore diameter of over 300mm that appeared to compress a nuclear blast into a directed energy 'slug' that would impact with the force between, at the discretion of the commander, of 11 kilotons all the way up to 22.5 megatons. It was capable of a shot every 5-11 seconds depending on the skill of the loader and how hot the chamber had gotten, compared to 15 seconds for his own guns. Worse, the main gun was capable of "mission flexible munitions" which had a dizzying array. Its armor was thicker than all the armor on Ekret's tank combined and made up of war-steel laminate. The rest of the weapons were point defense, mortars, vertical launch rocket systems, anti-infantry weapons.

"May I?" Ekret asked, moving toward the holotank and raising one paw toward the drive train specifications box.

"Of course, Armor High Most," The LTC said.

Ekret touched the box and watched the data spill out. It could move under counter-grav but was designed to move on the treads for a multitude of reasons, half of them psychological. It was capable of bursts of speed up to 180 kph and a sustained speed of 70 kph, which it was expected to do battle at. It could fire inside its own turning arc during a 90-degree turn. It carried the same crew as Ekret's tanks, with the exception of also carrying a maintenance/stores officer who ran something call the creation engine/nano-forge during battle.

It was a monster.

"How much do each of these cost?" Ekret asked, his mind boggling at what he was seeing.

"Roughly 255 million Terran Credits, mostly the resources shipment, creation of the parts, assembly. Not as expensive as, say, a Hercules Class War Titan, but still expensive," The Major said.

Ekret closed his eyes and thought a moment. If that was what the Terran military was going to field to help defend this planet, his tanks, even the heaviest ones, would be more than litter in front of the treads. Just the corona from that massive cannon passage would shred his tank's armor.

Insanely, that main gun could even hurt other tanks, shoot into near orbit, and maybe even hit a target on orbital approach.

"High Most?" The LTC asked.

"A moment," Ekret said. He thought quickly. They had not denigrated his men or his vehicles, just stated that there was a problem that was instantly obvious to Ekret the minute he saw one of their hyper-expensive massive war machines.

"What is equivelant to my armored vehicles?" Ekret asked, opening his eyes. "Do no be afraid of ruffling my fur, my men's lives depend on facts, not feelings."

The Terran's position shifted slightly and Ekret saw a couple of subtle nods, which the Terrans used to signify assent.

"Light attack craft. Primarily scouting and reconnaissance," The LTC said.

Ekret thought about what he'd read and witnessed looking at V Corps (Old Blood)'s record. He held up his hand for patience and closed his eyes. He looked for and found "Cav Scouts" in 3rd Armor and looked up their battle honors. Hundreds of them. He chose a battle at random and let it play out on fast forward in his mind. His implant heated with the amount of data and he shut down the link.

"Cavalry Scout is an honored and risky duty that often decides the order of battle," Ekret said, drawing himself up in pride. "My metal will be pleased to assist in such a manner."

The gathered up Terrans all nodded and he could see the gleam of respect in their eyes.

Ekret knew why. He'd seen the casualties but he'd also seen how vitally important they were.

War is not a place for pride, if one believes they are willing to pay any cost for victory, *Ekret thought to himself.* I will not sacrifice my men for my own pride. The Precursor munitions will not be stopped by a commander's pride, only the application of metal.

He waved the tank specs away. "Come, gentlebeings, let us plan."

3rd ARMOR DIVISION (OLD BLOOD) MEMO

Local Forces have agreed to act as light scout (Cav Scout) forces. Commander has a excellent ability to integrate new tactics into his skill set and does not react with pride when defeated in simulations. His "Heavy Armor" units are equivalent to Light Scout Vehicles. Will be integrating his forces with 3rd Armor. 3rd COSCOM is currently refitting their units to acceptable specifications while retaining existing abilities so as to not erode crew skill levels.

---NOTHING FOLLOWS---
3rd COSCOM (OLD BLOOD) MEMO

Local vehicles are in need of computer upgrade, VI upgrade, weapon upgrade, ablative armor additions, and power train upgrade. Am consulting with local commanders on comparable and compateble tech levels. The vehicles may be soft metal but their crews are experience and willing.

---NOTHING FOLLOWS---
SYSTEM MOST HIGH ORDERS

Armored Most High Ekret, you are to ensure that Unified Military Forces are retaining command of all units and areas of operation. Unified Intelligence Council and Unified Corporate Council both believe that the Terrans are over-estimating and overstating the level of their technology and their military's abilities.

Do not these aliens displace you from your honored command of Heavy Armor in the name of the Unified Military Forces and the Kestimet Corporation.

KESTIMET CORPORATION MEMO

Ekret, remember who holds your contract and who gives you your orders.

108th MILITARY INTELLIGENCE
ALL UNITS ALL COMMANDERS
IMP PRESENCE DETECTED IN OORT CLOUD
ATTACK IMMENENT
ATTACK IMMINENT
ATTACK IMMINENT
---NOTHING FOLLOWS---

The Lanaktallan was shaking with fury as Ekret approached. The Maintenance Second High Most's tendrils were curled, his crests inflating and deflating, and his hooves clattering on the concrete slab of the motor pool. His uniform was spotless, as always, and all four of his grasping hands were clean. He was in his near-dress uniform, badges and awards sparking as well as the silver decorations.

"High Most, I must protest most strongly the fact you are allowing these aliens access to our vehicles," The Maintenance

Second High Most, one Lowenmoo, complained.

"Protest all you want, it is happening," Ekret stated flatly, walking toward the large buildings where his tanks were kept. "The Terrans have offered to ensure that we are able to work within their tactical computer network as well as are able to co-ordinate with our forces. An offer I intended on taking them up on."

Lowenmoo shuddered with anger. "We do not need their help! They haven't even been rated on the level of their sapience! What could they have to teach or offer us?"

"Their plasma compression chambers are eighteen times more efficient that ours, cool down four times as fast, their barrels are 340% more durable than ours, and are capable of firing five times as fast at the same bore width and chamber weight," Ekret stated, still moving at a steady walk to the hangar. "Just for that alone I would gratefully invite them over to engage in inter-species sexual intercourse with their choice of my mother or sister."

The Lanaktallan inflated his crests with horror.

"That kind of firepower alone ends battles faster than our weapons. Their focusing arrays are stronger, increasing the plasma cannon's range, they use a laser 'tip' to heat the air so that it does not attenuate the plasma as much. Why haven't our military researchers come up with that simple of a method to in-crease range," Ekret asked. He saluted the door guards, who were standing next to the massive Terran warborgs who had taken up stations recently.

"I would not presume to know. That is outside and above our paygrade," The Lanaktallan harrumphed. It paused for a sec-ond. "And above your birth station, Heavy Armor Most High," the four legged creature said slyly to remind Ekret of 'his place' in the scheme of things.

"In combat one's station matters little, all that matters is one's will, skill, and equipment," Ekret stated. The Maintenance Second Most High harrumphed as they entered the hangar and were greeted with chaos.

Terrans swarmed everywhere. Moving about quickly, sometimes at a jog, sometimes running. Carrying parts, tools, equipment. Climbing on the tanks, working under them, on the sides, conversing with the crews, attaching equipment to the tanks, or opening sections to gain access to critical systems. They called out to one another with their voices and Ekret could tell that the air was thick with implant and com array discussions. He could see VR keyboards, manuals, schematics glimmering in the air and ass he watched one Terran turned his palm up to project a schematic for several interested technicians to lean forward and examine.

The maintenance officers, primarily Lanaktallan's, were all clustered against the back wall, staring at the humans and some of the other 'lesser' species as they worked.

"They are causing chaos, you must stop them, Heavy Armor High Most," The Lanaktallan said, wringing his four hands together.

Ekret's brain, without the help of his implant, quickly deduced what everyone was up to. He'd seen plenty of maintenance done after the battlefield when the maintenance techs were trying to get ready for the Corporate Inspection Most High's arrival.

"Yes, they are," Ekret mused, heading toward his own heavy tank. His crew were watching a Terran affix something to the inside of the rear glacis, where the crumple-zone airspace was located that was supposed to keep EFP rounds from gutting his tank.

"Most High," his gunner, Cheepeek, snapped.

"Relax," Ekret said, waving a paw. He climbed up the tank, ignoring the Lanaktallan's plaintive pleas to stop the Terrans. He looked at the driver. "How is our vehicle?"

The saurian blinked his clear inner eyelids twice then gestured for Ekret to follow him into the tank. Once they were both inside the saurian, Driver Second Class Sselssen made a gesture of irritation.

"The Terrans, they try to hide it, but they are angry with

our maintenance crews," He said.

"Why is that? Speak freely, we have been through too many battles together for you to worry about combing my fur," Ekret said.

"The Terrans claim we have armor and frame microfractures, that the alloy of our hull is showing stress, that our engine is not running at optimal performance, and that our computer systems are sadly lacking," Sselssen hissed. "Rather than rub my tail in it, their 'maintenance chief' ordered first our own crew to fix it, and when they refused, saying it was within company tolerances, he ordered his own men to carry out the repairs."

Ekret waited a moment. "And?"

Sselssen slapped his tailtip twice, a habit Ekret knew meant the other being was stressed. "They showed me, with our own instruments, how badly our vehicle has been maintained. I requested they repair our vehicle as if it was a Terran one and do you know what the 'maintenance chief' told me?"

Ekret sighed. "I assume he said no."

Sselssen slapped his tail again. "He told me, looking me right in my left eye: 'Bound by steel and blood, to lessen you is to lessen myself. Our lives are in one another's hands. It will be done.' and ordered his men to get to work."

Ekret cocked his head in confusion, then flicked his ears in assent. "All right. So..."

"Hi!' The voice interrupted their discussion. It came from the command panel and Ekret looked at it as Sselssen looked around the cramped tank compartment. A computer generated face, a blank icon usually used by the Unified Communications Agency, was on his command communication panel.

"Greetings," Ekret said.

"It's your aVI, a warboi," Zkukov whispered to him over the implant. "He's just been hashed, so he'll be curious about the tank."

The image jumped from display to display. Ekret motioned for Sselssen to relax. Finally the icon stopped and 'looked' at Ekret.

"Cav All the Way! It Will Be Done!" the image spoke and bobbed up and down while showing the rune for pleasure.

"Welcome aboard. You are installed to assist us?" Ekret asked.

"I work best with bio-troops," The 'warboi' chirped. "Together, we work the best. I compute a thirty percent increase in effectiveness."

Sselssen raised his tail curiously. "What if we were just moving toward the battle and I suddenly went to maximum acceleration, computer?"

"I would double-check the scans to see what I missed and assume your predator instinct had alerted you to a threat I cannot detect," The aVI said. "Did you know a human can tell if someone is staring at them even if the one staring at the human is hidden from sight and behind the human? Nobody knows why!"

Sselssen twitched his tail again. "That is very interesting. What should we call you?"

"Bouncy," Ekret said, watching the little icon for the aVI (advanced VI) bounce eagerly on the screen.

"I like that name," Bouncy answered.

"Indeed," Ekret looked at the VI's icon. "Is there anything else?"

"Our tank is in need of immediate repair, refurbishing, Service Life Extension, and refit," Bouncy said, sounding sad. "We are at less than 20% battle effective. Should I file a maintenance report?"

"Yes," Ekret said. "File it with the Terrans of 3rd COSCOM," he turned to Sselssen, "I shall be outside the tank. I wish to see the progress."

"As you wish, High Most," Sselseen said.

As Ekret climbed out he could see the VI, Bouncy the warboi, going through systems and running maintenance depot level diagnostics, somehow getting by the Corporate security lockouts.

The bay was still full of chaos, with the normal team still

against the far wall. They'd started clustering up by rank and Ekret knew they would soon be complaining.

A Terran who looked more cyborg than bio came up, nodding.

"General Trucker, 3rd Armor Division. You must be Armored High Most Ekret, the new Armored Scout Recon Division CO," The big Terran said.

Ekret avoided the instinct to cower down in the face of a predator's stare that intense.

"Say 'yes, sir' and don't salute," Zhukov suggested. The AI followed up by uploading Terran Confederate Military etiquette to Ekret. Ekret noticed it all seemed to be for keeping highly aggressive predators from going at each other with knives over rank disputes.

"Yes, sir," Ekret said.

The big Terran nodded. "Third COSCOM tells me that through no fault of your own, you're in need of depot maintenance," he said.

"Yes, sir, that is correct," Ekret answered.

"Do you have enough simulators for all your men? I noticed you have ten thousand vehicles divided up between heavy, medium, and light designations. Can you put all of your men in simulators?" General Trucker asked, watching the maintenance crews work.

Ekret shook his head. "Only twenty percent of my men are expected to take part in any conflict," he said.

"That may be how you are used to it, V Corps takes a different approach," The General said.

"My military liaison, Zhukov-442, made me aware of that," Ekret said.

"Four-four-two? Good man, that one. Steady head, innovative, works well with non-digitals, an excellent mentor for you during this integration period," The General mused. "You two getting along?"

"Yes, sir," Ekret said.

"Excellent," The General looked around the bay. "We'll get

you interlocked, Armored High Most, don't you worry about that."

Despite the fact that the Terran had been mostly bored looking, his voice calm and unruffled, Ekret believed him.

The first simulator practice had been a disaster. Ekret's unit had been virtually wiped out. His commanders had made every possible mistake. Worse, the 3rd Armored Division General himself had been riding in "tank" as they'd used VR to practice.

When he showed up at the After Action Briefing Ekret firmly believed he'd be dressed down at least, replaced at worst. He gathered up with the other Division commanders and waited as the General of V Corps, a Treana'ad by the name of General Nodra'ak stared at a fast forward reply in the holotank for almost ten minutes.

Finally the General stopped it at the words "END SIMULA-TION" and looked around.

"That went... suboptimal," The General said, his voice calm and unruffled and sounding more like a human's than a large mantis-like insect. He lit a small white stick, which Ekret had learned was some kind of stimulant and appetite suppressant and pain killer that was used through inhalation of the smoke.

Ekret waited for the lash to hit.

"General Trucker, care to explain what happened?" General Nodra'ak asked mildly, pointing with his "smoke."

Trucker lifted a can and spit some kind of cud juice into it before answering. "A cascade of failures that mistakes and bad decisions that happens in any unit's first integrated exercise," he shrugged. "We let our armored recon get chewed up and then acted all surprised when the 'enemy' flanked us and wiped out our logistics."

The burning white stick got jabbed at him and Ekret stood as straight as his hips and spine allowed him.

"What went wrong, Armored High Most?" General No-dra'ak asked.

"I outran my artillery support. Several of my commanders refused to listen to their vehicle VI's and called in airstrikes, orbital strikes, or artillery strikes on their own units. An entire brigade ran out in front of a moving BOLO company. When we took 15% casualties my men tried to withdraw, as is Unified Military Forces policy and the 'enemy' pounded us into scrap while we ran," Ekret said honestly.

The General lifted an antenna as he inhaled smoke. When Ekret finished speaking the General blew the smoke out of his mandibles and nodded. "Brutal, but truthful. I like that in an Armor officer," he jabbed the tube at the holotank. "Well, Unit-9823JWS, you have an explanation for what happened to an entire Brigade of my recon, Jaws?"

The slightly mechanical voice came out of the holotank. "We had not been loaded up with the proper IFF and they were mistaken for Precursor machines. I have remedied that by ordering my Brigade mates to load up allied vehicle profile and IFF files," there was a moment of calm. "I was unaware that command had not loaded them."

"You didn't ask for them either, Jaws," The General chided. "You're a brand new CO, that's why we're doing this shakedown."

The General turned to the 19th Artillery CO. "What happened with you? Why didn't you autocorrect."

"When my controller went to verify the coordinates, they were given the friendly units present override code," that General said.

Ekret felt himself bridle up. Those idiots hadn't passed the request through him and then had used a code normally use when a unit was being overrun?

"I shall rectify that, sir," Ekret stated.

"All right, gentlebeings," General Nodra'ak said. "Let's get to work. We have a long way to go."

Ekret found himself nodding.

He refused to embarrass himself or his men again.

"What happened, Ekret?" General Nodra'ak said, lighting his smoke.

"I should have asked for a sonar scan of that bay. It had been reported a Jotun crashed into the ocean, I didn't expect it to lunge up out of the ocean," Ekret admitted. "I didn't expect my commanders to retreat rather than open fire."

"Well, Ekret?" General Nodra'ak asked, bringing out his pack of 'cigarettes' that apparently were imported all the way from Terra.

"My men had turned off the VI's at the orders from their Brigade Commander and were unfamiliar with the map designation for minefield."

"How did I lose three quarters of my recon to friendly fire on the first day, Ekret?" General Nodra'ak asked, exhaling smoke from his mandibles.

"It all went to excrement, sir," Ekret said. "One of my Brigade commanders mistook a friendly unit for an enemy unit and opened fire. The rest of my Commanders panicked and tried to retreat or opened fire."

General Nodra'ak stared at him for a long moment, his compound eyes seeemingly serious. "If you want to replace commanders, High Most, now is the time."

Ekret watched the Lanaktallan officers leave, all threatening to destroy his career, all reminding him that he was just a neo-sapient and that he would rue the day he ever joined the UMF.

"What should I do, Zhukov?" Ekret asked.

"Promote from within, list 10% of your vehicles as combat replacements, begin training. Let it be known that any officer who fails in his duty shall be replaced. As High Most, you could have them executed, which I approve of, but Terran Military

Code of Uniform Justice prohibits. Just assign any failure officers to light tanks and put them in risky positions," The AI told him.

Ekret nodded.

The General lit his smoke and pointed at Ekret. "What happened?"

Ekret stood up as straight as possible. "I convinced the enemy through electronic warfare that my light tanks were BOLO's, pulling him out of position and into an artillery placed mine field where his anti-air could not counter our close air support. I then had my men go to full stealth and fall back to the rally point at Point Golf," Ekret said.

The General exhaled bluish smoke, turning to General Trucker. "So, General, how exactly did you lose half my heavy metal before even deployment?"

Trucker spit the cud-juice into the can and shook his head. "I didn't trust my recon and ordered the dropships to land us at Hotel, walking straight into an ambush."

Nodra'ak nodded, stalking around the hototank in a very human movement despite his four legs.

"We're getting better, gentlebeings," the Treana'ad growled. "A few more and we'll use our actual vehicles."

Ekret sat on the back of his tank, chewing his ration. Less than a hundred feet above him one of Combat Talon ripped across the sky, followed by a dozen of its comrades. Ekret watched the overpowered 'aircraft' go by, his ration tube in his mouth.

"Ten minutes, sir," Zhukov told him.

"Thank you, Zhukov," he said. He spit the ration tube into the churned up grass and climbed back in his tank. He looked at his crew and gave a Terran-esque smile. "Let's see what General Kli'kitik is trying to hide from everyone."

His crew gave back the same expressions. Bouncy jumped to the command console as Ekret's driver made sure the stealth systems the Terrans had installed were running *before* firing up his engine so he didn't 'attract a butt load of missiles' again.

"So, Jaws, what happened?" The General asked.

"I had not expected Most High Ekret to use his recon skimmers to drop depth charges on me as I crossed the channel," The BOLO answered. "He used stealth sheathing on the charges and the very first one 'detonated' between my hull and the barrel of my Hellbore. He delivered enough firepower to cripple a Jotun before I could surface."

The General nodded, moving to the next point.

Ekret felt a cold burning pride in his men.

Ekret sat on the edge of the hatch, chewing an empty ration tube and staring at all the maintenance crews running at top speed to correct the defects identified when the tank crews had inspected their vehicles that morning. Each tank crew helped their maintenance crew with the work, adding man-power to the job. Ekret ignored how many of his Armored unit had the V Corps blue triangles pentagon shaved into fur, tattooed onto skin, dyed into feathers, or scarred into scales. Their morale was high, even doing maintenance and constant drills. The tank crews had been trained to care for their tanks, doing the small jobs that were easy to do without special tools, including repairing hoverskirts and even replacing a broken fan-blade.

"Bouncy, what's on the agenda for the rest of the day?" Ekret asked, considering giving the crews the night off to go into town.

"I don't know. You're supposed to..." the aVI started to say. I suddenly bounced over to Ekret's panel and flashed it twice for attention. "Incoming message from TERMILINT!"

"Put it up and to my implant," Ekret said, spitting out the ration tube and sliding into his commander's seat.

Both had the same message: ATTACK IMMINENT! ALL TROOPS TO READY STATION! ATTACK IMMINENT! LOAD WAR-

PLANS AND GO TO BRAVO!

"Download the warplans, Bouncy," Ekret said, trigging the elevator to lift him out of the tank. "Sselssen, as soon as the maintenance techs give you the clearance, get this thing ready to roll!"

Ekret saw the humans were working faster somehow. Putting armor back on, tightening bolds, fixing hoverskirts. In some places ten or twenty humans swarmed a tank, ripping it apart, adding to it or replacing parts, and putting it back together.

"GREEN GREEN GREEN!" One of the Terrans at the back of Ekret's tank yelled, slapping it three times. The Terrans all scattered, running to tanks that only had a paw's count of techs working on it.

His crew climbed past him, dove into the hatch, and got into their positions.

"Zhukov, redesignate my unit as an HHQ Armored Cavalry Scout Brigade, redesignate the rest of my units as discussed," Ekret ordered.

"Redesignating," Zhukov said. "Third Armor Commander's compliments, sir. Signal when deployable."

"Most High," A signal over the implant broke in. Oh, great, it was Sa'altlikk, his Third Most High in charge of the light stealth tanks.

"Ekret, go ahead," he said. He had considered replacing the cud-chewer repeatedly, but his crew were excellent soldiers and he didn't want to mess it up.

Great, I'm starting to talk like the humans too, *he thought.*

"I object. We are a heavy armor division, with divisions of medium and light tanks. We are heavy armor, not some kind of reconnaissance force," Sa'altlikk moaned. "I request permission to rejoin the heavy tanks again, not this flotilla of floaters."

"Compared to Terran tanks, we're lucky we aren't considered ammunition," Ekret snapped. "Get off my implant and get your crew ready."

"We'll see what my cousin says about this," The Lanaktallan threatened before cutting out.

"I have disabled all non-military communications that are not routed through me, sir," Zhukov said. "Am maintaining proper communications net procedure. Additionally I have assigned a code string to ensure that Third High Most Sa'altlikk's vehicle is under proper EMCOM."

"Thank you, Zhukov," Ekret said.

He enjoyed the speed and efficiency of the AI.

Ekret turned and climbed back up on his tank, standing on the seat so his upper body was outside the tank's hull. He watched the Terran techs suddenly stream away, like a flock of birds, and the floor was completely clear except for the odd crewman running for his tank.

Ekret shook his head. It would have taken the normal maintenance crew almost an hour to make their way to the back wall where they were already huddled. They would have stopped for conversations, to establish dominance over each other or 'lesser species' or stopped to berate tank crewmen.

Instead, the hangar bay looked like it was deserted of everything but the tanks.

"Warplan loaded, sir," Zhukov suddenly said.

"Thank you, Zhukov," Ekret said. He ducked down and looked at his communications officer. "Open a unit wide channel."

"Open sir," the officer said.

"I helped. I shut down all communications outside each tank so they can't talk to other people!" the aVI, Bouncy, said.

"Yes, yes you did," The com-tech reassured it.

"All units, all units," Ekret said. His men were used to him abandoning honorifics. "The Precursors are fighting their way to our planet as they speak. The Corporate Military Council and our own Unified Military Services Council are still engaged in argument even as space shakes with the thunder of combat."

Ekret thumbed the activate rune for the movement plan to someplace called "Staging Point Bravo" and kept talking.

"The Terrans have dispensed with arguing and instead

are ordering their units, of which we are to consider ourselves part of, to protecting this world, these people, this system. We are still under my command, and I will not spend your lives without reason. You know this, I have proved this in a dozen battles with you," Ekret said. "But we are to act as part of a larger whole, so that we interlock together like a finely made engine. Like the whole of a tank we are greater than the sum of our parts."

"We are the First Armored Scout Cavalry Division. We shall find the enemy, seek him out, so that he may be destroyed. We do this in honor. Our scanners are tuned, our eyes are sharp, and our guns are ready.

"MOVE OUT!"

"IT WILL BE DONE!" roared back over the com-links.

Ekret noted that the formation the Terrans expected was an odd one. A staggered wedge with firing orders. It was one long practiced, but for his recon division to use it was odd.

It meant that it was real. The Precursors were here.

And expected to make landfall.

Ekret slid an empty ration tube out of his chest pocket and started chewing on the end.

TERMILCOM ALERT
FIFTY (50) GOLIATHS IN SYSTEM! DOUBLE ATTENDANT NUMBERS! PREPARE FOR BATTLE!
---NOTHING FOLLOWS---
V CORPS ALERT
Unknown number of Goliaths heading toward planet. Expected to be four (4) or more. Commanders, load battle plan Alpha-five-niner.

IT WILL BE DONE!
---NOTHING FOLLOWS---
UNIFIED MILITARY FORCES ALERT
The size of Precursor forces is too much to defend against. All commanders withdraw at your own discretion. All Third

High Most and above commanders and Company Executives or higher are permitted to retreat from the system at own discretion.

Ekret sat on the back of his tank, chewing on an empty ration tube, his palm turned up so his palm implant, which had only been put in a week before the attack happened, could display a wire-frame VR holo above his palm.

His unit had fought its way through the night. Getting close enough for his vehicle's upgraded scanners to spot the enemy then racing away. Positioning themselves to call in orbital strikes, artillery, close air strikes, or heavy bombing. Always moving, never stopping, never letting themselves get pinned down. Using their upgraded speed, their improved stealth, and their constant training to always be where the enemy didn't expect them and to never be where the enemy's fire was.

"So, I ordered you to scan that valley, not from the ridge, but from down inside the valley to prevent you from showing your profile to anyone on either side of that rise. I ordered you to use stealth drones in front of you at a range no further than one hundred meters," Ekret said, without taking his eyes from it. "Instead, you led an entire battalion of recon tanks up over the top of that hill, on top of the ridge, while running unstealthed drones at maximum speed into the valley."

The VR holo hissed, showing the Percursor fire ripping into the flanks of his men. Destroying a quarter of them before the lead vehicle turned and fled, turning its back to the Precursor. The other vehicles turned their rear to the fire and began to explode. According to the icons nearly thirty of the fifty light tanks had been destroyed without ever identifying what kind of Precursor force was in there.

Worse, the Precursors now knew that he knew they were there, and that he knew that they knew.

The drones had been wiped out. 108th Military Intelligence could guess at what was in that valley, but couldn't be sure.

Ekret didn't want to have happen to his men what had happened to Old Iron Feathers and mistake a Precursor vehicle for something else.

Clenching his fist and turning off the handy implant, Ekret turned in place, swinging his legs off the back of his tank, staring down on the ground. Sa'altlikk, the Third Most High, former CO of the 4th Light Armor Recon Battalion, was kneeling on the ground, all four of his legs folded underneath him. All four of his arms were bound painfully behind his back, and two of his six eyes were swollen.

"What happened, Sa'altlikk?" Ekret asked, still chewing on the empty ration tube.

"We were taking casualties! We had to withdraw!" the Lanaktallan protested.

"Rewind the holo a little bit. Why were you taking casualties?" Ekret tried.

"The enemy spotted us," Sa'altlikk moaned.

"Why did they spot you?" Ekret asked mildly, slowly drawing his sidearm.

"Their sensors must be better than we thought," Sa'altlikk said, his voice low and slow, all six eyes rolling in the sockets.

"Or, I don't know, could it have been you were silhouetted against the rising sun on top of a ridge I explicitly ordered you to stay away from?" Ekret asked.

Sa'altlikk's tongue came out and wetted his jowls and tendrils. "They must have spotted the drones?"

"You mean the high speed drones you used instead of the stealth drones I ordered?" Ekret said. He shook his head. "And then what did you do, instead of turning to face the enemy and backing off the ridge?"

"Our tanks go 22% faster moving forward than backward," the Third Most High tried.

"And your forward battle screens and armor would have ensured you survived the shots. Instead you ordered flank speed, which drains the battle screens, meaning each shot into your rear armor penetrated into interior spaces, as you had ordered the reactive armor disabled to, and I quote, save Corporate funds," Ekret said slowly. "Your decisions, from stop to finish, cost me thirty crews, experiences crews, beings I know personally, including your Executive Officer."

"We have replacements for the tanks. New crews can be drawn from a conscription order of the workers," Sa'altlikk answered.

"Welders and agricultural robot supervisors are *not tankers!*" Ekret snarled.

The Treana'ad are right, there's just something about the Terran snarl.

*"*Your ill advised decisions killed tankers," Ekret finished.

"There are a million more to take each one's place," the Lanaktallan said, repeating the line the UMF said as a way of instilling the knowledge that the UMF's legions were endless. "My cousin..." he tried.

"Is not here," Ekret said. He stared at the other officer. "That is three times, in a single day period, that you have displayed cowardice under fire."

"And? What will you do, Ekret? Send me back to the rear? I will just evacuate this pathetic dirt ball and leave you here to die facing the Precursors," The Lanaktallan answered. The bovine spit on the ground. "You dare not do..."

The pistol's retort was quiet compared to the thunder of the last few hours.

The hyper-velocity dart hit Sa'altlikk in the head, blowing it apart, dropping the Lanaktallan to the ground. One hoof kicked.

Ekret looked at the dead officer's crew. "Take command of your tank. We leave in ten minutes," he looked at the other gathered officers, noting the satisfaction on their faces, even the other Lanaktallan. "Cowardice has only one reward."

"It shall be done!" They all shouted, then turned as one

and started toward their tanks.

The tank jerked to the right, throwing Ekret hard against the command chair. The hypersonic rounds tore apart the trees behind him as the 150 ton bulk of his hovertank shattered the trees in front of him, the fans howling like damned souls.

Bouncy sent a tingle into his hands.

"Fire!" Ekret yelled unnecessarily as his gunner fired the main gun. Ekret knew that Bouncy had signaled the gunner to fire at the same moment as Ekret's hands had tingled.

"Shot out!" the gunner, Cheepeek, called out.

"Direct hit! Target killed!" Bouncy called out.

Sselssen yanked the tank into another dodge, bouncing deliberately off a bigger tree, the battle-screen exploding it into burning chunks. The hypervelocity shots tore apart a copse of trees instead of the tank.

"Got Trucker on the line!" Heslettek called out from the Com/EW/EMCOM spot.

"Ekret," the tank commander snapped.

"Trucker here, what have you got?" the Terran sounded stress.

"TARGET!" Bouncy yelled.

"Precursor heavy infantry with vehicles. No air support, no anti-aircraft!" Ekret called out.

"SHOT OUT!" Cheepeek yelled.

"226th Artillery is being jammed. I'll relay it to 221st!" Trucker yelled. In the background Ekret heard someone call out "MAIN GUN OUT!"

"GOOD HIT! GOOD HIT! STILL ACTIVE!"

The channel dissolved into static from Trucker's end.

"Ekret, can you hear me?" Trucker asked. "Gimme the grid!"

"SHOT OUT!"

Ekret felt Heslettek load it into his implant and he shot it to the big Terran General.

"Repeat," Trucker said and repeated the numbers. "All 168th elements, go to rapid fire, break that big bastard in half!" the Terran suddenly roared. DIRECT HIT! TARGET DOWN! Ekret saw an icon blink in his vision letting him know that the commo wasn't for him, the big Terran had simply not cut Ekret out of the link.

"Ekret, you still there?" Trucker asked.

"TARGET!"

"Still here, sir," Ekret said.

"SHOT OUT!"

"Ninety seconds, button up!" Trucker yelled. It sounded like the human was half deaf.

The tank jerked, moving again, jerking at Bouncy and Sselssen's commands.

"DIRECT HIT! TARGET DOWN!" Bouncy called out. Ekret had noticed that Bouncy looked more like him, only made of chrome and burning blue neon, with the V Corps logo on his head.

"Gimme HHQ Brigade!" Ekret yelled to Heslettek.

"TARGET!"

"Open channel," Heslettek called out.

"SHOT OUT!"

"All elements, ninety seconds! Incoming rainstorm!" Ekret called out over his comlink. He hit the stud to close the hatch, which he had left open to suck out the vapors and smoke from the plasma cannon venting slightly into the crew cabin. TARGET DOWN! The hatch slammed shut, no longer slowly whining shut but instead checking for any blockage with micro-pulse lasers then yanked down.

Ekret stomped the pedal that normally would override the gunner, bringing all his screens back to life. He ground the plas ration tube between his molars.

The forest was burning around them, his units were moving fast, blowing through the ambush. His last unit was almost clear, and following training, was rotating as they left the enemy, their battle-screens exploding trees as it deflected or absorbed shots. His units were all pocked, cratered, from the hypervelocity rounds.

But none of his tanks were mission-killed and none of his men were seriously injured.

His own tank was following, pouring fire into the enemy, who was trying to link up with a larger force that had heavy vehicles but couldn't move through the canyons where 1/32 was dug in.

"THIRTY SECONDS!" Bouncy squealed.

"SHOT OUT!"

"TARGET DESTROYED!" Bouncy added.

His men were clear and he signalled all stop, all power to forward and hull battle screens, and to ground down.

"INCOMING FUEL AIR AND ARMOR PENETRATORS!" Bouncy called out.

The forest erupted in fire.

here comes the rain, Ekret thought to himself.

Explosions blossomed on the starboard battle-screen as Ekret stood up, half out of the hatch, his helmet left below, and the Precursor aircraft shot by, winding around for another shot. The point defense roared at it but missed. The hoverfans roared, at max accel, as the 150 ton hovertank slid to starboard and Cheepeek cursed, trying to line up the shot. Sensors were useless, thermal masking smoke, droplet suspended microcrystal prisms, chaff, and more filling the air. Cheepeek had to rely on his optical sight. Bouncy was fully engaged helping Heslettek in keeping the EW running since air superiority was still in question.

The mag-lev had been built by the Precursors, from a Jotun that had slammed down into the bay to its Devestators and Destructors and Djinn. It was ferrying war vehicles, ammunition, supplies, and only the Precursor knew what.

Sselssen drove the tank straight through the wooden buildings, blowing through the (hopefully) empty housing, the battle-screen throwing away burning debris even as the tank's fans ground the debris into the dirt. Ekret winced, hoping no-being was taking shelter in the buildings. The battle-screen would do to flesh and bone what it did to wood and plasteel.

The tanks of 1/1 HHQ CO burst out of the wooden buildings, rotating and putting on the power to make a tight swinging curve so they were racing next to the train. The last tanks started pouring fire into the train cars, into the tracks, as they raced after their fellows. The trail was winding, moving between the high piles of old mining tailings from when the area had been an active lithium salt mine.

"ENGINE UP AHEAD!" Cheepeek yelled, his face pressed into the foam cushion on his sight. The avian already had thick scabs around his eyes and a cut on the side of his face from slamming around in the tank while using his sight.

"FIRE AT WILL!" Ekret bellowed over his comlink, using the 2cm four-barrel mag-acel coaxil on the train cars. It tore through the metal and something exploded, throwing debris against the battle-screen.

"SHOT OUT!" Cheepeek yelled.

The engine exploded, jumped the track, and the entirety of 1/1H yanked away from the mag-lev train as it began to derail. Several threw shots into cars coming at them, blowing the cars apart.

In a perfect world I'd have been able to stop the train, load it with atomics, and blow that Jotun sky high, *Ekret thought to himself.*

The aircraft came roaring back, and the gunner of 1/1-3 blew it out of the air with a main gun shot.

"Commander's compliments to crew of 1/1-3," Ekret sent over the voice-com.

The night burned around them as they raced for their next target area.

The air was full of the ticking of cooling osmium and warsteel as the tanks slowly cooled. The crews crawled over them, patching the fan housings where it needed, cleaning the air filters, checking the hoses, recompiling battle-programs under the watchful eye of the VI's, eating or drinking when they could, moving to the opposite side of their tank to eliminate waste, or just trying to relax. 144th Ordnance Company was reloading the tanks, passing up ammunition from their armored vehicles. They men and women in the power chassis worked fast, chattering to one another as they worked.

Ekret was chewing on an empty ration pack, staring up at the night sky. Streaks, blots of light, all lit up the dark violet sky. A bright flash the size of a credit chip let Ekret know that something big had just blown up.

He was listening to the chatter of this crews over his implant, the command codes the Terrans had loaded into it proving useful. They were in high spirits, even though 1/1-6 had caught a massive magnetic accelerated hypervelocity shot that had blown clear through the tank. The anti-spalling liner the Terrans had installed on the tanks had kept the crew alive, but the tank commander had been vaporized above his waist, the gunner had lost his tail, and the driver's armor was the only thing that had saved his life as the round punched out the other side.

One crew. One crew in over 24 hours, out of 8,000 tanks and crews.

Ekret knew his luck couldn't last forever, but right there, at that moment, the universe felt perfect to him.

Off in the distance the thunder of an orbital strike rumbled and a faint flash sped across the night sky.

A Terran heavy cruiser had gotten a shot at that Jotun and took it. From the chatter on Ekret's implant, the Jotun was suffering chain reaction explosions. Its point defense was down and the artillery units of V Corps had already plotted and let loose fire missions.

The night was perfect.

The ion bolt, fired from a 200mm cannon, slammed into the battlescreen, slamming Ekret painfully against the edge of his hatch. Ekret swung the 2cm autocannon around, snarling through bloody teeth, and triggered the coaxil.

The density collapsed metal shard sheered the armor away from the vehicle, ripping a deep gouge in the side. The hypervelocity rounds connected the coaxil and the armored vehicle for a second.

1/1-4 took the shot and the vehicle exploded, debris flashing on the battle-screens.

They were past and Ekret could see another vehicle, this one facing away. Ekret held down the trigger, hosed a burst into the machine even as Sselseen fluttered the fans and nudged the ground with the forward port fan, slewing the tank around.

The machine exploded as a mag-driven sabot slashed the edge of the port battle-screen, not disrupting it but instead bleeding energy into it which the battle-screens dumped into the capacitors of the tank.

Ekret snarled, the empty thin plas ration tube held between his teeth. He saw another vehicle and slashed the coaxil across it right before Cheekeet slammed a plasma cannon round into it.

They were past, all of 1/1H running for it, deploying chaff, jammers, microprism mist, and good old thermal masking smoke.

"Headcount," Ekret growled over his implant, his teeth still worrying the tube.

It came back.

No casualties.

"Break net, break net, Rapid Viper, do you read?" The message pushed across the entire net. It was Trucker himself. Behind the Terran's voice Ekret heard "SHOT OUT!"

Heslettek boosted the gain, deployed a com-drone, firing it into the low clouds that were dropping ash filled rain on them.

"Rapid Viper Six here," Ekret answered. "We hear you."

"You where TacCom says you are?" Trucker asked.

TARGET! Ekret wasn't sure if it came from Trucker's link or his.

Ekret checked the screens quickly. Only off by about a hundred meters, but that could matter. He thumbed the update icon. "Roger that, Papa Dragon."

"Listen close, you know that check you signed?" Trucker asked.

Shit, Ekret thought. Human cursewords were satisfying to let out in a human snarl. *That check. Oooh boy.*

"Roger that, sir," Ekret said. "Check cashing time, sir."

"Punch up 13th Evac Hospital," Trucker ordered. Bouncy threw it up as a pulse from Trucker ID'd it for the aVI. Ekret pinged he had it. "OK, there's a force of heavy metal heading in on it. They can't get out, I've got only one thing in range to get in the way of the heavy metal."

"You can count on us, sir," Ekret said.

SHOT OUT! rang in both Ekret's crew cabin and over Trucker's transmission.

"Passing data to your warboi," Trucker snapped. "I've got elements of 8th Infantry and 3rd Armor heading in, but they won't get there in time. Just slow them down, you don't have to slambang them toe to toe, Rapid Viper."

"We're on it, sir! Rapid Viper enroute and out," Ekret said.

Bouncy threw the scans up on the datapads that still worked around Ekret. Ekret pursed his lips. They were big machines. Two thousand to Ekret's two hundred. They outweighed him by a factor of 20 at least. The only good thing was they were track motivated with repulsor assist. Maser cannons on the front, plasma cannons on the side, a single magack at the back. Point defense was thick, though. No battle screens. Armor meters thick, though. No reactive armor, that was something. No indirect fire but forward facing rocket pods. They all had gunpods around them, vehicle sized drones mounting hypervelocity cannons.

They were outnumbered, counting the pods, thirty to one.

"All 1/1 elements, this is Rapid Viper Six, incoming battleplan update. Fire off masking and go to flank speed," Ekret said. He put what they were trying to protect. "Our wounded are there. 1/5 and 1/7's men are there. It's check cashing time, as the Terran's say."

Sselsseen whipped the tank around like it was a hockey puck on ice, gunned the fans. Cheapshot stroked his sole remaining feather for luck. Ekret put an empty plas ration tube in his mouth.

It was going to be an ugly fight. 13th Evac was just beyond some hills, which meant that they couldn't get their line of sight weapons on the incoming metal. The air superiority was still in question and most of the aircraft were busy pounding two different Jotuns that were spewing fire and molten metal.

Ekret worked up the plan as best he could. Warning drivers to stay low, ordering the warbois to go to maximum deflection on the topside battle screens, ordering the warbois to rehash the entire Battalion's crypto, ordering the gunners to load all the heavy war-shot they'd largely been saving.

He ordered them to focus on the tracks, the repulsors, knock them out and keep going, stay mobile, stay alive.

He finished the transmission with "It Will Be Done."

He got back a resounding reply from every tank.

It Will Be Done, Sir!

The two hundred and six tanks of 1/1 Recon roared through the afternoon, their fans churning the grass and bushes into puree and spraying it around. They hit the beginning of the hills and split up according to Ekret's warplan, going to full stealth.

The battle was ugly but it wasn't fast as Ekret's tanks caught the Precursor machines with their electronic pants down. Gunners, their skills razor sharp after two days of fighting, disabled nearly three times their number as they raced into the enemy, taking them from the rear.

TARGET!

FIRE!

became the watchword.

But the Precursors didn't die alone. Ekret watched as a tank went to the white cross of a mission kill. It still moved, though, gouting flames as the main gun kept firing. It took another hit, slewed the side, fired again, and blew up. A red X covered two. Then another. Then another.

Then 1/1 was clear, spinning in place, tilting the fans to push the tanks back toward the enemy as the guns fired. Roaring back in, their guns thundering, aimed at tracks or repulsor pods.

Ekret ran the coaxil, the same with Heslettek, blowing pods out of the air, raking the tracks, slamming plasma bolts and mag-shot against the armor.

Another mission kill, the driver slewed it out of the formation, bouncing off a Precursor machine, the tank spinning, but getting clear. It was burning its two fans, trying to keep air cushion up, but still firing its gun.

Sa'altlikk's old crew, put in a heavy tank after the light tank had blown a primary engine. They kept pouring fire into the Precursor vehicles until three of the enemy vehicles targeted the grounded tank.

It burst into flame.

And 1/1 was clear. The Precursor machines had abandoned their advance, stung too hard, over 25% of their forces and almost all the pods already destroyed. One Precursor machine tried to deploy a pod and somehow Sa'altlikk's old crew put one more plasma cannon shot downrange, hitting the open pod bay.

The Precursor blew up at the same time as the wounded UMF tank exploded into shards.

Back in, into the thunder and fire, the crash of metal and the scream of overloaded hoverfans, the stench of burning battle-screens and scorched metal.

1/1 came out of the other side, but this time the Precursors gave chase.

Ekret had planned for that and the tanks of 1/1 swam between the low hills, that had once been debris piles for a massive factory that had been reclaimed two centuries before.

"BLACK HORSE ENROUTE! HOLD THE LINE, BROTHERS!" came over the comlink.

"HEAVY METAL INCOMING!" roared the warborgs of 8th Infantry.

Ekret looked at his tactical display and knew if his men broke off the Precursor machines would pound 1/1's rear arcs with concentrated fire and not a single one of Ekret's men would survive getting out of the hills.

"Stick with the *fucking* war-plan, men!" Ekret roared over the comlink.

"IT WILL BE DONE! FOR THIRTEENTH!" his men roared back.

Ekret's men began making figure eights, turning the machines in circles, forcing them to try to go over the hills and firing into the underbellies of the Precursor machines.

The Precursors kept exploding, but not fast enough. Another tank was killed. One mission killed but then crushed beneath the treads of Precursor tank it had just gutted as gravity pulled the dead Precursor down the hill.

The commander was firing the coaxil even as the Precursor's treads slammed down on the tank.

A round hit, blowing through the battle-screen, slamming into the hull of the turret. The cupola rang but the spall lining held. A six inch deep glowing crater shown on the side of Ekret's tank, but Cheepeek "Cheapshot" slammed a plasma bolt back, blowing the track off. The Precursor vehicle slewed the side and Cheapshot slammed a bolt into its side, into a crater left by another tank.

The Precursor exploded.

A drone popped up and Ekret raked it with magshot, shattering it before it could deploy a weapon. It was still wet, greasy looking.

Sselseen whipped the tank around the dead carcass of

another Precursor, coming up behind a still moving Precursor machine.

"SHOT OUT!" Cheapshot trilled.

The return shot hit the side of Ekret's tank, throwing Viper-Six against the burning wreckage of another tank. The spalling liner worked but the shot still blew two of the fans out.

The second shot hit the engine and Bouncy blew the fusion engine free, flushing it with water. It flew out, toward a moving Precursor machine.

Heslettek raked the glowing fusion engine.

Sselseen pulled the tank around, slamming the injured side against another wreck, the vehicle rocking on its side slightly.

Bouncy put full power, everything he could get, into the starboard battle-screen, ignoring the heat and overload warnings.

Ekret hosed a drone.

Cheapshot hit the bottom of a tank that was clearing the hill with a roar.

The shells breached the mag-bottle and the fusion engine erupted.

Nuclear fire washed over Viper-Six, slamming it against the hill, dragging it along the dirt, spinning it, tearing away the last two fans.

Cheapshot fired another round, gutting another tank.

The tank went dead. Black. After a long moment red light clicked on, went off, then came on. Sparks were shooting from Cheapshot's scope. The avian gunner had blood running down his face and his prosthetic beak was cracked down the middle.

"I I I I I g-g-g-got that," Bouncy said.

The scope stopped shooting sparks.

The hull still rumbled with the battle roaring outside.

"Get me a screen, Bouncy," Ekret ordered.

"No can do, boss. "We're fused shut in here and running on emergency power backup batteries," Bouncy said. He stuttered several times. "I gotta drop into my surv vi vi vival core.

Sorry, boss."

"Ya did good, Bouncy. Get some rest," Ekret coughed. "Who's still alive."

"Me," Haslettek coughed.

"Here," Sselseen said. He coughed, blinking his transparent lids over his eyes.

"Present," Cheapshot hacked.

The little digital display on the yellow striped box wit the yellow handle next to Ekret's head flashed a smiley face.

Something crashed into the remains of Viper-Six, sending it spinning. The lights went out.

shit

They sat in the dark for a long moment.

"Sir, can you pass me the medical kit?" Cheapshot asked. "My face is torn up."

Ekret fumbled around until he found it, then passed it to his gunner. "Hear you go, Cheapshot. Good fight, no?"

"Best fight," they all said together.

Something glanced off their hull, bulging the side of crew compartment, but the anti-spalling liner held.

Sselseen grabbed the extinquisher and hosed down his controls.

"Just in case," The saurian said.

"No complaints from me," Ekret said, putting an empty ration tube in his teeth. "Wish we had a pack of glow in the dark dice or cards like the Terrans carry."

"Gonna trade for some," Cheapshot said in the darkness.

"Hand me the kit," Ekret said. There was some fumbling but he got the kit. He used it silently, listening to the battle outside and his crew being alive inside.

It went quiet. The crew was panting, the air thick. They took turns on the oxygen mask from the medkit, gasping and sweating between each hit.

Eventually, it ran out while the world still thundered through the hull.

There was a clank in the darkness. Ekret opened his eyes.

It was still dark inside.

"13th Evac SAR, hold on, brothers," was inducted to the interior.

There was a loud roar above Ekret and he shielded his eyes when the hatch was ripped free.

A UMF Air Mobile suit, with the red cresent on one side of the chest, the red cross on the other, was looking inside.

"Can you move, Most High?" Old Iron Feathers asked, shining his light on the slap-patch on the stump of his right leg.

"Yeah," Ekret said. He grabbed the handle on the yellow square, pulled it out, then twisted the handle. The cube popped free. "Don't forget our warboi."

"Leave none behind," Old Iron Feathers quoted as he deployed a pair of Purrbois.

Ekret looked at his new chrome foot. The Terrans had replaced his entire leg with a cyborg prosthetic. The armor on the leg had been pulled from his faithful tank.

His crew had survived.

Cheapshot had black chrome around his eyes, his eyes replaced with cybernetics. Sselseen had his tail regrown and his shoulder repaired. Haslettek had needed a new implant and both of his legs had been broken.

But they survived the brutal fight two days ago. They'd held off the Precursors, 1/1 taking heavy casualties but keeping them from sweeping over the hills to crash down the Medical Evac company.

Ekret looked up. The new tank was in front of him. He was carrying Bouncy's Survival Core.

"Let's get it on," Cheapshot said.

Together they moved to the tank, climbing inside. Ekret locked the box in place, hit the stud, and watched as Bouncy moved across the screens. Once everyone was buckled in, Ekret stood up in the hatch and nudged his implant.

"1/1's waiting, men," Ekret said, pulling an empty ration

tube from his pocket, where it had sat next to the glow in the dark dice, and put it between his teeth.

The tank moved smoothly away on its hoverfans.

V CORPS

Special Unit Commendation to 1/1 Recon for valor above and beyond the call of duty in the defense of 13th Evac hospital. Battle standard to be awarded. Permission for unit crest and unit motto (to be approved) is granted.

---NOTHING FOLLOWS---

THE BAD LANAKTALLAN

Ullmo'ok was a bad Lanaktallan. His mother and father had always told him so. He was uninterested in money for the most part, he was uninterested in power, he had little to no interest in politics, and he didn't care one way or another for rules. The last would have been understandable if it involved the first three in any way, but Ullmo'ok's idea of a fun evening was getting together with some friends, all of them from the UnCivilized species or the neo-sapients, hacking a car's computer, and roaring around the city in it.

The final straw had come when Ullmo'ok had gotten high on stim-grass, stripped naked, painted himself red with the crowd suppression paintgun, stolen a LawSec cruiser and driven it on a two hour chase that had culminated in Ullmo'ok deliberately crashing the armored vehicle into the river and standing on top of it as it sank, rearing up to show his genitals to the TriVid cameras, his jowls full of stimgrass. He'd had a gun in each hand, taken from the LawSec cruiser, and kept shooting potshots at the cameras until a LawSec sniper had tagged him with a stunner rifle. The sniper had been forced to shoot the young Lanaktallan three times to drop him.

It was put up to the jowls full of stimgrass.

His parents had been horrified. His friends had found it hilarious. LawSec had taken the bribe and looked the other way.

Ullmo'ok had been entertained. He'd *almost* felt something, standing on the roof the sinking LawSec vehicle. He'd come so close but the stunner had hit him. He'd felt something then, not the ravening nerve pain that the second shot brought, not the darkness that the third shot had dropped onto him, but he'd felt *something* he'd never felt before.

He had been sent to where his father's uncle was in charge of resource collection in a system in the Unified Outer Systems. His great-uncle was less than impressed that Ullmo'ok had gotten intoxicated during the flight and had fallen off the gangplank and onto the spaceport tarmac, laughing like a pair of bagpipes in a paint shaker, a bottle of alk-brew in each hand and a stimstick in his mouth.

His great-uncle had tried to put him in the offices, doing busy work and just moving files and papers around down in the mail room.

Ullmo'ok had convinced the neo-sapients who worked in the mail room to fight one another in the "Pit of Fists Swinging" for the reward of time off, vacation days, and raises.

His great-uncle moved him to the warehouse, where Ullmo'ok had put together a racing rally with the wheeled ground effect forklifts with "prizes" for the winners. After that was stopped by his great-uncle he arranged a 'hover smash' where workers drove old hoverlifts and crashed into one another with the winners getting prizes. Soon every hoverlift was covered in sheet metal and spikes and mesh. Ullmo'ok himself took part in them until finally he broke one of his arms when he was t-boned by another lift. Ullmo'ok's uncle sighed and sent the young Lanaktallan out to one of the mines as soon as he healed.

Ullmo'ok himself had *almost* felt something when the bones in his arm had snapped and he'd whipped his hoverlift around to slam the heavy weighted end into the worker's side. He'd *almost* felt something when his uncle had ordered his arm set without painkillers. He'd knocked out the Umtervian medic with one hit when he'd reacted to the pain and felt a little bit of *something* that he had been chasing.

At the mines, Ullmo'ok's uncle had despaired. Ullmo'ok had gotten bored with paperwork and supervision the first week and had bribed one of the workers to teach him to use a cargo-mech to load the raw ore into the transports. That had led to "Mech Bash" competitions where mechs smashed against each other, slamming each other with graspers or lifters, while an audience cheered. Within a month the cargo-mechs were covered in metal and spikes and painted garish colors.

A few workers were killed in the competitions, but Mech-Bash went on, with Ullmo'ok participating to the roar of the crowd.

Strangely, productivity was up. Incidents between the workers and CorpSec were down. Alcohol and drug use were up, black market trading of ration chips and CorpStore script was up, fighting was up, but the amount of lethal stabbings, shootings, beatings, and ambushes went down.

Ullmo'ok's uncle just swept all the Mech-Bash incidents under the rug. He purchased junk mechs from the other Corporate divisions, thinking maybe having older, battered, less maintained cargo-mechs would stop the Mech-Bash and having massive redundancy would replace the cargo-mechs when they failed.

Instead Ullmo'ok's band started stripping parts from the junk-mechs and adding them to the cargo mechs.

Then CorpSec reported that the junkyard where the old defunct corporate crowd control and law enforcement vehicles had been robbed.

Ullmo'ok's uncle knew exactly who had robbed it, but at least this time there was no evidence. The older Lanaktallan had boarded his executive hoverlimo and gone out to the mine, chewing narco-cud the whole way to ease his anxiety.

He could see two cargo-mechs battering each other as his hover-limo came in for a landing. As he watched in horror one of them opened up with a chain-gun that was the same type as the heavy crowd control vehicles from CorpSec used.

He could hear the roar of the crowd even through his armored limo's windows.

When he landed a small Puntimat neo-sapient lizard asked the older Lanaktallan if he wanted to purchase something called 'box seats' or if he wanted refreshments or to meet some of the 'Mech Slammers" personally.

The Uncle, who went by the name of Lo'omo'nan, har-rumphed and demanded to see his nephew. Lo'omo'nan found himself escorted by two young female Lanaktallan of lower caste, secretaries for the Corporation's mining facility, dressed scandalously so much of their udders showed. Instead of taking him directly to see his nephew Lo'omo'nan was taken to a seat protected by pressor beams and armaglass.

"Where, harrumph, is my nephew?" Lo'omo'nan asked, accepting the offer of a narcobrew.

One of the Lanaktallan females pointed out at the dirt field where a cargo-mech had just walked out. The cargo mech was covered in crude metal armor, garishly painted, with chain guns, a giant sawblade for a hand, and a crudely fashioned metal spiked fist replacing one of the graspers.

"He is right there, Most High Guest," the Lanaktallan fe-male informed the older male.

As Lo'omo'nan watched the cargo-mech raised all four arms, slamming the forearms together as the crowd roared.

The entire crowd roared so fiercely that Lo'omo'nan's ten-dril curled and his crests inflated defensively.

The battle was fierce and made Lo'omo'nan cringe and feel nauseous. His grand-nephew showed no hesitation, like a proper civilized being would, and instead charged his opponent and met him blow for blow. The battle ended when the other cargo-mech landed on its back with a crash and the crowd roared. Lo'omo'nan thought it strange that his nephew reached down one mechanical hand to help his opponent to their feet and raised the mech's hand with his own, to the roar of the crowd.

One of his female hanger-ons asked Lo'omo'nan if he wanted a Tri-Vid or VR chip of the battle as a souvenir.

Only 24 Corpscript.

Lo'omo'nan couldn't believe that the crowd had been chanting his family name at top volume. He himself avoided crowds, which all stared and muttered as his limo moved through. He saw his nephew pushing through the crowd, slapping extended hands with his four hands, cursing loudly, and swigging narco-brew handed to him. His nephew, Ullmo'ok, was sweaty, wearing only a cooling vest and a bandage over one of his side eyes, not even a sash to proclaim who he was and what his standing was. Lo'omo'nan watched, horrified, as one of the tall neosapient mammals, a two-legged Hikken, poured narcobrew on her fur covered mammary glands and his nephew pressed his sweaty face between them, shook his head, and made blubbering sounds.

The crowd around his nephew roared with glee.

Another worker being, another neosapient, stripped off her shirt, revealing scandalous flesh and fur, handing her shirt to Lo'omo'nan's nephew. Ullmo'ok wiped his face and chest and handed it back, the neo-sapient clutching it tight to her upper body, her eyes bright as she watched Lo'omo'nan's nephew swagger between a doorway.

Lo'omo'nan was led to his nephew's "office", taking a winding way. They moved through the maintenance bay where Lo'omo'nan saw maintenance techs working on the crudely armored and armed mechs. Past makeshift lounges and bars where Lo'omo'nan saw wealthy executives of the Corporation yelling, shaking fists, and shouting bets as the narcobrew flowed and the stimcud was chewed. Lo'omo'nan couldn't believe what he was seeing.

He *knew* that Lanaktallan, a senior executive with the Corporation, from distinguished family lineage, who's family was wealthy and powerful even by Unified Core Systems standards. The SEO was at the bar, shouting at the screen where two cargo-mechs brawled, a narcobrew in each hand of his four hands, while two small lemurian Welkret females combed the Lanaktallan's fur and rubbed his skin while *sitting on his back*. As Lo'omo'nan watched, the wealthy and powerful being turned at the waist to face the two on his back. The closer one took a deep drag off a stimstick held by the other one, put her hands on either side of the Lanaktallan's jowls, and blew the smoke directly into his nostrils.

Lo'omo'nan hurriedly clopped past that, closing his side and rear eyes so he didn't have to see such disgusting deviance carried on by members of his own species.

Finally he reached his nephew, who was sitting on a broken couch, a stimstick in his mouth, a Welkret female with a medikit tending to his bruises and small cuts on his hide. The younger Lanaktallan had his eyes closed, his hands at his sides, and Lo'omo'nan was horrified to see that his nephew was allowing two comely young Lanaktallan females manually stimulate him *sexually* as he relaxed and the Welkret tended to his wounds while loud music, prohibited by the Corporation, blared from speakers stacked in the corners.

"Nephew!" the elder Lanaktallan harrumphed, hoping the sound of his voice would put a stop to this degeneracy and debasement.

He was shocked and appalled that the two females didn't even look up, instead just leaned over his nephews back to entwine their jowl tendrils, their hands still busy. The Welkret ran the auto-suturer down a cut on his nephews flank. Everyone else cheered as an arm was torn free from a cargo-mech as the other yanked the arm straight and ravaged the joint with the chaingun.

"I perfected that move, you know, uncle," His nephew said, pointing at the screen with a half-empty narcobrew.

Lo'omo'nan yanked his attention from the huge display, normally used by executives to display data, and looked at his nephew, who was patting the rumps of the two females and shooing them away.

"Just what do you think you're doing?" Lo'omo'nan demanded of his nephew.

"Getting 'patched up' to use a phrase, Uncle," Ullmo'ok answered, taking a swig from his narcobrew. "My opponent was skilled and determined. I was proud to defeat him, Most Honored Uncle."

"Honored? Honored? You destroy the honor of our line, of our name, by brawling with these... these... neo-species," Lo'omo'nan sputtered, his tendrils tight with outrage.

"If you say so," Ullmo'ok said. He twitched slightly and the Welkret snapped at him to stay still so she could scrape the emergency coagulate off his skin and suture the wound.

"Your workers cause damage to company property, costing the mine credits, undoubtedly putting this whole facility into the red! If you don't care about our honor, what about our stockholders?" Lo'omo'nan barked as best he could, inflating his crests to establish dominance over his nephew.

His nephew ignored the crests, taking another swig. "Is it money you're worried about, uncle?" The younger Lanaktallan said slowly. He signified disappointment and resignation then made a tossing motion toward the older male. "View that if all you worry about is the profits."

Lo'omo'nan snorted and opened the datafile. It was a spreadsheet of company costs and expenses balanced against income, with man hours, and expenses and income broken down.

Ullmo'ok watched his uncle digest the data that seemed so important to the older Lanaktallan but was infinitely uninteresting to Ullmo'ok himself.

Anyone can turn a neo-sapient upside down and shake the credit chits from his pockets, *Ullmo'ok thought to himself.* Only the best can convince them to roar out his name in frenzied appreciation.

Lo'omo'nan couldn't believe what he was seeing. The entire facility was making more profit in a single planetary cycle than it ever had in its entire existence. Membership fees, drinks and narcotics, prostitution, viewing fees, entrance fees, income from TriVid and VR chips, GalNet broadcast on shady Netsites that were pay per view only, gambling, and more. The credits were pouring in, outstripping even the cost to black marketeers for weapons, armor, narcotics. Even outstripping worker payments, taxes, everything else. The books were then cooked, using the mining and refinery plant as cover. What the refinery actually made in profit could have been listed in the slush funds compared to what his nephew was bringing in from his illegal and immoral activities.

Even more startling was that Ullmo'ok had reported every drip and drop of income to the Unified Taxation Office and paid the taxes.

Ullmo'ok watched his uncle's tendrils tremble in pleasure and gave the equivalent of a sigh of envy. His uncle looked almost orgasmic, a feeling that Ullmo'ok chased but could only taste the bare edges of.

Only in the cockpit of his cargo-mech.

"You did all this?" Lo'omo'nan asked, surprised his nephew even understood how to do multi-column accounting.

Ullmo'ok snorted in amusement. "Hardly, uncle. I pay employees to do it and pay them well."

"What if one of the neo-sapients tries to cheat you or rob you?" Lo'omo'nan asked, sure his nephew didn't understand how to keep the neo-sapients in line.

"The first one that got greedy, I had chained to the fist of my cargo-mech and pasted him against the chest armor of my opponent with a few punches," Ullmo'ok said matter of factly, as if he wasn't talking about the brutal killing of another sentient being. Lo'omo'nan stared at his nephew in horror as the younger one gave the equivalent of a shrug. "It's one of the most downloaded and paid for clips. My opponent painted over the dark blue of the dried blood with bright blue paint to remind everyone of that battle. Since then, my employees only steal about 2%, which I'm willing to overlook."

Lo'omo'nan just stared in horror. Without another word he turned around and galloped back to his limo, returning to the capital with a promise to himself that as long as his nephew kept bringing in record profits the maniacal Lanaktallan could just stay at the remote facility.

Ullmo'ok looked at the being. Called a 'human' apparently.

A bipedal primate with the closely set forward facing eyes of a predator, thickly muscles, with hair only on its head and around its mouth, with five fingers instead of four. It was dressed in clothing covered with holograms that showed cartoon female humans chasing each other and hitting one another with blunt object. It made Ullmo'ok inflate his crests with amusement.

"You know, I can replace that eye with a cybereye in about an hour," the human said, using a universal translator. "No charge. Just have the medibot do it while we conduct business."

Ullmo'ok signified his agreement with one hand, his eyes only for what the human "Junker" had brought him.

Massive robot power armor. Armor meters thick. Bristling with weapons. Designed like a biped but just oozing malice. All of them designed to appear aggressive and menacing just sitting there with their fusion reactors pulled and weapons empty or disengaged.

A spider-bot climbed up Ullmo'ok's foreleg, then up his torso, then onto his head, settling over the empty socket of his right side eye.

Ullmo'ok ignored it. A medibot was nothing to grow anxious about. He mentally braced for pain. Pain was inevitable. Pain was good.

Pain was life.

"I've got some old Terran battle-cruiser battle-screens. That should protect the crowd from any missed shots as well as provide really slamming effects when they're hit. Nothing outside a nuclear penetrator can get through that class of shields, even though they're old tech. Pulled 'em off some blown-out ships back around Rigel-6," The Terran, human, Max-a-Millions said, slapping his hands together eagerly, the motion like he was brushing off dust but more animated and loud.

Ullmo'ok liked that body language. He tried it himself and found it much more satisfying than the handwringing of anticipation that most of his race used.

"That sounds sufficient," Ullmo'ok said, following the Terran's body language of nodding rather than inflating his crest in assent. He liked that too.

"Now, these mechs are civilian grade, usually used by frontier harsh environment worlds for heavy security. They'll rip a pirate ship to shreds, can go toe to toe with light armor, and can even take on your civilian government grade heavy armor units," Max said, pointing at one of the smaller mechs. "That one, right there? That can crush most heavy armor units used by your civilian governments with a single stomp. I wouldn't try taking on a Confed Mil-spec tank, that thing would rip you apart. But against anything you'll probably face? No contest."

Ullmo'ok nodded, admiring the lethal lines of the massive mech. He liked the one with the skull face, the big fists, and the retractable rotating sawblade sword in its forearm.

"So, how many do you want?" The human asked, rubbing his hands together. Ullmo'ok's implant told him that it was eagerness, not distress.

Ullmo'ok stared at all the mechs in the massive freighter's hold. Over a hundred of them. All heavily armored and armed.

"All of them."

The cartoon female humans frolicking on Max-a-Million's suit all waved their pom-poms with their eyes replaced by throbbing hearts.

CorpSec Chief Executive Officer Moolim'ak exited his armored LawSec wagon, adjusted his sash, and trotted forward. The small neo-sapients waiting for him performed the elaborate welcoming rituals that were his due. Two lower caste Lanaktallan females, their implants marking them as food service workers for refinery executives, both trotted forward to coo at him and rub him. A Welkret climbed up on his back and began rubbing soothing narco-cream into his four shoulder-blades. He liked her, she had strong, soft hands and knew how to rub his muscles just right to force knots from tension to relax.

The smell of hot lubricant, scorched metal, sweat, and anticipation filled the CorpSec CEO's nostrils and his tendrils shivered in anticipation.

He was a wealthy and powerful male of the Lanaktallan executive caste, even beyond this planet. Yes, he should arrest young Ullmo'ok and every being involved or served by the younger male's illegal activities, but Moolim'ak couldn't bring himself to even think about such a thing.

After all, where else would he see such amazing sights?

The sound of music, new music, harsh, demanding, thundering, aggressive and violent, poured over the CEO as he entered the Most High Class Executive Lounge. He merely used that entrance to gain access to the facility. He handed off his sash and badges of rank to the little Puntimat at the door, who was inside an armored cage and took all valuables and put them in registered locked boxes. The sign at the top of her armor-plast window stated a warning: "Not Responsible For Grabbed Stuff You Take In!" The CEO nodded at the warning, gave the little neo-sapient a week's worth the meal chits for the way she bobbed and groveled as she put his stuff away, and headed deeper into the facility.

He passed the other members of his race at the clean and immaculate feeling lounges, moving past that to where he preferred. The greasy, slightly dirty, shabby lounge where the neon glowed, the music was almost too loud, and more than once some of the neo-sapients and even members of his own race threw fists over the outcome of a match or a disagreement over which cargo-mech pilot was best.

A bunch of his CorpSec men, all lower executives, raised up narcobeer and cheered him. Moolim'ak signaled the being tending the bar to bring another round to the table and clopped over to his men. They all thanked him for getting them in to the Grand Mech Bash. Something new was promised, something grand, and the alien sounded hard driving music hinted at whatever it was, it was going to be big.

When the fireworks went off and the lights went out, Moolim'ak turned to watch the oversized vid display. Sure, the tables in the executive lounges had built-in holoprojectors, but the faded and transparent holos just didn't have the excitement of the vid screens.

The little Welkret on his back tapped him and he turned around to face her. She took a drag off her stimstick, put her other hand against his left-hand jowl, and slowly exhaled stimsmoke into his nostril. He inhaled deeply, gratefully, feeling the already activated stim surge into his bloodstream and shivered.

What stomped out onto the viewscreen, obviously shaking the ground of the arena, was something that Moolim'ak recognized, something he had seen in classified videos from the furious fighting against the Precursors over the last two months.

A human Warmech.

It raised its arms over its head, clasping the massive hands, and shook them while the crowd roared.

Moolim'ak was aghast. How had those war machines, some weighing as much as 500 tons, gotten to the planet? How had young Ullmo'ok gotten his grasping four hands on one? He stared as special effects froze the giant mechanized war machine, spun it around, put it in garish colors, and then detailed the weapons.

Sweat popped up on Moolim'ak's crests and he inflated them with agitation. That giant beast carried two 200mm autocannons just to start off with. It packed missiles, lasers, particle beams, something called a 'chainsword", and more. Its polyceramic warsteel laminate armor could shrug anything his entire CorpSec force could bring to bear and those autocannons would shred anything he could field.

"Yeah! Yeah!" One of his subordinates, a Senior Executive Officer cheered. "Slamsmash! Slamsmash!"

The little Welkret tapped Moolim'ak and when the CEO turned at the waist to face behind him the little mammal pressed both hands against his nose and slowly exhaled narcosmoke into first one then the other nostril. Moolim'ak closed his eyes and let the little neo-sapient put his four hands on her fur and start to stroke.

It soothed him, such degeneracy. It calmed him, indulging in such deviance. He would never do so in private or at work, but here, surrounded by pounding alien music, in a dimly lit grimy "sports-lounge", surrounded by his subordinates and other Mechbash fans, he indulged himself in vices that he would have never imagined as a young Lanaktallan in the Unified Core Systems where he had grown up.

He turned around, shifting his arms so he still reached behind him to stroke the Welkret, who tapped the inside of one arm with a narcojet, just in time to see the opponent. A giant warmech the same weight class, different weapons, painted in the garish colors of another competitor. This one armed with lasers, particle cannons, missiles, with point defense and other missile defenses.

It then pulled back, displaying the modified arena. Giant chunks of 'armor' made up of warsteel and battlesteel, glimmering energy fields, and other things to take cover behind. Plasma 'mines', auto-turrets, flamers, all kinds of hazards that the crowd could activate by throwing 'BashCash' at it in the form of work-chits, food chits, corp-script, Unified Systems Credits, even promises of favors.

The count-down started and Moolim'ak calmed his agitation by touching the little female in ways that a member of his species, his caste, his executive status probably shouldn't. He brought her around to his chest, cradling and stroking her in his four arms, while she blew clouds of narco-vape across his nose and balanced a mug of narcobrew on her stomach.

The battle started and Moolim'ak quickly forgot his agitation. Particle cannons thundered, autocannons shrieked, the shields screamed and sparked with misses that thrilled the crowd as they were only held off from certain death by the invisible hands of battle-screen projectors.

Ten fights, all between massive Terran Warmechs. Moolim'ak gambled and won as often as he lost, but by the time he was halfway through watching the fights he was cheering as often as everyone else. He broke a narcobrew bottle across the face of a Senior Executive Lanaktallan from Financial Services during the sixth fight, clasped hands with the same being and cheered during the seventh, the two males slapping each other's sides in shared joy as the mech they had bet on defeated the larger one. One of his subordinates put a fist in his eye and he responded by kicking the other male in the chest to the roar of the onlookers. He bought his defeated subordinate a large mug of the subordinate's favorite narcobrew to show how gracious he was in victory. The subordinate cheered Moolim'ak's name as they all left together and rode home in the same executive limo.

Ullmo'ok's uncle looked at the profits from the "New & Improved Mechbash!" and had to shuffle funds around at a Senior Executive level to hide the profits. He noticed the CEO of CorpSec had a swollen eye during a luncheon, but didn't pay it any mind, CorpSec types often had to put down riots.

The air was full of thunder as atmospheric craft roared overhead. More humans had arrived, to protect the system from a possible Precursor attack. Humans had sworn to protect the star system, had deployed massive amounts of war machines through space, around moons, on planets. Everywhere a Precursor might attack, might strike at the beings they so hated.

While other Lanaktallan had run in circles panicking, wringing their four hands, inflating and deflating their crests in fear, shaking their jowls in terror, bleating and crying out in anxiety, Ullmo'ok felt a tingling tremor deep inside. Actually felt it.

He invited Terrans to his Mechbash, comped them entrance, drinks, anything they wanted.

They had enjoyed it.

Ullmo'ok liked the Terrans he had met. Members of something called V Corps (Old Blood) that just made his tendrils coil in joy. Ullmo'ok had noticed that even their officers liked the dimmer, grimier looking lounges, more deviant and dangerous the better.

Two humans had pulled knives on each other, fighting on

the floor of one of the lounges over a Puntimat female they had both been petting. Neither one had been killed but they had been injured. Ullmo'ok had ordered the Welkret 'medicos' to not use painkillers on the Terrans to see how they reacted.

Every reaction to pain brought jeers from their fellow Terrans. One who had flinched had narcobrew poured over him by his fellows.

The two knife fighters were arm in arm, cheering, less than a fight later.

Ullmo'ok was fascinated by the Terrans.

They looked... looked...

alive.

Ullmo'ok envied them.

V CORPS COMMANDER'S MEMO

Attendance at Ullmo'ok Mech Bash Arena is permitted via recreation pass.

Please stop stabbing each other. It looks bad to our hosts when senior officers duel with knives over who gets to pet the furry xenospecies 'with great tits' no matter how much it amuses your subordinates. I appreciate a great set of mammary glands as much as the next species but rolling around on the floor while the enlisted pour narcobrew on you is undignified. Real officers use stun-pistols at twenty paces. While dueling is legal, please refrain from doing so unless it is vitally important, like who may have stolen your last pack of Terran cigarettes.

--General Nodra'ak, V Corps, Commanding

---NOTHING FOLLOWS---
KESTIMET CORPORATE MEMO

Attendance at this so called "Mech Bash" is strictly prohibited to all executives by order of Kestimet Corporate Headquarters, Core Worlds. Attendance to any of this illegal activity can result in a fine of up to three day's pay.

---NOTHING FOLLOWS---

The Terran was a big warborg, two tons of anodized black

warsteel, heavy weapons hidden inside his chassis and the magnetic power-inductors the size of Ullmo'ok's hand covered with a thin layer of armorplas, with an 8 pierced by an upright arrow marking both of his shoulders. His face shield was open, letting Ullmo'ok see the Terran's biological face that had been attached to a warsteel skull. While other Lanaktallan's might have been distressed by the cyborg it didn't bother Ullmo'ok at all. The Terran was one of Ullmo'ok's loyal customers over the last weeks the Terrans had been deploying their war material and getting ready for a possible Precursor attack.

"You might want to get off the planet soon, Ullmo'ok," the Terran said. It took a sip of narcobrew. "Good stuff."

"My appreciation of your enjoyment," Ullmo'ok answered, nodding. He liked Terran physical body language much better than he liked crest and tendril signals. "Why would I want to leave?"

The Terran sighed. "There's Imps in the Oort Cloud and that can only mean one thing."

"Precursors are coming," Ullmo'ok guessed. The big Terran nodded. "You advise me to flee?"

The Terran warborg slowly nodded. "It's going to get ugly, friend. The Precursors are going to come at this system with everything they can shake loose. This is an important extraction and refinery system," The warborg paused. "They're going to come straight at this facility."

Ullmo'ok nodded again. "That sounds logical. My uncle has sent some of CorpSec out here, some with heavy vehicles as CorpSec designates them. To protect this refinery from any rivals he says but I believed it to try to protect from any of my Bashmech pilots going rogue."

"The CorpSec vehicles won't last fifteen seconds against Precursor machines," the Terran answered.

"I have seen my Bashmech list them as light civilian defense vehicles," Ullmo'ok answered. He lifted his hands in an approximation of a shrug. "My Bashmech is a civilian version, I can only imagine what the Precursor machines must be like and even then, I am probably under-imagining them."

The Warborg nodded. "I faced off against some Precursors a few centuries ago. Not this brand, the other types, and they're a serious opponent. They don't stop and they linger to kill every living thing. To top it off, friend, they view your species as deserving to be wiped out."

Ullmo'ok shook his head. "I will not leave my loyal workers. They work hard for me, they fight harder."

The warborg sighed. "All right. Look, saying this is in the gray. I can probably get away with it because you're technically a CEO and a community leader. Nobody else outside of TERCON-FEDMIL knows this yet."

"One moment," Ullmo'ok said. He used his implant to turn off any surveillance devices, clear the surrounding rooms, and lock the doors. The big warborg nodded at the sound of the mag-locks engaging. "Go ahead."

"These things use psychic assault arrays. We don't mind that much, we're highly resistant to such things, but I don't know how your people will react," the warborg said. "They come at you, they're going to hit you with a psychic assault then slaughter your people while they're still alive and screaming."

Ullmo'ok thought a moment. "Is there a way for non-Terrans to protect themselves from this psychic assault?"

The warborg nodded. "Sure. Most of the Treana'ad officers have psychic shield implants, most vehicles have them, we've even got portable ones to protect camps and bases."

Ullmo'ok nodded. "Thank you for the information. It is most helpful. Can you guess at how long until the Precursors arrive?"

"Days? Weeks? With Imps in the Oort Cloud, we're being recon'd. It's not *if* they get here, it's *when* they get here," The warborg said. He stood up. "I should get back before I'm missed."

Ullmo'ok nodded, thinking carefully. He unlocked the door and ordered that the warborg be comp'd tonight's entertainment.

Psychic shielding, eh? The Terrans seem to have it commonly installed, that means they have it in abundance, he thought to himself. He signaled to the facilities computer to send two of his employees to him. One a structural engineer responsible for keeping the mine operational, the other a refinery expert.

They arrived quickly, both smelling of stim-sticks but they both had the obvious shakes from taking a quiksober. Ullmo'ot soothed their fears, handing them bottles of Terran narcobeer after he twisted the caps off. He turned down the music, then locked the doors.

"Honored Jumina'at," Ullmo'ok addressed the refinery master. The other being nervously signaled he was paying attention. "The humans call it warsteel, can we create and work it?"

The other Lanaktallan shook his heavy head. "No, honored Ullmo'ok. We can craft it but it immediately hardens and cannot be worked."

"What hyperalloy can we create that we can work with the tools available?" Ullmo'ok asked.

"Terran endosteel. We had the templates and industrial fabrication specifications," the refinery master said.

"Turn ten percent of our output to endosteel production. Keep it off the books. Offer triple-pay for anyone willing to work off the books shifts to produce it," Ullmo'ok said.

"As you wish, Most High," Jumina'at said.

"One another thing, Jumina'at," Ullmo'ok said. The subordinate looked nervous. "You have family on planet?"

"Yes, Most High," he answered.

"Bring them in. I will have vacation time authorized for them. Use one of the empty Executive Villas for them. Bring all of them," Ullmo'ok ordered.

Jumina'at didn't ask why, just nodded. Every one of Ullmo'ok's ideas had enriched him vastly and Jumina'at had ceased asking questions. He accepted his dismissal and left, Ullmo'ot locking the door again behind him.

"Za'almooint?" Ullmo'ok turned to the master engineer.

She nodded, still looking miserable from the quiksober shot. "Yes, Most High?" She stared at the male's robotic eye, fascinated by it. Supposedly Lanaktallan's were 'too advanced' to accept cybernetic prosthetics, but the eye had been there for weeks without problems.

Ullmo'ok used his personal holotank, a Terran version with excellent resolution and fidelity, to put up a map of one of the played out mines that wormed beneath the worker habs and the executive villas. "I want you to build shelters beneath these structures, in these mines, with fast access ports that can then be sealed and camouflaged until rescue can arrive."

The female Lanaktallan nodded slowly, getting up and moving around the holotank. "Shelters for how many people, Most High?"

"All of them. Plus another 10% redundancy, no, make it 20% redundancy and provide atmospheric, power, and food dispenser backups," Ullmo'ok ordered. "Triple pay for all who work on this. I want it done as soon as possible."

"As you will," she answered. "Will that be all?"

Ullmo'ok shook his head. "No, I have one other set of orders," he stated. He moved the scan to a set of played out mines a mile away. It had a large entry-cavern.

She curled her tendrils in confusion but waited.

"I want you to move all our spare parts, all our spare repair equipment, for the Bashmechs to this spot. We're going to be going back to cargo-mech fights for a little bit," he said. "Build these hollow buildings out of durachrome. Make sure the repair scaffolding is finished first."

"Which do I prioritize?"

"Concealed repair bays first, moving the parts second. I'll have different crews get the cargomech's ready to fight."

"Your customers won't like that," she warned.

"I'll play it up as a celebration of some type, offer reduced fees, that will quiet them," He said. He thought for a moment. "Send in Krekit. Personally, no datalink or com."

Za'almooint nodded and left, finding the Puntimat mechanic drinking narcobrew and puffing on a narcostick in one of the lounges, a pile of script, chits, and rations in front of him.

"Sober up, the Most High wants you right now," Za'almoo-int said.

The little Puntimat nodded, ordering a quiksober and getting up. He injected it into his arm as he hustled to where he knew The Boss would be watching the fights. When he went in he heard the door lock behind him and worried that The Boss knew that he'd been skimming money off the repair fees being charged the fighters.

"Sit, Honored High Mechanic," Ullmo'ok said, motioning at the comfortable seats. Krekit sat down, nervous, noting the unholstered needler pistol on the holotank. Ullmo'ok cracked open two Terran narcobeers and handed the little furry lizard one.

Krekit watched as Ullmo'ok brought up the schematics for his own Bashmech.

"Assign your less skilled techs to bringing the cargomechs back up to fighting status," Ullmo'ok stated. "Your best techs will have an assignment soon. They'll be making modifications to our Bashmechs."

"What kind?" Krekit asked, feeling a tingle of excitement.

"Right now, I'm not sure. Just have your men go over the technical documents for the Bashmechs and start doing eVR training from the datachips in the manuals. Even the stuff like a ruptured reactor shield," Ullmo'ok ordered. He handed another beer to the little fuzzy lizard. "Triple pay."

Krekit nodded, hustling out of the room.

Ullmo'ok opened his personal encrypted datalink address book, going over the various link addresses he had amassed. There, there was some contacts there were even at the Mechbash Arena.

He ordered in comely male and female members of all races, had them dress scandalously, then had his "office" arranged for effect. He then went out and took part in an "unscheduled match" to get *that* feeling again.

He needed his edge to meet with the beings he needed to meet with.

Uncle Lo'omo'nan;

I invite you to inspect the mines in a week or two. Please bring my aunt and my cousins, I have missed them dearly. I promise you won't be disappointed in what I wish to show you.

--Ullmo'ok

The Terran officer got out of the heavy cargo truck, walking toward where Ullmo'ok sat on the foot of his Bashmech, feeling the machine vibrate with power and menace. The Terran officer glanced up once then nodded before moving up to Ullmo'ok. The big Terran held out one crushing primate gripper and when Ullmo'ok shook it the primate increased the pressure, staring in Ullmo'ok's eyes.

Ullmo'ok held the stare, refusing to show any pain.

Pain was life.

The Terran officer nodded, grudgingly, and released Ullmo'ok's hand. Ullmo'ok ignored the pain of crushed muscle and bruised bone, the balloon-like feeling of swelling.

It was just pain.

"I got what you wanted. Psychic shielding for warmechs, updated molycirc packs, everything but warboi hashes. Even got you training eVR progs for your simulators. Uses the latest battle data we've got against the Precursor machines," the Terran said. "What do you have for me?"

"Here," the Lanaktallan said, motioning. Two Puntimat's ran forward each carrying a chip box. The idea had startled Ullmo'ok, it was simple, so easily done, and apparently brought in massive amounts of credits, chits, payment, and customers.

The first one was opened and the Terran removed one of the chips, checking it. The fifteen seconds was unlocked, the rest behind, surprisingly enough, civilian grade Terran cryptography. The Terran turned it off and put it back in the box. "Full eVR?" he asked. "That's important."

Ullmo'ok nodded. "That one's just sex," he opened the second case. "This one, my friend, will be your big money maker."

"Oh? Why? What do you have there?" the Terran asked.

"Everything from slowly eating a meal while sitting naked outside in the rain to feeling low power heated blowers drying one's fur to a slow kiss between two lovers. Urinating after the bladder has gotten excessively full, the first drink of water after going a full day without, the feel of an infant's soft fur or scales or skin beneath your warm hand. The gain was turned up to maximum, as broad spectrum as my techs could make it," Ullmo'ot said. He lifted his upper lip in the best approximation of a human smile as he could make. "Before you tell me that's worthless compared to xenospecies sex, let me tell you, a warborg offered me a year's pay for the eVR of a female Puntimat finishing a long run on a treadmill then carefully and slowing washing with shampoo beneath a stream of warm water before blow drying her fur slowly."

The Terran narrowed his eyes. He'd dealt with Lanaktallan before, but had never seen one who was so focused, almost predatory for an herbivore species that might, occasionally, eat meat. He thought for a moment, trying to decide if he could bluff this one or maybe apply a little bit of good old intimidation.

Ullmo'ok knew what the other was thinking. He pulled out a long thin stick of spiced and treated meat, something he saw the Terrans enjoy, slowly unwrapping the Slender James, and beginning to chew on the stick, coiling his feeding tendrils in pleasure. When he knew he had the Terrans attention he reached down and patted the gigantic foot of the "Pleasure & Glory" with his lower left hand.

The Terran quickly changed his opinion. He had been warned by the person who had put him on this nice bit of graft that *this* Lanaktallan was different but he hadn't believed it until he watched the way the Lanaktallan was not enjoying the meat stick but *knew* what kind of effect it had and was relishing every little bit of the transaction.

"All right. Deal," The Terran said. "Parts, ammunition, repair vehicles, the whole nine yards."

"Excellent, buddy," Lanaktallan said. He whistled, another Terran skill he'd spend days mastering. Puntimat worker ran forward while others drove cargo trucks up. Lanaktallan shook the other being's hand, and this time *he* squeezed as hard as possible, staring into the human's eyes, tilting his head so his side-cybereye was part of the stare.

The Terran, Major Taktaven, Delta Company, 108th Military Intelligence (Rangers) (Detached), smiled back. "Pleasure doing business with you."

Krekit looked up from where he was crouched behind Ullmo'ok's fighting cradle, the panel behind the cradle removed. The little Puntimat had a firmware analyzer in his hand and had an expression of satisfaction on his face.

"Well, we know what those interfaces we could never figure out are actually for now," Krekit said. "The psychic shielding booted up just fine, went through diagnostics, then stayed stable during your entire match."

Ullmo'ok nodded. "And the shielding inside the shelters?" he asked.

"Four days of constant activation and now we've got the right analytics and wavelengths to protect everyone," Krekit said. He used his tools to start reattaching the covers over the dense molycirc bricks. "The shelters are complete; they're being furnished and stocked as we speak."

"All right, outfit the rest of the Bashmechs with the psychic shielding," Ullmo'ok ordered.

Krekit hesitated a moment. "Honored Most High Ullmo'ok?" he asked.

"Yes, loyal one?" Ullmo'ok asked, stroking the controls to *Pleasure & Glory* like some men stroked their sleeping wife's hip, the same faraway look on his face.

"The Precursors are coming, aren't they?" Krekit asked.

"Yes. They are."

"Do you intend on fighting them?" Krekit asked.

"Do I intended to defend all of my loyal employees? Of course," Ullmo'ok said. "Your wife pulled a knife from my back and repaired my lung. Your daughter works hard to make sure the coin-girls and joyboys are all healthy and have thumpmen nearby. How could I not defend you?"

Krekit nodded. "My men, they have spoken. We will hide in the cavern and repair any damage we can."

"That pleases me to know," Ullmo'ok said.

And he meant it.

Lo'omo'nan exited his vehicle, moving over to where his nephew was dressed appropriately for once, surrounded by well-dressed sycophants and underlings like a proper Lanaktallan should be. Lo'omo'nan's wife and children exited the limo, looking around with parts disgust at being at a refinery/mining location/manufacturing facility, parts pleasure at seeing Ullmo'ok so improved.

They all oohed and aahed appreciatively during the tour. Lo'omo'nan noticed that beings came to his nephew frequently with updates, forms to be signed, introductions.

They were moving outside, preparing to leave, when Lo'omo'nan saw his nephew suddenly jerk upright and put his hand against the elaborate datalink on his temple and blink all six eyes.

"Repeat that," Ullmo'ok snapped. The authority and urgent focus in the two words made Lo'omo'nan and his family draw back from the young male Lanaktallan in slight fear. There was a second and Ullmo'ok took his hand from his implant, blinking his eyes, including the ugly looking cybertic one, and gave a reassuring gesture. Lo'omo'nan saw Tukna'rn security officers jogging toward them, holding weapons.

"Sorry, my apologies," Ullmo'ok said. He gestured toward the Executive Villas and made a motion. "Please, before you fly out, at least enjoy some refreshments."

"I'm sorry, Honored Nephew, we don't have the time,"

Lo'omo'nan answered, suddenly feeling nervous. "Perhaps another day."

Ullmo'ok sighed and looked at his uncle, slowly drawing a needler from a holster he kept beneath his sash pouch. The Tukna'rn security men leveled their weapons at Lo'omo'nan's Lanaktallan guards and then disarmed them.

"I'm sorry, aunt, uncle, cousins, but I'm afraid that my words were not a request. It is an insistence," Ullmo'on said, his voice violent sounding and menacing.

It reminded Lo'omo'nan of how stressed Terran's sounded.

"Ullo, dear? What do you mean, darling one?" Lo'omo'nan's wife asked, hugging herself in fear.

"I am sorry, most beloved aunt, but you must quickly come with my men. I will be remaining here," Ullmo'ok said. He stared at his aunt. "Do remember, though, that I do care deeply for all of you."

The guards barked and motioned and Lo'omo'nan and his family began moving.

As they clattered away, their hoofs clumping on the tarmac, Lo'omo'nan called out to his nephew. "I won't forget this betrayal as long as I live!"

Ullmo'ok didn't look back as more of his facility guards took the servants into 'custody'. Servants that had mysteriously brought along their families to see a perfectly normal mining facility. They all hid smiles as they hurried after Lo'omo'nan, and one signaled eternal affection at Ullmo'ok.

Ullmo'ok watched, listening to his implant.

ATTACK IMMINENT!
ATTACK IMMINENT!
ATTACK IMMINENT!

Ullmo'ok was strapped into *Pleasure & Glory*, the datalink plugged in, his feet on the pedals, his hands on the controls. The big Bashmech was vibrating faintly around him, the huge fusion engine at low power. The scaffolding around him was clear, his access ports were closed, his armor ready. The durachrome around the scaffolding made the repair scaffolding look as it was just some kind of material storage towers.

He could hear his gladiators talk to each other. Weeks in the simulators were one thing, but they could hear on the radios that Goliaths were landing vehicles on the planet. That the Terran vessels were engaged in pitched fighting. The UMF and the Kestimet Corporation had already taken massive casualties. Only a few units survived, most of them working carefully with the Terrans. His men were nervous but unafraid.

He was not nervous. He was not afraid.

Instead, he *felt* something. The way poets described a female's tendrils trembling, the way commercials made tasting their wares sound.

He wondered what it was.

"Hi!" a small voice said in his ear. It was on his personal comlink.

"Clear the channel," Ullmo'ok ordered, doing his best to imitate the Kestimet security jargon he'd picked up being arrested so many times.

"I'm your new friend," the voice said. Ullmo'ok opened his eyes in shock as something tore through his firewalls, through his security, and scanned his entire Bashmech in seconds. "Wow, good job on this. I should hash your security encryption though, you're using an old outdated one that the Precursors already cracked."

"Who are you?" Ullmo'ok asked sharply.

"Oh, I'm your new Warboi. Assigned by Third COSCOM Digital Warfare Command. Either I help you, and you let my friends help your friends..." There was a long pause. "Or V Corps has ordered me to slag your warmechs."

Ullmo'ok thought for a moment. "All right, new friend. I'll warn you, I am here to defend my loyal people. I will not stray far from this area."

"Okie-dokey," The voice answered. "Rehashing now."

His mech went to standby, booted up, shut down everything, then restarted again.

"Rehashed. I updated your systems with the latest IFF and targeting systems. I'm sending my brothers to help your friend," The little voice said.

"What do I call you?" Ullmo'ok wondered aloud.

"Dunno. That's up to you," the voice said. "Oh, V Corps is referring to you as 5th Light Armor Irregulars and limiting your operations to a ten-mile radius."

"All right," He thought for a second. One of his friends back in the Core Worlds talked like the computer program. His name had been long, but everyone had shorted it to "Tak" so that they could get a word in edgewise. "I'll call you Tak."

"Tak it is. I have General Trucker on secure comlink. He wants to speak to you."

A General? That was like a military Most High. Curious, Ullmo'ok opened the comlink.

"Fifth LAI? Do you read?" a Terran's rough voice sounded in his ear. Ullmo'ok could hear a nuclear cannon cut loose in the background.

"Yes," Ullmo'ok answered.

"All right. I'm sending you some air defense and point defense units and some warborg infantry. I'll keep those shelters of your locked down and defended, you just worry about any armor units that head your way," Trucker growled. In the background Ullmo'ot heard bellowed orders. "You stay out of our zone though, you get in my way I'll run you over just like ancient metal."

"Of course. Nothing personal," Ullmo'ok said. He'd seen more than a few black market Terran war TriVids in the past few months.

"Nothing personal," Trucker said. Suddenly the pitch of his voice changed. "Get those UMF areospace fighters out of there, tell them to get that blasted formation tighter or they're going to get raked out of the sky by that mass of Djinn! Tell that dumbass cow he's about to get slaughtered!"

Ullmo'ok knew Trucker was referring to a member of his species, but it did not bother him.

Cattle described most of the people Ullmo'ok met before the Terrans arrived.

"Look, 5th, I'll get you a dedicated data-stream and provide what support I can, but... TELL THAT DUMB BASTARD TO ACTIVATE HIS POINT DEFENSE!... but I've got my hands full. I wish you'd have interlocked with us earlier but... JEEZ-SUS SODOMIZING KEE-RICEST WILL SOMEONE KILL THAT THING? ... but I'll interlock you as best I can."

"I understand," Ollmo'ok replied. The sounds behind the Terran's voice and his bellowed commands made something inside Ollmo'ok's soul tingle. He opened a Slender James and chewed on it, filling his mouth with the taste of the greasy meat stick.

"Do your best, Fifth. Trucker out."

"Understood."

In his tank Trucker looked at his EW/EMCOM/Com-tech. "You sure we were talking to an Lanaktallan? He sounded like a damn answering service VI."

His tech nodded. "VI says he was an actual living being with almost 83% certainty."

"Huh," Trucker said, then took his mind back to the battle at hand.

Ullmo'ok was relaxing in his crash couch, keeping his men's moral up, ordering them to sleep in shifts.

Listening to his implant, which Tak was keeping him aware of what was happening as more and more Precursor ships made planetfall.

Nearly two hours later Tak woke him up, the vibration of his Bashmech lulling him to sleep.

"Got Confed troops on the horn, boss. They want to know which warehouses to conceal themselves in," Tak said.

Ullmo'ok rubbed his eyes. "What?"

"General Trucker sent some air defense and point defense vehicles to keep your area safe. He also sent ammunition trucks and counter-battery artillery units, including radar," Tak answered.

Ullmo'ok closed his eyes, visualizing the layout of the factory with his cybereye. He 'blinked' at the buildings, assigning them. "Tell the leader of the vehicles that the warehouses and vehicle hangers can be destroyed. *All* of the surface installations can be destroyed. Just defend the shelters."

Tak hummed for a moment. "They say OK. Well, they talk weird. You know, Terran military guys. They all talk funny."

"Wake me up if anything moves funny."

"Oky-Dokey!" Tak said.

Ullmo'ok closed his eyes, going back to sleep.

"BOSS! BOSS! WAKE UP!" Tak yelled.

Ullmo'ok opened his yes, lifting his two upper hands to rub at them. "Yes, Tak?"

"Trucker just signaled. You got a whole bunch of, and I quote, big nasty metal coming your way."

"Wake up the boys," Ullmo'ok said, bringing his big mech up to full readiness. He waited for each of his gladiators. Nearly eighty in all. Even the maintenance crews, led by Krekit checked in. Finally the Terran Confederate Military forces checked in.

Everyone was ready.

"It's time for the Ultimate Show," He said over the 'command channel'. "With the Ultimate Prize: living another day."

And put his mech in motion.

V CORPS COMMAND MEMO

Extensive civilian shelters outfitted with psychic shielding arrays at the Kestimet Hoolangenar Mountains Refinery. Estimated numbers of civilians in shelters in excess of 320,000. Area is protected by civilian grade medium warmechs.

8th Infantry has deployed a company of air and point defense units as well as battalion of artillery configured for counter-battery operations.

Support these guys when you can. The leader is a known and MILINT compromised black marketeer, but he's been good to our guys and is taking care of his people.

--General Nodra'ak, V Corps, Commanding

---NOTHING FOLLOWS---
KESTIMET INTERNAL MEMO

Lesser Most High Lo'omo'nan and his entire family as well as his servants have been kidnapped by his known law breaker nephew Ullmo'ok, who has seized control of the Hoolangenar Industrial Facility and may be planning on holding it for ransom.

At this time, do not speak to any press agents.

3rd ARMOR DIVISION BROADCAST

HERE THEY COME, BOYS!

---General Trucker, Commander

The massive duralloy doors, sheathed with endosteel and covered with radar scattering stealth paint opened with a screech that could be heard for over a mile. Out lumbered eighty mechs in the 450 to 500 ton range, all heavily armed and armored, piloted by beings who had dozens if not hundreds of arena battles under their belts. The pilots accelerated to a light jog, heading toward where the 'medium armored vehicles, mix of assault, air defense, self-propelled artillery, and anti-armor" were heading toward the industrial facility, accompanied by over three thousand infantry.

"OK, you want to disable the anti-armor first," Tak squealed, bouncing up and down. "Bring up your long range radar scanners."

Ullmo'ok realized he had no idea how the long range scanner worked. "Bring it up for me on screen five," he ordered, selecting the display that usually showed his point total. "Have the others bring up the long range radar on their point and ranking display."

"Um, Okie-dokie," Tak said. It was a bunch of concentric circles, with a line sweeping around in a clockwise direction fairly rapidly. At the far ring, at the top, where a narrow V terminated, a bunch of dots started showing. "We're six miles and closing."

"Not a problem," Ullmo'ok answered. He was calm, centered, that strange feeling of *lacking* something he had his entire life surrounding and filling him. "Hook me in to everyone else."

"Done. Go ahead," Tak said.

"All right. We've all fought in the arena, you know how to fight in your Bashmechs, we practiced in the simulators. We know we can take these guys," Ullmo'ok said. "Lets trashbash 'em up."

He paused, shooting a narco-stim into his arm before looking at Tak's display.

"Close the channel," he told Tak.

"Um, sure, boss," Tak said. After a moment Tak said: "Don't you have a warplan?"

"Yeah. Scrap 'em," Ullmo'ok said. "It's like any junker mechbash."

"Um, hang on," Tak said. Ullmo'ok say the communication light come on but didn't hear anything. After a minute the light went out. "Uh, boss, have you ever fought for real before?"

"Over three hundred matches. I can fight, Tak," Ullmo'ok said, feeling the narco-stim run through his veins, making his heart rate jump and easing his muscles. "Don't worry, we'll scrap these guys, go back for repair and reload, and wait for the next batch."

"Uh, are you sure, boss?" Tak asked.

Ullmo'ok sighed. "Yes, I'm sure. We ran a lot of simulations against the Terran Military Armed Services estimations of these machines. Even the ones we are heading toward."

"All right, boss," Tak sounded unsure to Ullmo'ok, but the aVI went silent.

The miles swept under his feet as the eighty mechs thundered toward the enemy.

"117 Artillery is dropping smoke and chaff to cover your advance and soften them up a little. They can only dedicate two companies, so it'll be light fire. When you exit cover you'll be a half mile from long to extreme range of your long range weaponry and 117 will cease fire," Tak said.

"All right," Ullmo'ok answered.

An alarm went off and the screen he usually showed himself the crowd on blanked to reveal another radar screen, this one tracking blue lines.

"What is that?" Ullmo'ok asked.

"That's point defense radar, boss," Tak said. "Um, those are friendly artillery rounds. I just told you about them."

"Ah, yes," Ullmo'ok said. He felt his tendrils tremble slightly and ignored it.

"Uh, ok, boss," Tak sounded really unsure and Ullmo'ok noticed that the transmission light came on again.

His forward radar was suddenly fogged out, like a solid wall had appeared.

"Pop a drone, boss," Tak said.

"Hey, my radar isn't working ahead of me," was the common thread of twenty of his men suddenly comlinking him.

"It's the stuff your aVI told you about," he reassured them. Half of them commented that they'd told the annoying little VI to be quiet.

"Boss, don't let them do that. I'm serious, I don't think that's a good idea," Tak said. "Turn on your EW suite, boss. Seriously, turn it on. Pop a drone and hit your EW."

"My what?" Ullmo'ok asked.

"For the sake of the Digital Omnimessiah and the Twelve Biological Apostles!" Tak yelled. Ullmo'ok saw a power drain he wasn't used to.

"Stop that, I balance my power load carefully," Ullmo'ok said. "Don't make me turn you off like the others."

"You guys shouldn't turn us off, boss! I'm serious, it's a really bad idea going into this fight!" Tak squealed.

"It will be all right. They know how to fight," Ullmo'ok reassured the aVI. Little Tak seemed like a very nervous sort. Ullmo'ok wondered for a moment if there was a way to give the little guy a narcojet hit or not.

They were into the cloud. A few of his fellow gladiators cursed, but they all ran through the smoke, coming out. Ullmo'ok noticed that his radar kept fuzzing and wavering.

Ullmo'ok's aVI suddenly carated all the dots on his radar, marking them with different shapes and colors.

"There's the anti-armor vehicles, boss! Get 'em!" the aVI squeaked.

"Yes," Ullmo'ok said. He activated his datalink to his men. "Kill the anti-armor first!" He clicked off his datalink and sped up, sprinting across the terrain. His men gave a shout over the datalink, breaking into a run with him.

"Boss, what are you doing? Boss?" the aVI squealed. "Turn on your battle-screens!"

"Moving to attack," Ullmo'ok answered. "I don't have battle-screens."

Lasers were being fired from the Precursor machines. He could see them now, heavy, blocky, bristling with weapons and thick with armor. They all moved on tracks that churned the ground, ran over small buildings, crushed houses and trees. They were making a straight line toward the mining facility.

"Uh, boss?" Tak asked. "Turn on your battle-screens!"

More lasers were lancing out, hitting the mechs charging them. Particle cannons, fired at extreme range joined in. Missiles started being fired from the machines, small ones, medium ones, seekers. Each mech's point defense shot down ones coming at them, picked off a few other, then went silent.

"Boss?" The aVI barked as Ullmo'ok's point defense went silent. A particle beam raked Ullmo'ok's leg but a quick glance showed Ullmo'ok that it hadn't done much more than minimal damage to his leg's thick armor.

"Yes?" Ullmo'ok asked. He was satisfied that his point defense knocked down not only all of the ones coming at him but ones aimed at others too.

"Activating battle-screens!" Tak yelled. Ullmo'ok saw his power take a hit and his viewscreens shimmered slightly.

"What is that? Stop that, I need that power for my guns!" Ullmo'ok barked. "Clear my vision."

"You *need* that power for your screens or you're gonna get splattered!" Tak shot back. "How do you *not* know this? I'm like three hours old! Gimme a sec to compensate for the screens."

The displays cleared up right as Ullmo'ok increased power and pushed his speed back up, more lasers and missiles hitting, but this time deflected or detonated by a shimmering field surrounding him.

"SHOOT!" Tak screamed.

Ullmo'ok jumped over a house, clearing it easily, and landed, raising his arms and triggering his missile launchers at the nearest set of tanks. Ullmo'ok knew missiles were point and shoot, the pilot's hand-eye mattering more than the computer reticle. The missiles, Terran military smart-weapons, shot out, blinked in surprised, armed, and impacted a second later before the VI's even went active. Both tanks shuddered, rocking back on their tracks, but continued forward, a half dozen craters in their forward glacis.

"BOSS! WHAT ARE YOU DOING?" Tak screamed as Ullmo'ok raked the leading rank of tanks with his 200mm autocannons, his whole mech shuddering as he raked his massive fists across the front of the Precursor tanks. Ullmo'ok fired lasers, covered some in plasma-napalm from his short range missile launchers, extended his sword and jumped into the air.

"BOSS! WHAT THE FUCK?" Tak shrieked as Ullmo'ok's massive feet slammed down on two enemy tanks, crushing them. He lunged forward and drove his sword through another tank, molten metal spraying from the impaled Precursor tank. He finished it off with a heavy laser shot as he yanked the chainsword free and turned to face the next one.

"Told you, going to mechbash these guys," Ullmo'ok said, feeling a slight trickle of something as two heavy cannon rounds his mech, forcing him back a step off the destroyed tanks.

He selected a single target and unloaded his two heavy missile pods, pouring a hundred heavy missiles into the front of the armor.

The missiles, normally long range smart missiles capable of dodging point defense, making popup attacks, or even circling wide to come around for another pass didn't even have a chance to completely unhash before they realized they were about to hit and armed the impact triggers.

The tank, a medium air defense tank with minimal armor, exploded into fury even as the missiles kept streaming into the fire, most of them barely able to fire up the sensors before they slammed into the ground and exploded. Most of the damage was from unburned fuel exploding and the sheer kinetic hit rather than their complex warheads designed to defeat heavy warmech armor.

"BOSS! THIS ISN'T AN ARENA FIGHT!" Tak shrieked. "WHAT THE FUCK, BOSS?"

A shot hit Ullmo'ok from the side and he turned in place, firing his autocannons as he did so, raking it across the front and sides of the robot tanks around him.

"Boss, you're losing men! I mean, *really* losing men! You gotta run!" Tak said. "Total armor is down by 50% and you're getting close to getting blow-through!"

Ullmo'ok bellowed and fired everything he had at a tank, his cockpit flushing with heat. Lasers, cannon shot, autocannon, and particle beams were raking at his mech. His point defense was overheating and he was losing armor fast.

"Boss, run!" Tak yelled. "I'm overwhelmed! I can't can't can't can't allocate screen-een-eens and point-tah-tah-tah defense-se-se."

"Everyone, back to base," Ullmo'ok said, finishing his turn and running out, stomping on tanks as he went, slashing right and left with his chainsword, firing his weapons into the side of the tanks. He got clear, running back into the remains of the smoke and chaff, confident the others were right behind him.

There was silence for a long time, broken only by the whirring of the cooling fans in the cockpit, the thud of his mech's feet, and the howl of his point defense going off.

He broke free of the smoke, running for the cave where the repair teams were.

"Close Air Support from 3-12 is coming in to clean it up," Tak said, his voice quiet. "117 is supporting them. They can dedicate the entire brigade now."

"All right," Ullmo'ok said.

It was silent for a long time. The small quarry that the cave opened up into came into view before Tak spoke again.

"That wasn't a sim or an arena fight, boss," Tak said.

"I know," Ullmo'ok answered.

"No, boss, I don't think you do," Tak said.

The aVI was quiet as Ullmo'ok slowed down and came to a stop in the quarry. Nearly a dozen of his fellow gladiator's mechs were already there, being worked on by mechanics. He was pleased to see how light the damage was, although it looked to him as if they'd taken a lot of damage to the rear quarter.

"I'm gonna talk to some friends," Tak said softly as Ullmo'ok started to shut down his mech.

"All right," Ullmo'ok said. The mech slowly shut down, a winding sound moaning through the cockpit. He popped the armored hatch and took a breath of fresh air. He could smell scorched and burnt metal, hot lubricant, and overheated cooling-cores. He breathed deep, relishing the cool air even though his bashmech was radiating heat. The ladder steps that he'd customized for his four legged form deployed and he moved down them. Mechanics were rushing forward with coolant hoses, grinders, welders and he moved past them.

Feeling the flush of victory from his first mass combat he moved toward where his fellow gladiators were, looking around for the narcobrew as he did so.

That was all right, but it still felt... lacking, *he thought to himself.*

"This is it?" Ullmo'ok asked, staring at the last mech to come in. It was stumbling junk, both legs ravaged down to the warsteel internal structures. Actuators were blown out, artificial muscle fiber was shredded or missing, armor was completely gone. The bashmech was stumbling junk, half of its weapons destroyed.

"That's it, boss," one of the mechanics said. "Everyone else is dead or had to eject."

"And got slaughtered by those machines before they could even get out of their ejection seats," One of his fellow gladiators, Mustlik, said, shaking his head. "If that bombing didn't happen and those aircraft hadn't have started pounding them, they would have gotten me too."

The Frestilek put his face in his hands and began crying. "I can't do it, Ullmo'ok, I can't go back into something like that again."

Ullmo'ok nodded, staring at the gladiator's mech. It had been ravaged by missile fire, laser beams, and particle beams. There was a hole clear through the lower torso on the mech, its skirting missing.

Only forty-three had made it back. The mechanics had told Ullmo'ok that eight of them were too damaged to return to service quickly, it would take a week or more working full time to fix them.

One of the other gladiators led Mustlik away, patting the smaller being on his back. The one leading Mustlik away glared at Ullmo'ot, clacking her beak in agitation.

"I will not go back either. I'm a Bashmech driver, not someone to race to the slaughter," she clacked.

Ullmo'ok shrugged. "I will not force anyone to fight who does not want to."

"Boss," Tak spoke up for the first time in hours.

"Yes?" Ullmo'ok answered, taking a sip off his narcobrew.

"We need to talk, somewhere private," the aVI said, it's

voice was deeper, less squeaky, and sounded very serious.

Ullmo'ok got up and moved to the old mine supervisor's office, resting on the sling-like chair.

"What?" Ullmo'ok asked, taking another drink.

"That happens again, and you're dead. Your family in those bunkers are dead," The aVI said.

Ullmo'ok gave the equivalent of a shrug. "All right."

"Boss, did you train at all?" Tak asked.

"Simulators. Against Terran VR representations of Precursor machines," Ullmo'ok said. He unwrapped a ration and shoved it into his mouth, pushing it into his jowls so he could chew it slowly. "True, we did better in the simulators, but I think we did well. We stopped them, didn't we?"

"That was *one battle*, boss. This is the eighty-sixth century, not a battlefield in Europe during the Bronze Age!" Tak said. "By the Digital Omnimessiah, boss, did all of you do solo fights in the simulators?"

"We trained at the same time. Why?" Ullmo'ok said.

"No, were all of you on the same VR battlefield?" Tak asked.

"No. We each watched the others to learn from them," Ullmo'ok answered. "We knew we could fight next to each other. We had fought one another, we knew each other's tactics."

"Arena tactics, boss," Tak said. "Arena tactics. This was *one battle* in a war that might last for months, years, depending on how much metal the Precursors are willing to bring to bear."

"We did well," Ullmo'ok said. "We outfought the..."

"No, boss, you didn't. Your entire force destroyed less than one hundred-twenty tanks, damaged only two hundred, and in return you lost almost fifty medium grade mechs," Tak interrupted. "You took over fifty percent casualties and only inflicted twenty-percent on the enemy. If it wasn't for 3-12 and 117 those Precursors would be digging your family out of those bunkers to tear them apart with their claws. Boss, you barely touched their infantry support."

Ullmo'ok frowned. He remembered destroying at least a

half dozen.

"Why didn't you shoot boss? Why?" Tak asked. His voice sounded close to tears. "Why didn't you order them to turn on their electronic warfare suites or battle-screens? Why did you sprint at them like that?"

Ullmo'ok thought. "It's how we fight."

"I had *friends* on those mechs, boss. You didn't know what you were doing and you ran straight into a meat grinder and got them all killed," Tak said. "I might only be eight hours old, but those were my *friends*, we were hashed together. Half of them died in their *sleep*, boss. Warbois, dying in their *sleep*."

"My condolences. I did not know your kind formed attachments so quickly," Ullmo'ok answered.

"Boss, what about your fellow gladiators?" Tak asked.

Ullmo'ok shrugged. "They died gloriously, in combat, just like they were all prepared to do in the arena."

There was silence a moment. "No, boss, they didn't."

There was silence a moment.

"You got them killed. You *wasted* them. I'm not sure if I want to be your warboi anymore."

And Tak was gone.

Ullmo'ok sat in the office, sipping his narcobrew, trying to understand what the aVI had been telling him.

"All right, hook me in," Ullmo'ok said, staring at the technician. The Puntimat nodded, reaching out and hitting the keyboard.

Ullmo'ok felt his awareness expand. He was over the battlefield, looking down, the feed from multiple Terran satellites all merged by the technicians. He had asked Tak to get him some data and Tak had reluctantly agreed.

He saw his mechs, in a ragged staggered line, charging forward. Some stumbled and recovered, some slid, a few almost tripped on buildings. He saw designations come up in a line in front of the mechs and then around the Precursor machines his mechs were running toward. He'd seen those markings on his radar and scanner screens and queried his implant.

Artillery markers. Type, estimated time to impact, unit of origin, target.

Ullmo'ot loaded the information in his datalink into Qik-RAM, so it would automatically come to mind when he saw those markings again.

The artillery shells started hitting, creating a solid look-ing barrier of white smoke, chaff, and EM jammers. Other artil-lery rounds, anti-armor and fuel air, started detonating among the tanks.

He saw his mechs charge through the smoke, saw new icons pop up. According to his datalink that meant 117 Field Ar-tillery Brigade had stopped firing. By the time they came out of the smoke the last of the rounds had hit.

Most of the infantry had been destroyed by the fuel-air.

He stopped the replay, then watched from each cockpit.

Each gladiator fought like masters. Putting fire into the tanks, raking them with autocannons, lasers, missiles, baller-inas in a ballet of death. Each one that went down fell to super-ior numbers, going down yelling and firing. Some ejected, their mechs smashed to junk.

After the last one, he rewound the sim and played it again.

He watched his own mech and that of the gladiators sprint into the Precursor tanks. Four of the mechs stopped, firing missiles from just outside the smoke. Firing heavy lasers and the lighter autocannons that didn't kick so badly and could stay on target. One went down from a lucky particle beam that punched through the cockpit.

The rest, the seventy-five, charged in, laying about them with their weapons in a frenzy. Three times Ullmo'ok saw a mech accidentally hit another one. Once from the rear, blowing the friendly mech apart. The tanks began concentrating on the mechs inside their own formation, shifting rapidly. The slower anti-tank vehicles maneuvered, getting shots on the mechs.

Less than thirty of them had their battle-screens and the electronic warfare suite activated. Most of them only had one or the other. As he watched they were pounded on, hammered, reduced to scrap. One, then two, then more began to run away. Those without battle-screens barely made it halfway to the smoke before getting destroyed.

Only some of them ejected.

He saw himself give tell the others to run. Only a dozen made it, most of those staggering. The ones that had stayed by the fading wall of smoke turned and ran when they saw Ullmo'ok coming.

He kept watched as artillery started hammering the tanks, followed by aircraft roaring in to drop heavy explosives. It took six passes, and two of the aircraft were blown out of the sky, and another artillery barrage before the Precursor tanks were stopped.

The sim ended and Ullmo'ok gasped as he opened his eyes. The techs were looking at him and he motioned for a narco-brew. After he had a few drinks to settle down he nodded.

"Load up the file Tak got me. I want to see it. I *need* to know," Ullmo'ok stated.

The world vanished in a dazzle of pixels, loading back up another composite view. This time was fifty light military grade mechs, roughly the same firepower and armor and shielding as his own. They were advancing on nearly three times what Ullmo'ok and his force had attacked.

He had asked Tak to find him a sim like this, as close to what his own battle had been like between forces and terrain.

He watched as they didn't sprint through the cloud, they walked, a slow steady metronome of steps. He saw drones pop up. He had drones on his own mech, but hadn't used them. From the cloud was fired heavy missiles. His datalink implant identified them as long range missiles. He watched them streak in, going to evasive maneuvers, hugging low to the ground, only popping up at the last second to hit the top of the Precursor vehicles. The mechs fired staggered, one set then another while the first reloaded, keeping the area flooded with missiles. The more enemy tanks that were destroyed, the more gaps appeared in the point defense, the more missiles hit. A few of the light mechs fired off smoke and chaff of their own, keeping the mechs surrounded by the cloud. More drones popped up, getting targeting data for the mechs. Artillery joined in, the rounds impacting with more accuracy thanks to the drones. The mechs expended 20% of their missile loads and stopped firing.

The smoke started to clear and the mechs began advancing on the tattered remained of the tanks, firing long range weapons. Only a few of the tanks had the reach to strike back. Ullmo'ok noted that the light mechs worked in teams, three to five each concentrating on the heavier tanks till it exploded.

They moved through the wreckage, pausing at each wreck, firing short range but powerful plasma guns, the type that the gladiators used to augment fist punches, into the shattered Precursor mechs.

The replay sim ended as the mechs moved on.

It didn't seem like a proper battle to Ullmo'ok, who was used to getting in his foe's face. It seemed almost dishonorable.

Until he saw the casualties.

None. Hardly any armor damage. Less than 20% of munitions used, including the drones.

That group of mechs were still fighting, still engaged in combat. They had only been reloaded once during the day and had not needed to stop to be repaired.

"End sim," Ullmo'ok said. When the world cleared he lifted up his narcobrew and took a long drink off of it. "Get the Bashmech pilots still willing to fight."

The mechanic nodded as Ullmo'ok went into his datalink, looking for anything that would help him.

Twenty-five bashmech pilots, that was all he had left willing to fight.

"All right, boss, we'll listen. For now," The leader, Frestilek named Cranten, said, his voice serious.

"I made a mistake," Ullmo'ok said honestly. The others all nodded in agreement. "We trained in the simulators, we trained in the arena, but we did not train together. Worse, I found a quote from a long ago Terran leader that summed up what happened.

"Simulation training is nothing like field exercise training. Field exercise training is nothing like battle. Battle is nothing like war. Men must be trained to work with one another, to know what the man on his left and right will do, to know and understand how an army makes war. Warriors die gloriously in battle, soldiers win wars."

Ullmo'ok finished the quote and stared at his fellow gladiators for a long moment. "I trained us for one on one fighting, we practiced in our mechs, but we did not do what Terrans call field exercise, and this is why I led you all to your deaths. We should have trained, all together, to work as one. Like cogs in a well made machine," he finished.

"Watch the recording I sent you. Look it over. See how the Terrans fight, how a military fights, how soldiers fight," Ullmo'ok said. He heaved a deep breath. "Then decide if you still wish to fight with me, because that is how we must fight and there is no time for practice."

The others nodded, slowly breaking away from the group, leaving Ullmo'ok alone.

"Boss?" Tak said quietly.

"Yes?" Ullmo'ok asked.

"You don't have long," Tak said.

"How long?" Ullmo'ok asked.

"A few hours. The Precursors, that Jotun nearby, he sent more. A lot more. All light armor units and robotic infantry, but a lot of them. They're carrying close range anti-tank weaponry," Tak said. "Boss, you can't stop them, not if you fight like that again."

V CORPS MEMO

TO: aVI-4236a55z24 "Tak"

Request for reassignment denied. Train them up, teach them to fight. You have access to the training library, use it. Help these people help themselves.

---NOTHING FOLLOWS---

KESTIMET DEFENDS REFINERY SUCCESSFULLY

Kistimet CorpSec forces successfully defended the refinery held by the outlaw Ullmo'ok, despite the lack of Terran military forces. CorpSec has reported only minimal casualties while destroying the entire Precursor force of thousands sent to attack the critical facility, perhaps offered the valuable refinery by the outlaw Ullmo'ok.

CorpSec wishes to remind all Corporation Citizens and Employees that they are only contracted to protect you if you are in a designated shelter.

---NOTHING FOLLOWS---

Ullmo'ok looked at his gathered up Bashmech pilots, all of them taking deep drinks of their narcobrews before setting the mugs down. He could see they were worried, anxious, afraid. He wondered, for a moment, what it was like for them, then mentally shrugged and got down to business.

"There's a lot of Precursor machines heading for us. Apparently they are all carrying heavy short range missiles, even the robot infantry," he told them.

"So they're going to chew us up like a cargomech against a bashmech," Woxtow muttered.

"If we go in like we did, then yes," Ullmo'ok said. "Did you all review the record I sent you?"

They all nodded.

"Did you see what we did wrong?" Ullmo'ok asked.

"We took arena bashmechs into a military fight?" Susxto guessed.

Ullmo'ok nodded. "I had us take arena mechs to a war. Most of our weapons are modified, adjusted, calibrated for the arena. Some of our weapons are still on low power. The mechanics are fixing them, putting them back to their original standards."

"The Terrans should have warned us! Should have protected us better," Ixnartray said.

"Perhaps," Ullmo'ok agreed. He pointed at the speaker. "Tak, tell us what we would need to learn to fight like the Terrans."

The little speaker vibrated for a second. "OK, boss. You would need to learn radio procedure, maneuver and fire formations, weapon ranges, effective warboi use, how to use variable munitions, rank structure, mission planning, how to use satellite and recon drones, first aid, how to interlock a war plan, logistics support, how to call in close air support and artillery, how to..."

"That's good, Tak," Ullmo'ok said, seeing that half his pilots were already lost and confused. "How long does it take the Terrans to train a bashmech pilot?"

"It takes nearly a year to train a warmech pilot and that is after taking a year to teach them the basics," Tak added. "That's not counting sim, VR, and eVR time. Then a warmech pilot would be sent somewhere to do basic combat operations in a hazardous environment for two to three years."

"Much longer than we had," Ullmo'ok stated. "Make no mistake, individually we fought brilliantly. We're all brave, we're all skilled, but we made a mistake."

"What mistake is that?" Klemikit asked.

"We didn't listen to or talk to the warbois," Ullmo'ok said. "Mine told me to turn on battle-screens, kept asking me for my warplan, told me to turn on my electronic warfare, didn't understand what we were doing."

"Then let them pilot the bashmechs," Susxto said. "He can have mine."

"It doesn't work that way, boss," Tak said. Susxto looked at the speaker. "I can run the reactor, focus the battle-screens, run your commo, help with targeting, fire weapons when you tell me, keep your EW at max performance, but, to be honest, if you tried to have me pilot the mech I'd fall down. I don't have legs."

Ullmo'ok nodded. "He's never had a body. He doesn't know how to move. He handles stuff that we don't do instinctively because those are *his* instincts. He doesn't have all the wiring we do that we use just to stand up and keep our balance."

Susxto sat back down, looking mollified.

"But why didn't the Terran government stop us?" Ixnartray asked. "They had to have known we'd get massacred. It's the government's job to keep us safe."

"Because they aren't our parents," Ullmo'ok stated. When everyone looked at him confused he gave the equivalent of a shrug. "I looked at the Terran Confederacy legal code. I can sum it up for those of us who grew up under the Unified Tyrants as one simple sentence."

Ullmo'ok took a long drink, waiting for the others to say something.

"What?" Ixnartray finally asked.

"Do as you will as long as you do no harm to others," Ullmo'ok said. "If you dance in traffic and get killed the Terran government just lists your cause of death as being stupid. If you play with a rock cutter charge and chew on it and blow your head off, it is not the fault of the charge maker, the mine, or even your parents, it is your fault. There's protections for the mentally unstable or defective, for some children, but by and large, the Terran government just doesn't care. It doesn't pretend to care. I even lets you know it doesn't care. It expects you to take care of yourself if you are able."

All of his bashmech pilots looked at one another, confusion on their faces.

"Local governments might care, but the Terran Confederacy does not," Ullmo'ok shrugged.

"But... but..." Woxtow started, then stopped. "Who will keep us safe? What if a corporation put out a defective product? Who would protect us from it?"

"That is different. The corporation would be punished if

they did so knowingly, punished if they did not recall the product. But should you have been warned, go behind the government's back, acquire that product anyway, and your feet fall off, then that is your fault," Ullmo'ok said. He shrugged. "I find it reassuring."

"But, but, how will we stay safe without the government to protect us?" Ixnartray asked.

Ullmo'ok stared at the other being. "Do you remember what we do?"

Ixnartray shrugged. "Pilot bashmechs."

"Illegally. We gamble. Illegally. We sell drugs. Illegally. Rent out joyboys and coingirls. Illegally. We curse the government for stopping us from having fun. We call ourselves outlaws and gangsters. We boast we are beyond the government and now you want them to save you?" Ullmo'ok laughed like bagpipes being jumped on by a gorilla. "We are indeed intelligent life."

"Uhh, boss?" Tax said.

"Yes?" Ullmo'ok looked at the speaker.

"I got General Trucker on the line. He wants to know if you can talk."

"Put him through," Ullmo'ok wanted to know just how angry the Terran was.

"Ullmo'ok, can you hear me?" The Terran asked. There was a lot of static.

"Yes," Ullmo'ok answered.

"Good, good. Listen, you've got a whole shit-pot of light metal heading your way. That Jotun wants that refinery and it looks like it wants it intact. You did better than I thought against the last group. At least you went out and engaged them," the signal fuzzed out for a moment.

"Dammit, can you hear me, Ullmo'ok?"

"I can hear you."

"All right. They can't take that refinery intact. If you can't fight, you let me know, and I'll scrap the whole place with atomics and park a Bolo on it. I'll use airbursts so your shelters stay intact, but I'll have to wipe that refinery off the map. If you and your men want to fight, engage them at range," Trucker said.

"If my men and I should fail, what will you do?" Ullmo'ok asked.

"I'll do what I've planned to do since the beginning. I'll blow it off the map with a 1.2 megaton thermonuclear airburst and park a Bolo over it," Trucker said. "Then, after the battle's over, I'll dig your families out once the Precursors are defeated."

"Excellent. The shelters can withstand that. My men and I are willing to fight," Ullmo'ok said.

"Listen, I can't spare you a combat leadership AI. You don't have the bandwidth out there. Your aVI's are the next best thing, but they can't do it without you. I know you're not soldiers, but do your best," the signal fuzzed over, devolving to dot and dash codes, a high pitched static sound, then some sounds like metal being stressed and then the tension released.

"I'm trying to get him back," Tak said.

"Go to your bashmechs. I will be there shortly. We will do our best to fight well," Ullmo'ok said.

The other bashmech pilots nodded, the clump breaking up and streamed away.

"...read me? Ullmo'ok, do you read me?" Trucker's voice came back.

"Yes," Ullmo'ok said.

"Listen, I don't know what your government is telling you, but this is an all hands on deck situation. If I had my way I'd be having 8th Infantry handing out rifles to your plant workers and having the rest of the civilians rolling bandages and loading magazines. Our plans estimated twelve Goliaths. Fifty-plus hit us across the system. We still aren't interlocked with your government and corporate forces. Your government refused to let us put ammunition on the ground so we're running the nano-forges and creation engines till the slush spills out. There's no more heavy metal to back us up and I put out a call that even includes idiots and civilian irregulars," Trucker said. "If I'd known how it was going to go down, I'd have disregarded protocol and interlocked you earlier despite your government saying they could handle anything that came across the boundary zone."

"Understood," Ullmo'ok said. The Terrans had thrown the dice with their warplan but come up triple-fours.

"Do your best, Ullmo'ok. Every Precursor you turn to scrap helps. It's that bad," Trucker said. "Trucker, out."

"Goodbye," Ullmo'ok said, standing up. He drained his narcobrew and headed out of the cave, blinking at the sunlight. The Terrans had misjudged. "Tak, prep *Pleasure & Glory* for combat operations please."

"Ok, boss," Tak said. "Boss, do you think it's really that bad?"

"He would not lie to me. There is no profit or advantage in it," Ullmo'ok answered.

"Do you think he'll really use atomics?" Tak asked.

"I would."

"Boss, we don't have any artillery or close air support and the sat-links are down," Tak said. "You're going to want to start loading EW-rounds in your missile banks after this. I should have thought of it."

"It's all right. You cannot account for everything. We shall do our best," Ullmo'ok said. He tabbed a narcostim into his leg and checked his screens. The layout was strange, but Ullmo'ok knew he'd quickly get used to it. He wasn't like every other Lanaktallan who brayed and moaned when things changed. He wasn't a good Lanaktallan, he knew that. There was something wrong with him, everyone said so. He couldn't bring himself to care about what good Lanaktallan's cared about.

But he could keep the Precursors from digging his aunt and uncle and cousins out of the shelters and tearing them apart.

"It's raining. Lots of vaporized metal and ash in the droplets. That will fuzz your sensors a little depending on the range. I will compensate as best I can, boss," Tak said. "Two miles to target."

"All bashmechs, slow to a walk. Calibrate for long range," Ullmo'ok said. "Ready drones for launch. Warbois will pilot them."

He was surprised that Ixnartray did not remind him that he was not the boss of her.

"There's close to ten thousand of them. Whew," Tak said. "Drones ready."

"Everyone, launch your drones. Let's get a look at the enemy," Ullmo'ok said. "Remember to put the feed on a screen and look at it."

The drones popped up from the launchers that had previously been used to launch fireworks. Ullmo'ok watched, slightly disinterested, as the fast little aircraft activated their cameras and moved into position. Ullmo'ok could tell that the warbois had discussed their plans with one another. Some went wide, some went high, some stayed low, and others swept forward in a fast line. His own mech chugged out three, 5% of his total load of drones.

The landscape was different than it looked on the maps. There was a valley where they had not been, nearly a mile across. A large gouge ripped through the earth in the middle of the valley, creating a canyon nearly a hundred meters deep. The Precursor robots had been forced by terrain to split their forces. They were crossing what looked like smooth stone, broken by slight ripples.

"What caused that?" Ullmo'ok asked.

"Orbital strike," Tak answered. "Caught one of the Jotun's big boys out in the open. A mobile refinery heading toward you. What's left of it is at the bottom of the canyon."

"I see," Ullmo'ok said.

The Precursor robots were mostly hover, with what looked like crude copies of Terrans hanging off every surface, holding tight to missile launcher tubes. There were things that looked like crustaceans, things with tracks, things that walked on long stilt legs, others that slowly turned as they hovered.

Simulations usually showed the Precursors using hundreds or thousands of the same craft. Ullmo'ok made a small note to himself to change the parameters on his sims.

"Recommendations?" Ullmo'ok asked. Tak had been created to fight wars, Ullmo'ok felt it would be foolish to disregard his knowledge. He would ask Woxtow what the best fruit narco-brew was as Woxtow was an expert in that knowledge.

Only a fool disregarded the knowledge, expertise, and skill of another.

"Chaff mortars first. Since we know the wavelengths of the chaff we use missiles to start off with. Run EW suites, if they respond with heavy missile fire, pop more chaff and flares," Tak said. "Keep them at a distance, they look to all have short and medium range weaponry," Tak hummed a second. "This was tailor made to slaughter you if you tried the same tactics."

"Logical," Ullmo'ok stated. He opened a channel. "Missile volleys first. Let the warbois select the targets and allocate the missiles. You launch and watch."

"Boss, we really like doing this. We're used to helping," Tak said. "Give the word, we're ready."

"All bashmechs check your number. Even will fire, then odd will fire, that way someone is always firing missiles," Ullmo'ok ordered.

The drones were getting wiped out, but they were transmitting more than enough data. They'd identified to the point defense radar's wavelength, transmitting it to the mech's warbois, which loaded the scanner data into the mortar shells. The mortars thumped, previously used for fireworks and colored smoke, and the mortar shells dropped down. The Precursor machine's point defense hit a lot of them, but that still let the chaff deploy, degrading their point defense and letting more spread their chaff.

The screen got a little fuzzy but because the warbois knew the wavelengths the chaff had been designed to foul, the warbois could compensate and tell the missiles what to look for.

The mechs, all 450-500 tons of war machine, all began firing missile volleys. One group firing while the next reloaded.

The missiles screamed out, unable to use stealth like their stellar counterparts, instead just relying on speed and bare bones maneuvering as they went hypersonic, roaring in at over Mach-10. While the Precursor machines were nearly blind the missiles could see clearly through the small hole in the chaff's scanner defeating jamming.

"We should start mixing EW warheads," Tak suggested.

"What are those?" Ullmo'ok asked, feeling his mech shudder as it launched missiles. He'd noticed another reason for the staggered volley, it let his mech cool slightly between launches.

"Strobes, chaff, jammers, screamers, coughers, magic mirrors, stuff like that. Gives them false readings, jams up their sensors, tries to infect them with computer viruses through scanner input. It's to make your missiles more effective," Tak said.

"Yeah, do that," Ullmo'ok said.

"Um, how about one in twenty, we don't have many loaded," Tak said.

"Yes," Ullmo'ok said, watching the different feeds. He had expected the warbois to aim at all the front ones, instead the missiles were slipping in between enemy EW and point defense, knocking bigger and bigger holes in the point defense net.

"This does not feel right," Jestrix said suddenly.

"You would prefer the last fight? By all means, run down there, we will use the data of your death to plan our assault," Ullmo'ot stated.

Jestrix didn't answer.

Ullmo'ok noticed that some of the infantry robots were trying to use their missiles as point defense, but in a section of the grid they were scanning around as if they were blind. "Do you see that, Tak?"

"What?" Tak asked.

"Grid D-7, the infantry robots look blind," Ullmo'ok said.

"Got the wavelength, gonna see if it works. Other warbois are loading it now. Firing."

Ullmo'ok watched as it looked like all the robotic infantry suddenly went blind.

"Enemy is entering extreme range from direct fire weapons," Tak said.

"What's our missile count?" Ullmo'ok asked.

"We're at ninety percent still," Tak said.

"Back up, keep firing," Ullmo'ok ordered. "Activate battle-screens and EW. Fire long range energy weapons, don't consume ammo this far out."

"Will do, boss," Tak said. "Everyone acknowleges."

More and more gaps were appearing in point defense, the infantry weapons were obviously single shot, slow missiles, that the incoming missiles just rolled to avoid. The infantry robots began firing with their additional weapons, lasers and plasma, but obviously could not see.

Several times Ullmo'ok's targeting reticle flashed yellow and he took the shot with heavy lasers or particle beam cannons. His arena skills came in handy here, making difficult shots quickly, knowing how to cycle his weapons to keep his heat manageable.

"They're retreating," Tak said.

"Move forward," Ullmo'ok ordered.

"Boss?" Tak said.

"Yes?"

"Pop a drone, sweep it around behind them. It might be an ambush. Precursors don't care about casualty numbers beyond resource expenditure and gain," Tak said. "Remember that Jotun wants the refinery and the mines."

"Understood. Do so," Ullmo'ok ordered. He watched the drone launch, configure for stealth, and sweep around low and slow.

"See, boss, what did I tell you?" Tak said. The machines hiding just beyond the hills and beyond the range of sensors were massive. Large flattened eggs bristling with weapons. "You would have walked right into that."

"I see," Ullmo'ok said. He examining the data the drone was streaming back. Heavier weapons than his mech mounted, thicker point defense, thicker armor. The machines were heavier than his own mech, which was the largest of the bashmechs. The drone beeped excitedly and sent back the wavelengths the Precursor machines were using.

That narrow gap he'd left for his own missiles.

"What if we did this: fire EW with the same profile as we were using for the entire first wave, then drive in behind them, firing off EW in our gap, and drive the missiles through that way?" Ullmo'ok suggested.

"Lemme talk to the boys, boss. Keep up the fire but don't advance, OK?" Tak said.

"Everyone, keep up missile fire, do not advance. They have more hiding, trying to lure us in," Ullmo'ok ordered.

He waited, feeling bored, watching the missiles pounding the Precursor machines.

He felt nothing.

"OK, boss, we've got it figured out," Tak said. It showed a quick sim of the attack. It looked fine to Ullmo'ok. "Should we do it?"

"Go ahead," Ullmo'ok said. He gave a sigh and injected a straight stim into his leg. He was getting sleepy from boredom. He watched as the missiles reconfigured firing order then launched. they went in at the bigger machines in two prongs, EW leading the way. The Precursors held off on firing their point defense, obviously intending on luring the missiles in for better targeting data. When the second wave of EW cut loose it became obvious the big machines were blind. The missiles rolled, chose their targets, then shifted into a straight line.

"Why are they doing that?" Ullmo'ok asked.

"Follow the Leader targeting," Tak answered.

The missiles all drove in on the same point, the crater getting deeper and deeper until finally the last ten or so of the long-range missiles pounded into the interior of the Precursor machine. Fire and vaporized metal gouted out of the wound. Five of the machines exploded. The rest of them turned to face the two directions the missiles had streaked in from. There were twenty left.

"Fire again. Reverse the targeting EW," Ullmo'ok ordered.

"Oh, good idea, boss," Tak said. The second set began to launch.

"Fire a third set immediately after, double volley, maximum acceleration, straight into their face. No EW, just speed and warhead," Ullmo'ok ordered.

"OK, boss," Tak said.

The second volley was slowly approaching, hugging the ground, swerving around obstacles. The third volley roared out, bypassing the retreating combat machines. Less than 10% were knocked out.

The second volley activated the EW drones and went to supersonic immediately afterwards. At the same time the third volley went hypersonic.

The Precursor machines, hit from three sides, their jammers off bandwidth and their seekers using the wrong scanner data, had their point defense system fall apart. The missiles hammered in, over half of the vehicles exploding.

"Same thing, reverse, add a fourth on a high parabolic arc," Ullmo'ok answered.

"Boss, our ammo levels," Tak reminded.

"I'll send half back for reload while the rest of us stand guard, then we'll switch off," Ullmo'ok said. "We have no sat-scans or other battlefield data. It relies on our eyes," Ullmo'ok stated.

"If you're sure," Tak said.

"What would be your advice?" Ullmo'ok said.

"Umm, I don't know," Tak said.

"Then let us try my way," Ullmo'ok said.

The third 'volley' tore into the massive machines with even better effect. Ullmo'ok watched as the last of them exploded, then ordered a fourth volley to clean up the last of the original machines. He sighed and sent back half of his pilots to reload their ammo.

He felt nothing.

"That did not feel proper," Trekez said, staring at his mech, which was being reloaded with ammunition. "It lacked glory and honor."

Ullmo'ok drew his pistol, ignoring the sudden hiss of worry from the onlookers, and tossed it to Trekez. "There you go. Feel free to put that in your mouth. At least then nobody else will get killed and your bashmech will still be available for the same effect."

"I didn't mean..." Trekez said, carefully putting the needler on the table.

"It is all right, friend. I realize what you mean," Ullmo'ok said, walking over to the table. He picked up a narcobrew bottle and cracked it open, putting the needler back in his pocket with his two lower hands. He offered Trekez the bottle and when the other being took it grabbed himself one out of the plas case.

"Doesn't the lack of glory bother you? You, who fought the hardest for glory?" Illtrek asked.

Ullmo'ok shrugged. "What is the use of glory or honor is nobody survives to witness it? Who do we point our finger at and call out to witness us, if the Precursors kill everyone? We will help the Terrans destroy this menace and rebuild the Arena. If we fall, then we witness one another and perhaps the Terrans will witness what we did in historical TriVids," Ullmo'ok took a swig of narcobrew.

"My parents, my siblings, my husbands, my broodcarriers, my podlings, they are all in the shelters. I care not for honor and glory, I care only for them," Plunketi'ik said, lifting up her narcobrew. "If I must die and this Trucker must use atomics to scour away the factory so the Precursors no longer care, then that is what must be done. I am with you, Mooky."

"I thank you," Ullmo'ok said, nodding. "I will force none to fight who do not wish to. Nap, eat, while your bashmechs are reloaded."

Ullmo'ok turned away, walking to the nearby holotank.

"Tak, show me a replay of the battle. Point out what you see," Ullmo'ok ordered.

More battles followed, mostly the Jotun sending more mechanized minions to take the factory and Ullmo'ok wiping them out with missiles and long-range weaponry. It was becoming almost mechanical, something Ullmo'ok felt could be done by a machine, not even requiring as complex programming as Tak.

It was the eighth day that things went sideways, to use a Terran term.

"Precursor forces down to 15% remaining," Tak said. Ullmo'ok noticed that even the aVI seemed bored. "Missile and indirect fire munitions down to 60%."

"Keep up the pressure. We'll rotate out and reload now, we can finish off the remainder even at one-third strength," Ullmo'ok ordered.

"Gotcha, boss," Tak said. "Sixteen heading back, eight staying. Going to rapid fire."

The last of the Precursor machines fell easily, even as his ammunition levels dropped. Ullmo'ok joined the other eight in moving through the wreckage, using lasers to destroy any power source, destroy any possibly active Precursor machines.

"Boss, I have incoming aircraft. They're not even trying to be sneaky about it," Tak said.

"How so?" Ullmo'ok asked.

"They're broadcasting ID and flying in the normal flight paths. They say they're CorpSec and Planetary Executors," Tak said. "They're hailing you."

"Put it up on display-seven," Ullmo'ok said, focusing his cybereye on it.

A Lanaktallan, his crests inflated, his sash covered in decorations, appeared on the screen. He looked at Ullmo'ok, clad in his cooling vest and body-blanket only and curled his tendrils in disgust. The sight of the cybereye made the Lanaktallan look physically ill.

"May I help you?" Ullmo'ok asked, firing a laser into the cracked hull of a weird looking crab with treads.

"I am Second Most High Executor Pru'thestic, in command of CorpSec and Executor forces," the Lanaktallan snapped. "Shut down your engines and present yourself for arrest."

"Why would I do that?" Ullmo'ok asked, watching the ships swoop down. They landed, outside the debris field, and the sides lowered to allow being in powered armor to exit the craft.

"The Planetary Corporate Council and the Planetary Executor Council will take control of those shelters you illegally built and put them to proper use," The Executor huffed. "You will be placed under arrest and remanded for summary execution as a know criminal who has now been caught in possession of illegal technology and weaponry."

"I will not allow them to eject my podlings for the shelters just so Corporate Executives can take their place," Plunketi'ik snarled over the comlink.

"And if I object?" Ullmo'ok asked. He turned his bashmech to face the dropships, aware that the other eight mechs were moving up next to him, keeping far enough apart their battle-screens wouldn't rub together.

"Then you will be destroyed," the Executor stated, his tendrils shaking with excitement.

Ullmo'ok felt something. That *thing* he had felt so long just out of reach.

"Come then," Ullmo'ok answered, his voice cold and distant. "Witness us."

8th INFANTRY DIVISION MEMO

We're still getting pushed back but the tempo is slowing. Looks like the Precursors have been forced to start manufacturing reinforcements and replacements. They're going to be desperate for resources soon. Keep up the pressure.

---NOTHING FOLLOWS---

144th ORDNANCE COMPANY

We've got the breathing room to reload the ammo stores of the 5th Irregulars. Our creation engines and nano-forges can cool down and de-slush on the way. They could probably use actual ammunition instead of civilian versions. Will head out once we're done reloading 1st Armored Recon.

---NOTHING FOLLOWS---

KESTIMET DEFENDS REFINERY SUCCESSFULLY THROUGH THE NIGHT!

Kistimet CorpSec forces, working with Planetary Executor forces, have held off heavy attacks by the Precursor forces throughout the last day and night at the Hoolangenar Industrial Facility, managing to clear the area. The Corpsec and Executor forces intend on engaging the criminal Ullmo'ok and liberating the facility and the shelters beneath in just hours.

The government shelters beneath the facility should be open to Senior Executives and higher soon.

---NOTHING FOLLOWS---

The Second Most High expected the illegal fighters in the mechs to charge his dropships. He nearly two-thousand power armor ready to swarm the nine patchworking looking mechs in front him to pry the pilots out so they could be summarily executed. He was personally looking forward to exiting the cramped shelters in the center of the Executor Headquarters and moving to what seismic scouting had shown to be heavy and elaborate shelters beneath the mining facility. He already knew he'd use his planetary authority to order the Terran anti-aircraft and point defense units to either leave or follow his orders, then eject the rabble and useless drones from the shelter so those who, by right, should have been in those shelters could take their rightful places.

Ullmo'ok didn't bother charging, just opened the armored covers for his missiles launchers and started firing. The power-armor, barely taller than his foot, he raked with long range lasers and particle beams.

Armor exploded, the missiles, programmed to hammer through Precursor armor, sliced through the dropships like butter as the point defense barely had time to come online before the hypersonic missiles started blowing huge holes in the ships.

The *feeling* flickered and died as three quarters of the dropships exploded into shards, the shrapnel ripping through the still forming ranks of power armor. Autocannons, lasers, particle beams, magshot rounds, all ripped into the power armor as the mech pilots triggered a second salvo.

A few power armor groups charged, using their jump-packs to take to the air in big hops.

The mech pilots swept them out of the sky with lasers and autocannons.

Within seconds the armor was fleeing back to the dropships, several of the surviving handful of dropships attempting to take off only for the third volley of missiles to smash into them, collapsing deflector shields, overwhelming point defense that was more used to thrown home-made explosives that hypersonic missiles in a long stream or screaming swirling missiles, some of which exploded into submunitions that kicked in grav generators and slammed tungsten steel tips into the hulls of the dropships at nearly Mach-20.

"Goodbye, Executor," Ullmo'ok said emotionlessly to the image of the Second Most High. He then opened up with his rotating autocannon, slamming the 200mm shells, fired one every half second as the barrels rotated, into the hull. The single burst blew through the entire ship, exiting out the other side to slam against the next one.

He knew that his uncle, his aunt, his cousins, so young and innocent, would remain in their shelters as he raked the last of the power armor infantry with his non-consumable munition weapons.

He *felt* something then, a flicker, something. He didn't know what, but he *felt* for a second.

"All enemy down," Tak reported. "I don't think that went the way they expected."

"If it did, it was a poor plan," Ullmo'ok stated. "All pilots, back to the chokepoint. The Jotun undoubtedly hopes that we are damaged."

The other eight pilots just flashed icons for assent, following him back.

Plunketi'ik raked the shattered ranks of power armor once more just for good measure before turning and following Ullmo'ok. Her broodcarriers were swollen with squirming podlings grown from the eggs she had deposited and her husbands fertilized. She would not allow some pampered Executive who had looked down on the streets she had fought and clawed to survive on to take their place.

If she was fated to die, then so be it. Her husbands would sing her glory to the podlings.

The nine mechs, shimmering with heat, moved back to the end of the valley and waited.

Ullmo'ok was almost ready to radio back and find out what was taking so long when Tak spoke up.

"We've got satellite again. That mad-lad Trucker put a half-dozen Bolos in orbit! He did it, he actually did it!" Tak laughed. "Oh, and 144th Ordnance is arriving. They say they're going to load us up with munitions! They've even got maintenance techs and parts!"

"All right, everyone, let's head back," Ullmo'ok ordered.

Everyone was silent as they marched back. Gone was the chatter, the jokes, the usual talk. Instead, Ullmo'ok had noted that everyone appeared to be exhausted, even though they had been getting rest. He didn't feel tired, just bored.

"Tak?" Ullmo'ok asked.

"Yeah, boss, what's up?" Tak asked.

"Can you check everyone's vitals? I worry they may be tired," Ullmo'ok said.

"Yeah, just a second," Tak said. After a moment he answered. "A little tired, no more than normal."

"Why do they seem so exhausted? Why are they all so silent. Usually Destrixal can not stay silent but he has said hardly two sentences since the first battle," Ullmo'ok said. "Is it, what was it called, a bioweapon?"

There was silence for moment. "Boss, do you not know about battle-fatigue?"

"Battles make you tired? Of course, that's why I insist they nap or sleep between," Ullmo'ok said. "That's why I suggested stims before battle."

"Well, it's, wait, you did what?" Tak said. "Boss, that's not a good idea. It's not a good idea even with a professional standing force."

"Why not?" Ullmo'ok asked, looking at the unused stim-pack sticking out of his pouch.

"It messes with your body chemistry, and I mean real bad. Just a few minutes of combat can leave you exhausted for a day or two, that's why sleep is so important to commanders," Tak said. "Boss, you guys aren't trained for this. You need to start rotating."

"Like with the ammunition?" Ullmo'ok asked.

"Like that. Only take like half of your force out, just have the rest on standby, eating or sleeping," Tak said. "Some of them will feel too tired to drink liquid or even eat."

"Oh," Ullmo'ok said. He felt fine, he had assumed the other did to. "Who should I have sleep?"

Tak sighed. "I don't know. According to my files, have the ones who took the most damage get some sleep. They're going to be the most tired."

"I shall follow your advice, warboi," Ullmo'ok stated.

He wished he had a narcobrew.

"Captain Megran, 144th Ordnance Company. You must be Ullmo'ok," The Terran said. It still struck Ullmo'ok as odd when he saw a human who wasn't a warborg. The Terran had on body armor, with strength enhancement and a backpack more like a hump on his back, but nothing like the heavy body of a warborg. His face was fuzzy, orange and white, with a muzzle adorned with whiskers and a black nose, his mouth full of sharp pointed round canine teeth.

"I am known as such," Ullmo'ok said. He looked around at where humans were running everywhere. Some carrying technical looking equipment that must have outweighted them by five or six times. Some in massive cargo-mech frames were grabbing blocks of missiles and cannon and magshot and moving them over.

"This is all mil-spec ammo. Variable mission configurable missile warheads, all in the hypersonic range, mission configurable mortar rounds, same with your cannon and magshot rounds," The Terran said. "I'm having my men make sure your VI's know how to use them."

"We have advanced virtual intelligences," Ullmo'ok said.

The Terran raised one eyebrow. "Really?"

"Yes," Ullmo'ok said.

There was silence for a moment before the human cleared his throat. "Well, then. We'll reload your stores, some medical supplies and a medical VI, drop you some food and water, and get moving. We've got an armor brigade down to slush," the human said.

"Very well," Ullmo'ok said.

The Terran turned away, shaking his head and flicking his ears. He'd dealt with Lanaktallans before and usually they were blowing saliva, rattling those tendrils around, raising and lowering their crests, and shaking their jowls. That one had just been still, his eyes dead and empty, more life in his cybernetic eye.

He's probably just tired, Captain Megran thought to himself, wishing he could scratch the base of his tail through the armor.

Ullmo'ok moved over to where the narcobrew and the food was strewn out on a table. He took a bottle of brew and some condensed nutri-cud and watched the humans run around. It looked like complete anarchy to him but within a half hour the Terran who had talked to him came walking up.

"You're good to go. We can't drop a nano-forge or a creation engine here, too much metal in the rocks, they'd start doing extraction without taking a few hours to put up the proper shielding and running the proper protocols," the Terran said, his whiskers trembling. "Same reason we can't drop you an AI core, the AI would get drunk from the EM scatter in the metal without enough shielding and our nano-forges are mostly slush."

"Very well," Ullmo'ok said.

The Terran looked at him a moment, then shrugged and headed toward his vehicle. A sleek looking hovercraft with a quad-barrel ion-slug rapid fire gun on the back, a Terran leaning against it with a white stick in his mouth, blowing smoke and watching the sky.

Ullmo'ok knocked on the table with his almost empty bottle, getting his pilot's attention. Once he was sure he had it he spit out the plastic fiber wadding of the synth-cud on the ground and looked at them.

"Everyone get some sleep. We have satellites now to watch the Precursors for us," Ullmo'ok said. "I will wake you if you are needed. From now on, we only go out in groups of twelve with a leader."

They all nodded, breaking up, and Ullmo'ok watched them leave. He moved over the Most High Mechanic, Krekit, was looking over the ammunition and stores. Ullmo'ok noticed the smaller being had a headset on, obviously speaking to his own aVI.

"How well are we now stocked?" Ullmo'ok asked.

Krekit looked up, nodding. "Really well. These missiles, they're something else, boss. Our tubes can fire them, luckily."

"And the parts?" Ullmo'ok asked.

"A little problem there. If we have to fix a knee, we'll have to replace both actuators or you'll run with a limp because these are top-shelf stuff," Krekit said. He wiped his hands on his coveralls and stood up, shading his eyes. "You sure we'll get warning if anyone's coming?"

"I am sure," Ullmo'ok said. He looked around. "I must

go and speak to another. Ensure the mechs are loaded and repaired."

Krekit nodded. "Sure, boss, sure."

Ullmo'ok clopped away, heading into the office where Tak had been brave enough to tell him that he had failed. He moved in, picked up the shielded communicator normally used to talk to Corporate Headquarters in the capital, and plugged it in. He dialed in the com-code he'd memorized, leaned back in the sitting sling, and waited.

His uncle's face appeared. "Apartment 2621."

"Uncle," Ullmo'ok said, reaching out and touching the screen. He could *almost* feel something. Something he'd felt when he'd watched his thumpmen escort his uncle to the shelters.

"Ullmo'ok," his uncle said. Ullmo'ok expected the older Lanaktallan to inflate his crests, curl his tendrils, and shake his jowls in rage. Instead the older male looked behind him, then looked back at the screen. "Are you well?"

Ullmo'ok nodded. "I am uninjured."

"Is it terrible up there? The news says that the planetary forces are defeating the Precursors across all fronts and that they will be defeated in a matter of days," his uncle said. He paused. "That is not true, is it?"

Ullmo'ok shook his head. "No, uncle. It is not. Even the humans are fighting hard. The factory..."

"To the bowels of the dying ones with the factory, Ullmo'ok. How are you?" the older male repeated.

"I am uninjured," Ullmo'ok said. "I wished to know that you and our family are not suffering."

The older Ullmo'ok's tendrils trembled with something Ullmo'ok didn't understand. "It is crowded, it is noisy at times, but your Secmen are keeping order. We are not suffering. But what about you?"

Ullmo'ok shrugged again. "I will fight to defend the shelters. Not only are you there, but loyal workers and their families. Families of my bashmech pilots."

His uncle stayed silent, reaching out with all four hands and touching the screen at the corners. "Please, nephew, be careful."

Ullmo'ok shrugged again. "It will be what it will be, uncle. I shall fight hard to prevent the Precursors from reaching you. Should I fall, the Terrans have stated they will protect you."

"You, you managed to make a deal with the Terrans?" his uncle asked.

"No. They value you and the others and will seek to protect you," Ullmo'ok said. "No deal. No bargain. Just they have sworn to witness what I and my pilots do here and to protect you."

"Looey, who is that?" Ullmo'ok heard his aunt ask. Something inside him *twisted* and he felt something for a moment.

"Tell her it was just the thumpmen," Ullmo'ok said. "Stay alive, uncle."

Before his uncle could reply he unplugged the communications device.

The feeling went away and he picked up a half-empty bottle of whiskey and took a long drink.

"Boss? Are you all right?" Tak asked.

"Of course," Ullmo'ok said, finishing off the bottle and setting it on the desk. He tabbed a narco injector into his arm. "Why wouldn't I be?"

"Just checking. You should get some sleep," Tak said.

"I have things that must be done. You should get some rest, defrag, recompile, and sector-check yourself," Ullmo'ok said, sliding out of the sling.

"All right, boss. Call me if you need me," Tak said.

"I will," Ullmo'ok promised, clopping his way through the deserted refinery office.

The fifteenth day dawned as Ullmo'ok stood at the edge of the valley, staring at the hell beyond. The Jotun had pushed more vehicles, and more, and more at his bashmechs. Tak had told him that the Jotun had been forced to allocated his heavy combat robots to defend against the Terran combat vehicles.

Now the entire valley was nothing but broken, scorched, carbonized, and melted metal. Slagged internals of robots.

And a pair of dead bashmechs.

"I screwed up. I didn't fall back fast enough when the aircraft came in," Plunketi'ik said, shaking her head. "Zikmack and Trekez got caught by their bombing run. Half my bashmechs got seriously damaged and I've had to send them back for repair."

"Were they witnessed?" Ullmo'ok asked carefully.

"Yes," Plunketi'ik said softly. "Hail our dead," She said. She fired a single hypersonic missile, no guidance, no warhead, just a dead missile on a high parabolic arc that left a white trail in the sky as it sped toward the Jotun and vanished in the distance.

"Did they have family in the shelters?" Ullmo'ok stared at the destroyed valley that had once been the site of luxury vacation homes for wealthy executives.

The river was full of toxic runoff from the battles.

"Yes. Both did," Plunketi'ik said.

"Then they will live on," Ullmo'ok said.

"Boss, boss!" Tak suddenly broke into the somber moment. "TAKE A KNEE!"

"What?" Ullmo'ok asked. He heard Plunketi'ik's warboi yell the same thing.

"This!" Tak threw a wire-frame on all his screens. Down on one knee, arms covering the chest, face tilted down, hands over the face, leaning slightly forward.

Ullmo'ok took the position, feeling shattered Precursor machine crumble even further under his knee.

"Why do we..." Ullmo'ok started. A bright flash tore open the sky and Tak turned the screens off and the cockpit completely opaque.

A rumble started. His speakers howled with static. Sparks shot from his forward control panel. The rumble got harder and suddenly a shock wave hit him from the front. He actually felt his mech slide back a few meters, something moving its 500 ton bulk backwards like an adult pushing back a defiant child.

There was a split second of calm, then the blast hit again, harder, and Ullmo'ok found himself leaning forward.

"EJECTING MISSILE BAY! DIGITAL OMNIMESSIAH PROTECT US!" Tak screamed out.

Another space, then a third shockwave, this one lifting him slightly, giving him a brief feeling of weightlessness. Impacts hit his battle-screens and Ullmo'ok was sure that it was the wreckage of the Precursor vehicles being thrown against his bashmech by some giant hand.

Ullmo'ok *felt* something inside. Just for a second.

His mech hit the ground and he narrowly avoided putting a hand out to stabilize himself before Tak got the gyros under control.

"HERE COMES THE BOOM, BOSS!" Tak screamed and Ullmo'ok could hear the fear in the aVI's voice.

The roar, the explosion, wasn't a sound. It was a physical thing, a fist that slammed into his bashmech with steel covered knuckles. He managed to keep on one knee, managed to keep upright. Light shined through cracks he didn't even know where there around his modified cockpit cover. He saw his battle-screens fail right before his screens dissolved into static.

Tak screamed in agony.

The radiation meters inside the cockpit began to howl. Two vidpanels blew out, showering Ullmo'oks flanks with vizplaz. Static howled through Ullmo'ok's implant and his cybereye suddenly went white and shut down.

His mech went dead. Shut down.

It was silent, just the ticking of cooling metal, not even the faint hum of the fusion reactor. Ullmo'ok sat there, looking around in curiosity as his cybereye reboot, failed, reboot again and came on, shot with static that slowly cleared. His cockpit cover was cracked in two places, the foot thick armorplas crazed white and shot through with spiderwebs.

Carefully, slowly, Ullmo'ok restarted his bashmech.

It took five times before it started up sluggishly. The

fusion reactor had to be flushed twice before it would start, the mag-bottle projectors overloaded and charged, ionized, the circuitry full of stray charges.

"B-b-b-b-b-boss?" Tak asked. "Boss, you alive?"

"I am intact," Ullmo'ok said. "You screamed. It sounded like pain."

Tak made a sound that reminded Ullmo'ok of a cough. "Particle sleet. Someone saw a chance and hit the Jotun with an battery. That missile Plunketi'ik fired found a spot not covered by battlescreens and actually hit the Jotun's hull. Some wiseass in orbit made a snapshot at it," Tak coughed again. "A plasma wave phased motion gun from near orbit or a near C velocity shell or a main ion cannon from a battleship."

"It hurt?" Ullmo'ok asked.

"That was a 1.4 kilowatt EMP at the end, boss, it was like getting hit in the face with by a mech-fist to you. It blew straight through the particle shields, took down the battle-screens, wrecked up everything," Tak said. He buzzed a second. "I'm all hashed up. Sector errors, CRC errors, I'm pretty fragmented."

"Is it safe to stand up?" Ullmo'ok asked.

"Y-yeah, boss, it should be," Tak said. "I had to eject the missiles and plasma rounds. Take it easy."

"Defrag and perform maintenance on yourself, Tak," Ullmo'ok said, standing the mech up slowly. Only one of his displays worked, a small one for drone feeds, and Ullmo'ot shifted his forward view to it. It was nothing but static so he rebooted his screens.

Triggering his datalink he brought up the com-codes for the seven bashmech pilots that had been with him and dialed them.

Only four answered.

"Follow me. We need repair," Ullmo'ok said.

"Frextik'ik's ammunition exploded. He didn't eject his ammunition in time," Plunketi'ik said. "I can see Uskralet's mech, it's torn apart."

"What happened?" Vemtre asked.

"Orbit shot. They took a shot at the Jotun," Ullmo'ok told them. His display cleared up just in time for him to look at where the Jotun was. "Your missile revealed a gap in the Jotun's defenses. Our dead were witnessed."

"By the Forgotten Brood Mothers," Pluketi'ik said slowly, and Ullmo'ok knew she was seeing it too.

The clouds were gone, swept away by the blast. A huge mushroom cloud had formed, with other clouds riding up. Black and red, with fires burning in the huge cloud at the top, lightning flickering in them. The whole sky looked like it was burning.

"I think they got it," Woxtow said softly.

"Let us hope. Do not count the credits before the end of the match," Ullmo'ok warned. "Let us return, we need repair and refit."

The others, used to Ullmo'ok's calm voice and unshakable demeanor, followed him as they slowly trudged back. The trees were burning, what few buildings that remained were flattened. Debris from the valley had crashed into the landscape, the heavier and larger pieces first. Smoke covered everything, dust and small debris hanging in the air.

"My warboi is stuttering, he sounds drunk," Woxtow said.

"Order him to defrag and recompile," Ullmo'ok said.

They moved through the shattered day, Ullmo'ok piloting his damaged bashmech by a single screen that barely worked, until they reached the quarry. Twice more the rumble of great explosions washed over them.

In the quarry the stacks of ammo were tipped over, the cranes at the edge of the quarry fallen into it. Four of the bashmechs were on their backs. One was getting up slowly. Another was gutted, the chassis burning from where the missiles inside had detonated. Fires were still being put out and Ullmo'ok noted that it looked like everything had been pushed slightly toward the far side of the quarry. Ullmo'ok stopped and powered down his mech, noting that the survival core case for Tak no longer shined the green light, just a yellow one that slowly flashed. He tried to open the cockpit but the motors just sputtered and clattered on stripped gears.

Ullmo'ok had to have the mechanics remove his canopy.

The air smelled of seared metal, smoke, and pulverized rock.

Seeing the clouds in the distance with the naked eye, not on a small screen, was impressive, Ullmo'ok noted. Other bashmech pilots got out and just stared, their jaws hanging down. A few, like Woxtow, starting crying.

Ullmo'ok went into the office to check the status of the shelters. He had to go back out, get a battery, and attach it to the lone comlink he could find that still worked once he applied power.

They were fine. They'd barely felt the shock.

Still, he stood by the desk, thinking for a long time in the darkness. The power was still out. The only connection to the shelters was the single shielded hard line and a single freight elevator that still had power and was protected by a ten meter thick endosteel shutter. After a moment he made his decision, going out to the mechanics.

"I need some parts and your help," he told Krekit. The mechanic nodded.

Together they set to work.

It was raining. The clouds heavy and dark. The rain was full of ash, leaving sticky black streaks on everything.

The mechanics were still working on the bashmechs, replacing armor, damaged molecular circuitry, replacing actuators that had frozen up from the sleet of particles or from an impact of debris. Bashmechs were being reloaded as Ullmo'ok stared at his remaining pilots.

He was down to ten pilots. Several pilots had been killed by the shockwave, picked up and thrown against something hard enough to kill them. Some could not fight any more, unable to stop weeping. Some had died in the blast at the canyon.

He considered it worth it to kill the Jotun.

"We must keep fighting," Ullmo'ok said.

Half of them flinched.

"Those who cannot, retreat to the shelters," Ullmo'ok ordered. "Be with your families. You will witness those who stay."

Three left. Ullmo'ok touched each one on the shoulder and bid them farewell.

"Krekit, send all but your essential mechanics to the shelters," Ullmo'ok ordered. "Once the bashmechs are repaired and reloaded, you and the others will retreat to the shelters."

"Boss, you're going to need us," Krekit said. He waved at the mechs. "You're gonna get damaged, need us."

Ullmo'ok shook his head. "No, friend Krekit. We will not."

He turned to Plunketi'ik. "Go to the shelter, be with your podlings and your family."

Plunketi'ik shook her head. "No. I will not hide below while others fight to protect my family."

Ullmo'ok frowned. "They will need you down there."

"They will need me more up here," The female stared at Ullmo'ok for a long moment. "Boss, I've been with you since we were welding metal to forklifts. Since you were paying me to punch other Telkan in the face down in the mail room. I *know* you. There are some things you don't understand, and this is one."

"Very well. I thank you," Ullmo'ok said. She was right, some things he just did not understand. He understood loyalty though, and Plunketi'ik had denied telling the Executors and CorpSec who had stolen an entire batch of narcobrew, sitting in the cell right next to Ullmo'ok until his uncle had used his connections to set them both free.

Moving over to the table he picked up another wad of synth-cud, jamming it into his jaws. He chewed it slowly, looking at the entrance to the cave. There was a crack in it. A big one. One of the engineers had put a strut in place to ensure the cave stayed open and beings were moving the ammo into the cave with the rest of it.

Looking back toward the Jotun he could see the clouds start to spread out.

The sky looked bloody and bruised.

"Boss? You there, boss?" Tak suddenly asked over the com-link.

"I am here," Ullmo'ok said.

"I'm all better now, boss," Tak said. "I was really torn up by that EMP and those particle bursts, I'm better now."

"Good," Ullmo'ok said. "Run diagnostics on *Pleasure & Glory*, please."

"Sure, boss," Tak said. After a few minutes his voice came back. "Boss, why is there a shielded, encrypted, high speed data-link connected to my survival core? What is that for?"

"A manual suggested it, friend Tak," Ullmo'ok lied. Lying to friends was wrong, but Ullmo'ok had come to understand Tak.

"Oh. OK. The *Glory*'s really beat up. She's fully loaded, they've got her largely repaired, but there's some serious armor damage to the arms and your shock absorbers on your crash couch are blown out," Tak said.

"Very well. Inform the mechanics," Ullmo'ok said. He spit out the mess of plas-strings, the cud empty, and grabbed a narco-brew.

Something was happening. He was sure of it.

He stared off into the distance, where the Jotun was burn-ing.

"BOSS! BOSS!" Tak's voice got his attention.

"Yes?" Ullmo'ok asked, opening his eyes.

"I was looking through a couple of drones that survived the blast, we've got trouble, boss!" Tak said.

"What type?" Ullmo'ok asked, getting to his feet.

"Metal incoming! LOTS of metal incoming! They're pour-ing out of the Juton! It's an army!" Tak said. "I'm seeing everything. Repair bots, infantry, big bug bots, some flying with anti-grav, some on treads, some just pulling themselves with one arm."

"They want the refinery. To repair and bring back to life their god-machine," Ullmo'ok said. He whistled to get the attention of his pilots. Most of them were asleep and he sent a whistle through their comlinks.

"Start *Glory*," Ullmo'ok told Tak, then looked at his pilots. "The enemy are coming."

"How many?" Woxtow asked.

"All of them," Ullmo'ok answered. "If you cannot pilot, retreat to the shelter."

Three more blanched and left. One was Rask-talik, who's chest rings were broken and was having problems breathing.

That left five of them.

"Krekit," Ullmo'ok said through his link.

"Yeah?" The engineer asked.

"Take your people, hide in the cave, the Precursors are coming. All of them," Ullmo'ok ordered.

"Your mech isn't finished, boss," Krekit said.

"Obey me," was all Ullmo'ok said.

"All right, boss, we'll hide out at the back of the cave," Krekit said.

The mechanics and workers streamed by, running for the cave, as the bashmech pilots ran for their machines. Ullmo'ok stared at the burning horizon and idly injected the inside of his upper right arm with a narcostim, tossing the container behind him.

He walked to *Glory* and looked at it.

His pilot's couch was still exposed.

"Boss, you can't pilot this. They're going to be here in minutes," Tak said.

"Do not fear," Ullmo'ok said.

The sky screamed and Ullmo'ok looked up to see shafts of light streaking across the sky, terminating in greasy looking clouds. He heard a weird fluttering and saw rockets firing toward the Jotun.

"Point defense and counter-battery, boss," Tak said. "The Terran military is trying to help, but you're at the edge of their defense range."

"Tell them we will be there soon," Ullmo'ok said, climbing the ladder. He didn't bother to retract it, just sat back in his couch and leaned back, feeling his mech synch up with his brain. He lifted on hand, grabbed the ladder, and tore it away.

Moving over the pile of armor he bent down, grabbing a piece, then bending it in his bashmech's hands. Walking slowly he moved to Woxtow.

"Use your light laser and weld this to my mech," he ordered. He slammed the piece in place, bending it, flexing it with the power of his mech's hand.

"You sure?" Woxtow asked.

"I am sure," Ullmo'ok said.

"All right, boss," Woxtow said.

Ullmo'ok heard the hiss of the laser, moving his hand away when Woxtow told him to. He buckled down his restraining straps as Woxtow finished the job. His screens were sufficient. He moved the HUD from his missing canopy to his cybernetic eyes.

"There almost here, boss," Tak said.

"I am ready," Ullmo'ok said. He opened the link. "Get ready."

He turned to the cave, checking with thermals to ensure that nobody was near.

He used a laser to slice through the beam and the entrance collapsed. He fired a single particle beam cannon into the cliff face above the collapsed entrance, bringing more rock down.

"Boss, boss, what are you doing," Krekit asked.

"Stay safe. Go into the shelter, weld shut the door behind you. Someone will come and help you," Ullmo'ok. "You are a faithful employee, Krekit."

"Thank you, boss," Krekit said.

Ullmo'ok cut the link, turning and facing the far side of the quarry, where the switchback led down into it.

"Follow me, we will join the Terrans, and there," Ullmo'ok said. "There, they will witness us as we will them."

His five cohorts followed him, waiting as he used a laser on the last of the ammunition and parts, reducing everything to wreckage.

"They're coming, boss," Tak said.

The sky was full of tracers and puffs of explosions. Metal fragments had started falling from the sky. Ullmo'ok led his comrades to the large parking lot, which had once held hauler trucks, cargo-lifters, executive cars, and factory worker buses.

Now there was only a half-dozen Terran vehicles, all of them firing skyward.

Ullmo'ok wished he had the comlink for the Terrans but pushed that away.

Wishes were for children.

Together, they stood and faced the direction the machines would be coming from.

"Destroy the buildings," Ullmo'ok ordered.

Together, the last six pilots of the Arena reduced the buildings to slag, using laser and particle beams.

"Boss, here they come," Tak said.

The machines swarmed out of the wreckage and through the alleys.

There was no time to talk. The six pilots fired missiles, pouring them into the oncoming machines. Short range missiles for the rushers, long range to hammer the oncoming ranks. Lasers and particle beams shrieked and thundered through the air.

For every Precursor Ullmo'ok and his comrades killed, twenty more, a hundred more, filled the gap.

Slowly the machines gained ground. Coming closer and closer. The Terran vehicle's ammo ran dry and Ullmo'ok ordered them over his loudspeakers, which he entertained the crowd with so long ago, to retreat. He used a phrase he had Terrans say on the TriVid.

"Get out of here, boys, there's nothing you can do."

Two Terran vehicles stayed, laser point defense vehicles, their lasers raking long range missiles out of the sky.

As the Precursor machines advanced, now onto the tarmac of the parking lots, pushing past the wreckage of the public transit buses, the missiles got closer and closer, a waterfall slowly overwhelming the defenses of the Terran vehicles.

The Precursors were close enough to fight back. Battle-screens flared and rippled as lasers and cannon shells pried at them with deadly fingers, looking for some way in.

Ilktakna'ak went down first, a heavy cannon shot blowing through his failing and already damaged battle-screen, the liquid stream of the explosively forged penetrator hitting dead center of his cockpit and exiting from the back in a fan of liquid metal.

Ullmo'ok opened up with his autocannons, going to maximum fire rate, ignoring heat warnings, raking the encroaching line of vehicles with armor piercing discarding sabot rounds, sweeping it back and forth. His missile bays ran empty and slammed the protective covers shut.

One of the Terran vehicles exploded.

Missile salvos started landing on that side, blowing Neeklum apart as his mech took an entire volley of heavy missiles.

Ullmo'ok avenged his lost pilot with a trio of particle beams, stomped the overheating override, and kept fighting.

"Boss, we're going to get overrun!" Tak yelled.

"Yes," Ullmo'ok answered.

A warborg pulled its way free of the Terran wreckage, grabbing the slightly intact four-barrel point defense gun, plugging the power cable into its leg, and opened fire, laying 2cm laser fire into the oncoming Precursors.

Ullmo'ok added his own fire, sweeping across the still advancing metal horde.

"Boss, on our right!" Tak called.

The other Terran vehicle blew up.

Ullmo'ok turned, seeing more Precursor vehicles rush out, firing as they came. Ullmo'ok couldn't stem the tide as the sudden rush let them overwhelm Dwenstil's battle-screen and pour fire into them.

The Precursors were on them. Ullmo'ok was aware of the Terran warborg fighting, still firing the point defense gun like it was a sidearm, the beam bright and eyewatering, when he was swarmed over.

Woxtow went down next, screaming "WITNESS ME!" as crablike Precursor machines swarmed up his body, tearing off armor, firing lasers from their mouths.

Ullmo'ok heard him scream, turned, and washed over the downed mech with plasma, cutting off Woxtow's scream and destroying the crab bots. Alarms went off and his battle-screens went down.

"Back to back!" Plunketi'ik yelled. "My battle-screens are down!"

Ullmo'ok took two steps back, feeling his armor thud against hers.

Together they fired, raking the Precursor machines, who attacked as if they were insane. Swarming over the smoking wreckage of their own dead with their eagerness to get at the last two warriors fighting back to back.

"Boss, we're out of ammo, we're overheating, we have to withdraw!" Tak yelled. "You've got like 3 autocannon rounds left."

"Goodbye, Tak, you are faithful," Ullmo'ok said, slapping the red button he had helped wire into the cockpit.

"Boss... no... what are you.. don't... what are... wat?" Tak vanished, the automatic maintenance transfer sending him into his own survival core. The transmitter went live, sending Tak to a spare survival core that Ullmo'ok had prepared.

A survival core that by now would be being delivered to his uncle.

"I will see my podlings soon," Plunketi'ik gasped. "My mech's going to shut down. They're going to pull me from the

225

cockpit and pull me apart."

"Face me," Ullmo'ok ordered.

When he could see Plunketi'ik's cockpit on his reticle he lifted his arm.

"Join your podlings without pain, old friend," Ullmo'ok said. Plunketi'ik's mech stood straight up, Precursor machines crawling up its torso and legs.

He knew she was raising her chin in defiance as she dropped her arm. Ullmo'ok fired his last three autocannon rounds.

Heat flushed into his cockpit as Plunketi'ik's mech tipped over backwards, atomized metal streaming from the back of her bashmech like blood. Ullmo'ok extended the sword and started laying around him, firing lasers, PPC's, smashing the Precursor machines underfoot.

As he fought, he activated his datalink. His uncle's face appeared in his cybereye.

"I will be with you soon, uncle," was all he said before terminating the link.

The Precursor's were crawling on him as a barrage of missiles got past his overworked point defense and EW. His mech shuddered, stepped back, the overheated gyros siezed.

Ullmo'ok landed on his back, feeling something snap between his torso and body.

He couldn't feel his legs.

His mech's power failed. The heat was baking him and he could smell his own hair and flesh burning.

At least he couldn't feel it.

He opened the com-link.

"Trucker, come in Trucker," he gasped. His lower lungs weren't working, he could feel blood oozing up his long-throat. "Come in, Trucker."

Something was prying off his makeshift armor.

"Trucker, come in, Trucker," he gasped, pulling the needler out from where he kept it under his pouch. With another hand he pulled a handful of narcostims out and injected them into his chest. "Come in, Trucker!"

The armor screamed as it bent.

"Trucker here. Is that you Ullmo'ok?"

The armor bent far enough for a red-eyed tentacle with graspers to try to slide in. Ullmo'ok fired the needler, smashing the eye. He was able to breath, barely, without pain.

"Yes. Do it."

"Do what?" Trucker asked.

"Atomics. Do it," Ullmo'ok gapsed. "You can't help us. Do it."

Trucker dropped the line. Ullmo'ok slapped the engine start button twice, shooting two more Precursors that tried to get in.

His mech started and he struggled to his feet as what looked like a metal octopus ripped away the canopy.

The damaged laser still packed enough of a punch to blow the Precursor machine off the front of his cockpit even if it blistered his flesh and burnt away his hair. He was blind in his front eyes so he turned his head, using his mechanical eyes, and kept firing, not screaming, just shooting. Even as the Precursors smashed his weaponry he kept fighting. Even when the chainsword bound up and shattered inside the chassis of a Precursor mech twice Ullmo'ok's size.

He was still shooting as a Precursor pulled his torso out of the cockpit, his lower body staying strapped in, when the world went white.

V CORPS MEMO

5th Irregulars earned battle standard and awards due to their defense of the Hoolangenar Industrial Facility shelters. Will review after action is completed. Bolo-31673SCR is on site, reports the shelters are intact if sealed.

---NOTHING FOLLOWS---
HOOLANGENAR INDUSTRIAL FACILITY DESTROYED!

Yesterday the criminal Ullmo'ok detonated the industrial

facility's fusion reactor, destroying the Executor and Corporate Security who had been defending it from the Precursor threat, destroying the Hoolangenar Industrial Facility and the shelters both.

Tune in later for an official Kestimet Corporation Office of Public Affairs statement.

RUN, PODLING, RUN

The streets were full of smoke, random debris that swirled in the wind, corpses torn apart and left scattered, destroyed Precursor drones, and rubble that had spilled from where buildings had collapsed. The entire city was full of the sounds of explosions, the high pitched thrumming and screaming of energy weapons, the roar of rockets and missiles, and the wailing of the frightened, trapped in buildings or huddling in the rubble, that had grown so loud that it even could be heard over the combat between the Terran military and the Precursor machines.

The little Telkan ran on short little legs, her fur filthy and matted, her huge eyes wide and watering with tears, her tunic torn and filthy, a ragged tattered doll held tight to her body even though it was missing an arm. She was crying as she ran, terror pushing her exhausted body further down the street, her broodmother's words echoing through her mind.

Run, podling, don't look back! the warm, soft, good smelling, and loving broodmother had yelled to the little Telkan as the machines that bit and stung crashed through the window and into the little store they had been hiding inside.

So she ran. Past the bodies, her little brain editing them out, running past the fires burning in the street, past the holes in the ground, climbing over the rubble and sobbing as she did as she'd been told.

run!

She wanted her mother, her father, the broodmothers, the other podlings, but all she had was Mister Kikik, her stuffy, and the broodmother had told her, screaming it as the pinchy machines...

Run!

Her soft feet were bleeding from cuts where rubble has sliced into her delicate walking pads, but still, she kept going, crying, scrambling, holding tight to Mister Kikik as she ran. She scraped her knee and got up, running. She cut her hand scrambling up rubble and kept running. Fire burst up from a hole in the ground, scorching her fur, but she didn't stop.

RUN!

She came to a stop, screaming, when a huge metal snake, as wide as the street, crashed through the building, little pieces of rubble bouncing around her as she ducked and covered her head with one arm, screaming. The snake was twisting in the street and she saw it had hundreds, thousands of legs. It held something in its mouth, in the big pinchers, something that was struggling. She screamed, knowing it was going to hurt it, knowing the many legged snake was bad. She turned to run and saw them.

Pinchies.

She looked around wildly, looking for a way out. There was only walls on either side, pinchies running at her on their spider legs, and the huge snake thrashing around.

"KILL YOU! SKIN YOU! EAT YOU!" a voice roared through the translator necklace she wore.

She screamed, crouching down, holding Mister Kikik tight, covering her head with one arm. She was sure it was the pinchies yelling it.

The snake crashed down behind her and she screamed again, staring at the pinchy's running at her.

"YOU! AREN'T! NOTHING" she heard roar out from behind her, her necklace translating it. "EAT THIS!" There was an explosion behind her.

The pinchies were halfway at her and she turned to look behind her.

A big metal man was standing up, breaking the pinchers holding onto him. Bigger than daddy, but with two arms and two legs and a head with two eyes just like her and daddy. No tendrils or weird faces, just a flat face. He didn't have soft fur, not like mommy or broodmommy, or daddy, he was made of black metal and his eyes were bright glowy green.

"CHRIST, KID, LOOK OUT!" the metal man yelled, raising an arm.

She screamed, turned around, and ducked, covering her head, curling over Mister Kikik, holding him tight with her sore arm.

There was a thrumming noise, a loud noise, like when the food heaty (that she wasn't allowed to play with) was on, and she felt heat on her head that made her fur crinkle and made her get all wet and gross with sweat.

She saw the pinchies get touched by blue flickering light with a white core, the flickering light making them pop with bright flashes. She heard thudding footsteps and the big metal man moved in front of her, his hand cocked back strangely and the blue light coming from a tube sticking out of his palm.

She wondered if it hurt his handpad. She looked away, the light hurting her sensitive eyes.

The light stopped and she opened her eyes and looked up.

The big metal man was looking down at her and she saw that the metal man had tears in his metal skin like she had in her tunic. Silver fluid, like the red blood that filled her scrapes and ran into the fur on her arms and legs, filled up the tears in his metal skin. A big knife was sticking out of his arm and as she watched it slid back inside with a snap.

"You OK, kid?" The big metal man asked.

She nodded, her eyes wide as she stared at him.

"Where's your parents?" The metal man asked.

"The pinchies got my broodmommy," the little girl said, starting to sniffle again. "She yelled for me to run so I ran as far and as fast as I could," she sobbed. "The pinchies chased me."

"You're OK, kid. Let's find somewhere safe for you," the metal man said. He looked up. "This is Char-3381, does anyone read me? This is Char-3381, does anyone read me?"

"Who are you talking to?" she asked. "Is Char your name? Or is the numbers? That's a funny name."

The metal man looked down. "You can hear that?"

"Yes," The little girl said, hugging Mister Kikik close.

The metal man turned around and knelt down. "Can you see the back of my head?"

The little girl stood on her tiptoes. "Yes. You have a pinchy stuck in it."

The big metal man tried to reach back to his head but wasn't quite able to reach it. He gave a sigh.

"Honey, I need you to climb up on my back, OK?" he said. He sat down.

"OK," the little girl said. Her sniffles were stopping. She climbed up, standing on his legs, then pulling herself up. She whined a little when her arm hurt. "Now what?"

"Can you pull the piece of metal out of my head?" he asked.

She wrapped her paw around it, tried to squeeze and stopped. "It's sharp. You're really hot, do metal men get sickies?"

"No, we don't. All right," he sighed. He looked around. "I'm not even sure where I am. My GPS is out."

"Oh," she said. She climbed down and sat on a big rock in the street. "I'm lost too."

"Lost my rifle too. Autocannon's empty. Out of mass, overheating and slushed out. Battle-screen's down," the big metal man stood up. "And half my onboards are out."

He turned around and looked down at her. "Why aren't you in a shelter?"

She shrugged. "Momma tried, the people at the shelter told us that we belonged in the street and called my momma a bad name," she started sobbing. "We walked a ways and were in the crowd, hoping to get into a different one and there were really loud bangs from trucks with the people mommy always said to do what they say. People started screaming. Brood-mommy grabbed me and we ran."

She held tight to Mister Kikik. "There was a loud noise and everyone, even mommy and daddy and the other brood-mommies and the other podlings, all popped like balloons when the light touched them. There was light coming from some big trucks."

"Digital H. Christ, kid," The big metal man said. "I'm sorry."

The little girl sobbed and hugged Mister Kikik harder. "Broodmommy hid us in a store, even though she did a bad thing and broke a window with a rock. We've been in there during all the noise. Even when the big light came."

The big metal man knelt down. "You've been in that shop for five days? Have you even eaten?"

The little girl nodded. "Broodmommy fed me. She ran out of milk yesterday though. I'm hungry and thirsty."

The little girl looked up, tears coming from her large expressive eyes. "I want my broodmommy."

"It's OK, kid," the big metal man said. "I've got you. What's your name?"

"Podling," She said. "We don't have names yet."

"Can you eat regular food or only broodmommy milk?" The big metal man asked, standing up and looking around.

"I can eat big people food. I'm almost old enough to have a name," The little podling said, looking up.

"There, we can get you something to eat there," The big metal man said, pointing at a shop.

The little girl looked at the front of the shop and shook her head. "There's no podling sign. That's for the Masters."

"Not today, kid, you're with me," The big metal man said. He took a couple steps and stopped. "Oops, that's not good."

"What?" The little girl looked around.

The metal man moved over to a big car, the important kind that mommy said to always look out for, grabbed a door, and ripped it open with a scream of metal.

"Get in, kid, and hurry," The metal man said. "Sit in the back and in the middle of the seat. Don't look."

The podling nodded, hurrying up. She sat on the seat and buckled the seat harness.

"Don't look. Look down. Don't look, sweetie," The big

metal man said, then closed the door.

She could hear the wailing coming. The wailers screamed, and ran down the street, some breaking windows, some hitting people, others throwing rocks. She didn't know why they wailed, they just did. She saw them ripping each others clothing sometimes, still wailing. Even masters were part of the wailers. They were all blackened, with owies all over, their hair falling out and icky sores on their faces.

The wailing got louder and she covered her ears, bending over and squeezing her eyes shut.

"Get off me! Don't touch me! Get your slimy hands off me!" The metal man roared.

Glass broke, making her open her eyes, and some landed at her feet. She closed her eyes, squeezing them shut. She heard metal crunch, heard screaming, and terrible noises. The wailing got so loud it hurt her ears, and still the metal man yelled at them to stop touching him, get off of him, keep their hands to themselves. There was banging on the metal, more glass broke, and it felt like someone was jumping on the car.

Then the wailing slowly faded away.

It was quiet for a second and the door opened. She squeezed her eyes shut.

"Don't look, honey. I'll have to pull the roof off a little bit, but don't look, okay?" the metal man said.

"I won't. Promise," she said.

"OK. Be good," he said. She heard metal scream and could smell the air.

It smelled like blood.

She felt the harness unclick and the metal man lifted her up. His hands and arm were really hot.

"Are you sickie?" She asked.

"No sweetie, I'm just overheated," The metal man said. "Keep your eyes closed, hold onto your doll."

"He's Mister Kikik," the podling said.

"Hold onto Mister Kikik," The metal man said. He started walking, then running. It felt like she was flying, being held by the metal man, as he ran through the streets. He suddenly stopped and there was the noise of glass breaking and metal tearing.

She was carefully set in a chair. "OK, sweetie, you can open your eyes."

She looked around. It was a food shop, where masters and important people that you did what they said right away would eat. The big metal man had moved over to a food dispenser and had ripped open the front of it.

"It's nutripaste," he said, letting it pour from the broken machine and into a big bowl.

"You're gonna be in trouble," She said. "I don't want you to be in trouble."

"I'm already in trouble," The metal man said.

"OK," the little podling said, and started slurping down the nutripaste. It didn't taste like anything but it made her tummy feel better. The metal man moved over under where water was falling from a pipe, standing in the water. Pieces popped up with a hiss and she saw steam start to come off of him. She chewed a little on the bowl to ease the ache in her gums, watching. After a bit the pieces closed again and the big metal man came over to her.

"We need to move, kid," The metal man said. "The Precursors are all over the place. We need to get out of city. I'm hurt inside, I can't use my slush, can't run a diagnostic."

"Will a hug help?" She asked. Broodmommy would hug her when she was scared. The metal man didn't have a broodmommy with him.

"It won't hurt, kid," The metal man said. She grabbed his thick leg and hugged it, feeling how warm it was and liking how it vibrated. She let go and looked up.

"Will you carry me?" She asked.

The metal man nodded, picking up her and Mister Kikik. She went out in the street and started running. She felt like she was flying again as they ran. He kept dodging around the stuff that loomed out of the smoke, jumping over some of it.

The podling suddenly felt embarrassed.

"Metal man?" She said.

"Yes, sweetie?" The metal man said.

"I pooped myself. I'm sorry," she said. She rubbed her fur and some came off. Her skin was red looking and hurt. "My fur's coming off."

"You'll be all right. It's rad-sick, I'll get you to the medics and they'll patch you up," The metal man said. Somehow he ran faster.

He started stumbling, staggering, and the podling looked up at him. His green eyes, glowing in the dark, were fixed ahead.

"Are you all right, Mister Metal Man?" The podling asked.

"The goo around my thinky stuff is running out. I'm leaking, kid," the metal man said. "Medics. Get you to the medics," he said, his voice barely audible over the sounds of the war torn city.

They kept moving, the metal man lurching side to side, getting warmer and warmer. The metal man suddenly stopped, pushing the podling under a car.

"No come out. No look," he said. He stood up and she heard it.

A monster.

"Here! Here! Right here!" he yelled.

There was a crash.

"THREE THREE TWO INFANTRY!" the metal man roared.

There was the bright light, blue, and more light, some of it red, some green.

"KILL YOU!"

A giant hand hit the street next to the burnt out car and the podling closed her eyes, holding tight to Mister Kikik.

"SKIN YOU!"

There was another crash. A loud shriek and a clap of thunder that hurt the podling's ears.

"EAT YOU!" the metal man bellowed.

There was a heavy crash, then silence.

The car suddenly flipped off of her and the podling

screamed, looking up.

The metal man stood there. His head was smushed, one eye popped out and dangling from wires. His body looked smashed, wires poking out and goop leaking out.

"Podling," The metal man rumbled.

The podling held her arms up, Mister Kikik in her hand.

The metal man reached down, picking up the podling. The podling noticed that the big knife was broken, part of it bent away from the metal man's hand.

"Medics," The metal man said, his voice squeaking at the end.

He cradled her close and started running.

She looked behind her. It was another metal man, all brown metal, covered in holes, its head twisted off and a burning hold in its back. One foot was kicking but it didn't move.

It was *really* big.

"Podling," The metal man said as they ran through the smoke.

"Yes, Mister Metal Man," the little girl asked.

"Sick. Medic. Run," He said.

"Yes, Mister Metal Man, broodmommy said run," she said. She hugged the metal man's arm, feeling how hot it was. His chest was warm too, like broodmommy's.

"Run," Mister Metal Man said.

They kept running, through the streets, around the burning cars.

"Sick. Medic."

The podling hugged the metal man. Goo had oozed out of him. Some red, some pink, some silver, some blue.

"Podling. Sick. Medic." he kept repeating as he ran.

She hugged his arm tight. Once she threw up on him. Still she hugged him, willing him to be OK, willing the hug to make him all better.

The metal man stopped, looking up with his one green eye. He put his hand up and fired that bright blue light. Once. Twice. Three times.

The howl of a vehicle sounded, the vehicle coming closer. The metal man shot once, twice, three times again, straight up in the air.

The vehicle landed. More metal men jumped out. They had flashing red lights on their shoulders.

"Poooooodliiiiing," metal man said, the word drawing out and like a moan.

The vibration stopped. She looked up. His eyes were dark.

The new metal men ran up, red shapes on their chests. They had to pull Mister Metal Man's arm away, and they took her to the flying vehicle. She cried, reaching out for the metal man, as the vehicle went up in the air. She cried out for him, as they stuck a needle on a tube in her arm. She struggled, holding onto Mister Kikik as they put a mask on her face, reaching out for the metal man as the vehicle rose into the air.

He stood in the middle of an intersection, unmoving.

The smoke swirled around him, and he was gone.

She came there often, after she was named, after she grew up. She had looked it up, where Lance Corporal Char-3381 of the Terran Confederate Marine Corps had finally died.

She would stand on the corner, staring at the middle of the street as the ground-cars went by.

She never forgot him. Even when her patchy fur turned gray. Even when her whiskers drooped. Even when her own podling's podlings had to help her go there.

And she took Mister Kikik with her each time.

TERRAN CONFEDERATE MARINE CORPS

Lance Corporal Char-3381 is post-posthumously awarded the Marine Silver Star, for actions above and beyond the call of duty. Charr-3381, severely wounded, carried an orphaned Telkan podling suffering from radiation poisoning, beyond the city of Shur'rima'an, signaling a passing medical evacuation unit to the podling's distress. During his travels he engaged two super-heavy Precursor infantry units, upholding his duty, defeating them single-handedly in defense of the podling.

Despite a cracked brain case, despite being out of neural fluid, he kept moving, and by his valor and actions, the Telkan podling was evacuated from the city.

Lance Corporal Char-3381 was pronounced SUDS dead at the scene. His body was recovered and his tissue remains were buried with all Marine Corps honors on Terra.

---NOTHING FOLLOWS---

QUEST OF THE BLACK HEART

She was Queen Glad-Real-All, and she had been born whole.

A daughter of the Mad Angel Terrasol, he of the flaming warsteel sword and wings of flowing magic. She was born knowing the spells and incantations of life, of the sublime traceries of the blood code, of the how and the why all life together.

She knew of her people's ancient history, as inscribed by the ancient seer Toll-Klien, which translated to Child of the Toll, which she secretly knew was Child of the Price that Must Be Paid. She knew of triumph and loss, of how even her magic could be twisted to blasphemy and others would seek her power for their own.

She knew the songs of power to commune with the Arch-Angels of Warsteel that patrolled the far heavens to ensure that those who dwelt within her realm were inviolate from powers beyond.

Queen Glad-Real-All knew of the heroism of little people, at the difference a single being could make, knew that heroism and will and steel could carry the day even when all appeared to be lost.

She knew to never give up.

She was Queen Glad-Real-All, and she had been born whole.

Serving her were her Wood Elves, that she had touched and ensured that they knew the songs and incantations when they were born whole. She whispered to them in their sleep as they grew so that when they were born they knew their job in shepherding life across her domain.

She was Queen Glad-Real-All, all who knew of her loved her.

His name was Ukk-uk-huk and he was content.

The Overseers had came to his world when he was but a tadpole. The older members of his pool had all been killed when the Leebawans had tried to resist. He had watched as his people's little spaceport had been wiped away to be replaced by a giant smoking place that generated electricity for the cities of the Overseers, even as the Overseers destroyed the small towns and places of his people.

He had watched the Overseers destroy muddy banks where tadpole eggs should have hatched. He had seen them tear apart his world, cut down the beautiful silent forests where his small people had always marveled that living things grew so big.

They had learned the ways of space, learned to create ships that could travel between the stars, and for that, the Overseers had come and his people were doomed.

Then had come the metal ones. They had killed everything, destroyed everything.

Then had come the Terrans. Savage primates that reminded Ukk-uk-huk of the lemurs of the Southern continent, extinct now, as the Overseers had disliked their funny games and playful pranks. They had smashed the machines, taught Ukk's people to smash the machines. To scream and rage and not huddle in their burrows waiting to die.

Like the lemurs of the southern continent.

Ukk-uk-huk's people had blockaded and forbidden the southern continent for hundreds of years, to give the lemurs time to grow like Ukk's people had grown.

Now they were gone.

The Overseers had returned and the Terrans had told the Leebawans that they had to decide what would happen.

Ukk himself chased the Overseer in charge of "Incendiary Population Control Methods" down and shoved a spear made of a stick and a Terran Marine KaBar through the Overseers torso, pinning him there until the Leebawan females came with knives and hot coals.

Since then he had been content with his life. He guarded the Wood Elf Elanteer-1 when the strange being walked around. The Wood Elf, a servant of the Great Elven Queen Glad-Real-All, was curious about Ukk's world. Had wanted to see fish, taste plants (even the ones that weren't good), squish his feet in mud, and taste the waters. Elanteer-1 cared for Ukk's world, and Ukk had seen him weeping over dead fish and small crustaceans as if they were his own children.

When Ukk had told Elanteer that when he was tadpole there were many more of the small rainbow fish in the creeks Elanteer had sat with him and sang a song, one that the Wood Elf made up.

A month later Ukk had seen thousands of tiny rainbow fish in the creeks, darting around eating the algae that had bloomed in the old way.

It was then that Ukk began to believe in magic.

A year went by. Slowly. Around Ukk the world seemed to come to life. The Terrans rarely showed themselves, landing only at the small space port, and only going to talk to the Wood Elves or the Elven Queen unless invited by the Leebawans.

Ukk remembered when he had encountered the Terrans. Watched them save tadpoles and brood mothers and wounded Leebawans. How they had taught him the meaning of jawnconnor time. They had awaken a rage within the Leebawans, had watched, approvingly, as the Leebawens had driven the Overseers away with flame, spears, and a willingness to die on the Overseers guns if only they could drive their spear deep into the Overseer's body.

It felt good to rest in the algae rich mud and listen to Elanteer sing his songs of magic, holding tight to his magic spear where a Terran Marine KaBar gleamed in silent menace.

The Obscene One came from beyond. The Arch Angels of Warsteel and Fire had warned Queen Glad-Real-All that it was coming. Had warned her that it would attempt to bring black heretical magic to her world to twist her work. That they would attempt to slip past the Arch Angels and bring doom upon her kingdom.

She had thought he had been born whole. She had thought that she, Glad-Real-All the Elven Queen, had known all the spells, incantations, and rituals there was to know.

But the Gan-Dolph had been reborn Gray, and had taken her to a secret grove while she lay dreaming, unclad, next to her dreaming pool, her fingers trailing in the gently swirling water whose currents streamed her hair out beyond her.

There the Gan-Dolph had taught her spells left behind from the War of the Genome. From the War of Blood Code. Had shown her the ancient and great magics that were hidden even from her sight.

He had bid her to protect this world and its small, injured people. As if she would do anything other.

She could *feel* the Obscene One. Could feel his rapacious hunger, feel his raw hatred, and knew that this is why she had been born whole into such power, why she had been entrusted with the Sacred Fire and the Songs of the Seven Seals.

The Obscene One wished a ATCG War and the Elven Queen was willing.

This world, these small peoples she was shepherding and restoring even from extinction, were her charges and she would not let them go into the Dark Night.

Glad-Real-All sang the songs and summoned the birthing pools deep in the swamps of hydraulic fluid and battery acid around the slowly decaying machines of the Ancient Enemy's Great Iron Furnaces. There, she created new life, sang the songs to bring them into the world.

The trees she had grown, used great magics to accelerate

the growth, she whispered to in order to produce spores that she would need. She touched the algae across the world and whispered a long song of ATCG to its strands. She touched the Leebawans themselves and changed a single piece of dormant code to make it into a marker.

A way to tell the People from the Enemy.

She prepared Leebaw for war.

The Void Creature seeded the waves of attacks and slowed down. There was no hurry. There were few emissions from the world. It was not sure why it had been called. There were some ships around the world, not many, but not enough to face it.

It had wiped away this world before, a hundred times, and would do so again.

The ships around had launched missiles, but they had missed its great presence by kilometers, vainly attempting to get closer with gravitics pulses even as they peered at its bulk with LIDAR and RADAR.

Rear Admiral Jonathon E reached out with his mind, through his datalink, and grabbed the bars of the ship's wheel in front of him, looking down at his gestalt vision of the crews of his twelve vessel flotilla. He had laid in the fire plans. Dig the C+ shells deep, sweep the enemy from the skies with his cannon.

Around him the ocean sparkled as sea birds floated on air currents, singing songs and telling tales of the enemy's movements.

He had been raised in Texas, on the coast, and his gestalt image reflected it.

"OPEN FIRE!" he roared.

"WEAPONS FREE!" the cannoneers roared, yanking their lanyards.

The three massive battleships fired their main guns, C + Cannons, fired in carefully arranged sequence to keep from warping the keel. The Heavy Cruisers fired their Plasma Wave

Phased Motions guns, the giant pistons hammering at one gun then the other so the dual gunned ships could fire without tearing itself apart.

"VOLLEY ONE AWAY, SUH!" his Treana'ad Gunnery Officer called out. Admiral E preferred to have him appear dressed as if he was an ancient Terra pirate, dressed in blue with little caps with red tassels from the feared Londown Pirate Navy.

The cannon crews busied themselves, in their blue pants and white shirts, looking snappy as they reloaded the cannons.

"Get me the results, Scan," he ordered the two men working over a map with compasses and sextants.

"Direct hits. Target Alpha-One is heeling to starboard," the Treana'ad in the Crow's Nest called out.

"WEAPONS FREE!" the cannoneers roared, yanking the lanyards again.

The first salvo had wounded it badly. The shells impacting *inside* its armor, turning flesh and sinew, organs and tissue, into expanding bubbles of agony.

The creature screamed across the void in the voices it knew would be heard.

SUBMIT OR BE DESTROYED

The roar back staggered it, agony across its mind.

EAT ALL THE DICKS

The roar was feral, cruel, full of malice, hatred, and rage. It burned across the creature's mind, burning away synapses, snapping dendrites, seering axioms.

The second salvo hit, smashing deep. The creature reeled, an explosion of tissue from the great 'foot' it used to crawl through space itself.

This was impossible.

It was losing.

It reached out and gave the orders to the smallest of itself.

Reproduce one of its kind.

When beings through of the TerraSol Fleets they thought only of massive ships, huge weapons, gigantic shells, cliffsides of armor. They thought of fleets in the hundreds, thousands of ships, spreading out to engage the fleets of the enemy. Of the areospace fighters, bombers, intro-atmospheric ships that could operate in space or atmosphere with equal ease. Of dropships pounding the dirt in plumes of radioactive retrorockets to disgorge the ground forces.

When they thought of the ground forces they thought of the great firebases of the Army, the pounding artillery, the smashing tanks, of infantry dug in so that the enemy would have to use its own bones to dig them out. They thought of the Marines, the Mechaneks advancing through atomic fire, through the hell of the enemy's guns, landing in drop-pods that slammed to the ground and shattered the enemy.

But there was another battle that was always fought. One that didn't make for good Tri-D Drama, that didn't have vast militaries moving across the landscape even though the troops were deployed in such great numbers that it required scientific annotation to list.

Nanophage Texarkana-8817 numbered in the 6.43134×10^{38} in the upper atmosphere, hanging up above the jetstreams and soaking up the energy that cascaded across the ionosphere.

The Elven Queen knew it as Angrist, Keeper of the Upper Air.

It was the first assaulted. Spores from space fell far enough their shells ablated away. They were designed to reflect UV rays back into space or absorb them, to dim the amount of sunlight that fell upon the world.

Angrist fell upon them, their blade-like protein shells piercing the spores, rupturing them so they fell as scattered genetic debris to burn up on the air currents.

Layer after layer of warriors, or weapons, most too small to see with the naked eye, fought against the incoming tide of weapons of the Obscene One.

Glad-Real-All the Elven Queen sang her songs, performed her incantations.

The Arch Angels of War Steel in the Sky Beyond Sky were winning the battle against the Demons and Unclean Ones of the Darkness Beyond.

The battle for sea, land, and air, fell on her. On her mastery of incantations, spells, and rituals.

She reached out, to her Wood Elves, and led them in song.

In the quiet spaces, in burrows, the Leebawans sang with them, providing croaking counterpoint to songs they did not understand but respected.

Glad-Real-All, Elven Queen of Air and Ocean and Land and Sky sang her songs, guiding her soldiers as the battle raged on.

Larger creatures now sleeted into the atmosphere. 73% of them had been swept from the sky by carefully planned fire patterns of slushed out defense vehicles, a testament to Admiral E's tactical ability and the ability of his gunnery crews, but that left 27% of tens of millions sleeting into the atmosphere.

Some opened wings, gliding on the air currents, looking for where their primitive brains told them to land to hatch the life squirming inside of them.

Others fell like darts, slamming deep into earth or ocean, breaking apart as the impact woke the creatures inside.

All of them were met by Queen Glad-Real-All, Lady of the Blood Code, Keeper of the Sacred Flame, and her warriors.

Creatures the size of a dog, covered in hard chitin armor, with four blade-arms and a long tongue, shouldered their way out of the husk of the giant seed-pod that had brought them and scrambled from the crater.

The moss they stepped on shot rhizome tendrils into their feet, sucking at their nutrients. The nutrients letting them push more rhizome into the creatures. Tendrils slid from out of the joints in their hard chitin armor.

An inhalation to screech filled their lungs full of pollen. The rush of air down the throat caused the pollen to explode into life. Shooting roots into lung tissue.

Most of them burst before they got five feet. Some never made it out of the crater.

One, tougher than the others, managed to drag itself nearly ten feet, its bladearms scraping at the dust.

It touched a seed. The seed felt it and vegetable matter clenched, heating the drop of water into steam. The steam expanded.

Driving needle thin spikes through the creature. The seed drank deep and felt the corpse fall upon it.

A single tendril of green pushed up, petals opening, seeking the sun.

In the ocean great creatures that fed on algae swept through the vast beds of Obscene Things, scooping them up in their krill nets. The great creatures felt the hunger and swept on, searching for more to eat.

Everywhere the invading corrupted life touched down, they found soldiers waiting for them.

Airborne viruses swarmed a field of bacterial, slicing through them, injecting their own DNA, ripping and tearing at the DNA code.

Bacteria was inhaled by a giant creature, found the lung tissue, and massively bred.

The giant creatures that had unfolded themselves from the drop-shells they had rode to the planet's surface inhaled less than a dozen times.

And drowned in their own lung tissue.

The Wood Elves had been born whole. They knew the songs. They knew the incantations. They knew the spells and rituals.

The Leebawan had been born in mud and misery but had learned glory and the brightness of life once again. They sang with the Wood Elves.

All of them sang to the direction of their conductor, the

Elven Queen Glad-Real-All.

In one spot a massive creature crashed down, the fiery impact of the meteor giving time for the life inside to establish itself. It drove roots deep, cracking bedrock to look for what it hungered for. It quickly developed giant book lungs to stir and clean the air. It shuddered with the pain of the infections that wracked its body, but still it grew. Biological battle-screen projectors swelled to life, protecting the infection from even orbital guns.

A shell began to form, allowing the tissue inside to form without constant attack. It sent out tentacles that, even as they died, left behind soil more condusive to the new life than the old.

A single blot that in a week had grown to over a hundred miles wide.

Ukk-uk-huk followed Elanteer-3 to meet the Great Elven Queen. He was dressed in armor, plates taken from Overseer armor, can carrying his spear with the deadly blade. He shivered at her awe. She was coldly beautiful, unworldly, and moved with a grace that made him want to weep.

Ukk-uk-huk, bravest of all the Leebaw People the Elven Queen said, reaching down and touching him. **Are you ready to risk life and limb for your people again?**

"Yes, oh Queen," Ukk said, looking up at her beauty.

Though it may cost you your life? Queen Glad-Real-All asked.

"For my People, I will do the jawnconnor even if I must die," Ukk responded.

I have a quest for thee, noble one. Journey through the Unclean Lands, find the Citadel of Death, invade it, and stab the Heart of Darkness with this, your spear she said.

She grasped the spear and it warped in his hand. Great crystals wrapped around the stick and he could see a gold and silver fluid flowing around the stick.

"As you wish," Ukk said.

His people were a small one that none had ever cared about before.

The Lady had brought back the fish both great and small, had returned the birds that sangs and screeched, had even called up again the little lizards that Ukk remembered from his youth.

With you shall travel my servants, Elanteer the Brave, Karl the Undying Mechanek. to guide and keep you during your travels and troubles, the Queen said.

From beneath moss stood up a great black warsteel Mechanek, its armor breached but its eyes still red. Mushrooms bloomed from the cracks in its shoulders and backs, crystals grew from the rents in its chest and legs, a burning sword in its hand.

Elanteer was clad in armor of crystal and living lace. Armed with a sword of crystal and wood.

Together Ukk-uk-huk and his two companions headed for the Heart of Darkness. The touch of the Elven Queen burned upon Ukk's brow.

The pulsing mass within the shell sensed the three when they approached. It sent its warriors against the trio, but none could prevail. It tensed within its shell, knowing the armor was proof against any weapon that could be brought against it.

Their footsteps left behind spores that attacked the bio-mass the Pulsing One had carefully nutured on the ground, that had eaten into the soil. Spreading in moments, connecting to one another, creating a path that the rest of the vegetation used to assault the Pulsing One's territory.

The great black creature, clad in crystal and fungus, raised its fiery sword and struck, tearing a great hole into the side of the Pulsing One's citadel.

The three entered the spaces beyond. They crushed and destroyed the organs they found, severed the nerve cables that writhed in their way, smashed the creatures that the Pulsing

One sent to fight.

The Black Knight fell to a huge creature with massive bladearms that managed to shatter the crystal protecting the rents in his chest. He died with his fist around the creature's heart. He gave out a great trumpet-like death cry that shook the entire Obscene Citadel. In his death nanospores poured from the mushrooms, streamed from the rents in his armor, turning the tissue everywhere black as the Rohan Class nanospores attacked the tissue of the Pulsing One.

Ukk was wounded by a skinny creature with a stinger that fell from the ceiling and clung to his back, jabbing the stinger deep into his side. Elanteer swept it off Ukk's back with his sword.

Together the Elf and Leewbawan struggled on. Fever gripped Ukk, but Elanteer half carried him onward. They fought deeper and deeper into the Obscene Citadel, until, finally, they reached the Heart of Darkness.

It was a great pulsating organ, like twisting coral piled high.

The last of the Pulsating One's soldiers attacked.

Elanteer stood between Ukk and the foul creatures that burst from blister-like sacks inside the great cavity, his own sword of crystal and wood in one hand and the burning warsteel of the Black Knight in the other. He danced a dance of death, singing out his own death song as he did so, the blades flashing as he killed one after another.

Ukk dove into the black viscous fluid around the brain. It burned his skin, tried to dissolve his transparent inner eyelids, but he felt the Queen's touch on his brow and pressed on, one hand tight around his spear.

Ukk scrambled up the pedestal of bone and sinew the great pulsating mass sat atop of, used his claws on his hands to climb the mass itself.

As he reached the top Elanteer fell beneath the last of his

enemies, their blades in one another's hearts.

Ukk lifted the spear over his head, the same spear he had carried the night he had learned of jawnconnor, and thrust down into the mass.

It ripped through the outer shell, the magic of the Marine KaBar tearing through the hard chitin. As is drove deep into the neural tissue beyond the crystal cracked, leaking the gold and silver fluid.

The creature screamed, once, before the nanites shredded it, absorbed its genomic code, and transmitted it to the Queen.

Ukk rolled on his back and stared upwards as the shell split and the fibrous tissue gave way until he could see the stars.

There he laid.

He watched the stars, breathing heavy, his body wracked with fever. As the two moons rose he saw a delicate creature fly from the trees on gossamer wings. It lifted him up, and carried him to the tree.

There, it sang songs of healing and love, nursing him back to health.

Eventually Elanteer-5, who had been born whole, came for him.

Ukk limped back with Elanterr-5, who had been born whole with the scar down his face that Elanteer-3 had received from a great creature, until he saw his old burrow. It had soft moss inside and the Leebawan gratefully sunk down onto it.

In his hand, he held his spear. The stick he had gathered that fateful night, the KaBar he had been given as a gift.

The others croaked and clicked to him to tell them what he had seen, what he had done, but he found he had no words.

He lived out the rest of his life, long by the standards of his people, hopping beside Elanteer, even as the Wood Elf was re-born whole.

He never forgot the lessons of jawnconnor or the quest to pierce the black heart.

And he never let go of his spear.

A lesson he taught the tadpoles.

QUEEN GLAD-REAL-ALL 2871
INFESTATION ELIMATED
OBSCENE ONE DEFEATED
TERRAFORMING CONTINUES
RESTORING BIOSPHERE TO PRE-LANAKTALLAN STATUS
---NOTHING FOLLOWS---

THE LOST DAUGHTERS OF TERRASOL

It started out like a lot of things in late Pre-Glassing Terra.

As an InfoNet/SolNet joke on an image board. It spread to VR social media rooms, then to cosplay, then to fashion as it made the migration across SolNet. It managed to even do the most elusive of migrations, from SolNet insider joke to 'normie culture' until it was referenced in Tri-Vee and movies and even the news.

The Extinction Agenda Attack had left the majority of the TerraSol Colonies and Terra itself a dangerous wildland, full of aggressive and deadly plants, aggressive and deadly animals, all coded to find humanity a delicious source of protein.

It was an ugly time. Humanity retreated to fortress cities, hab-complexes, even domed cities. Resources had to be conserved, metered out, and carefully shepherded to ensure survival. Humanity did not doubt its survival, they put their faith in the human spirit, ingenuity, and scientific pursuits.

People found a way to grin, even if it was a grimace, during these terrible times.

It started out as a single image. A bit of dark humor after the loss of cats and dogs only a few decades prior. Someone had found it on one of the old archive sites that had scanned the internet and ensured that data wasn't lost. A feline in a mech made of boxes with the word "Mad Cat" on it. Then another image joined it, a cat in an exo-suit with a gun that read "Free to a Bad Home", then another cat image and another and another.

The laughter was tinged with sadness, but there was laughter all the same.

Since the Friend Plague nobody had dared to try hybrid splicing. Everyone knew the Dogboys had died enmasse, which had led to a deep mourning.

Still, someone will eventually try something even if it might kill them.

And teenagers, even girls, aren't exactly known for risk/ reward assessment.

The teenage girl who succeeded quickly broadcast across SolNet which hybrid tweak she had used.

Thousands copied her as the clique spread from a few isolated individuals on SolNet to eventually normie media.

The movie "Reign of the Cat-Girls" was slated. The casting call went out and tens of thousands of teenage girls flocked to their Netcams to record a casting call answer.

The wealthy individual bankrolling the project to cater to his spoiled daughter made a decision that he would not survive to see the end result of.

He decided that rather than use computer generated crowds and armies, he'd hire *all* the cat-girls and have it be a novel work with minimal sfx-generated characters. The producers, directors, and writers tried to talk him out of it, but he offered to return them to Hollywood and drop them out of a shuttle where they could fight the plants and animals driven mad by the Extinction Agenda Attack.

They bowed to his whims.

After all, the wealth businessman had computed the cost and realized that it would be cheaper to pay for all of them to be hybridized and then do a thousand shoots than it would be to hire a professional sfx company to create them.

Word got around that *Reign* would be almost entirely live action. Only special effects where it was needed to protect the health and safety of the actors and actresses.

He sent one of his luxury liners on a swan tour of the Sol-

System, gathering up the girls.

Fifteen thousand cat girls signed contracts, boarded the liner, had minor adjustment tweaks to their chimeric line, and were given voice coaching and acting classes. They were taught how to use the armor, which was prototypes the wealthy businessman was trying to sell to the Republic, during the months the vessel made its voyage.

Video of the cat-girls training in the armor hit SolNet and garnered millions of views.

The business magnate had already made back the investment for the movie *Reign* on the ads watched by those who viewed the "Inside the *Reign*" webumentary videos.

By the time the ship reached the shining blue jewel of Ganymede, the business magnate had even made back the research and development costs for the power armor and weapons.

Personally, he wondered if perhaps he had been born to bankroll entertainment projects. The Republic had turned down his armor, citing that it was too bulky, too ugly, that focus groups preferred the sleek black armor of the Republic, the battlesteel loricated plate armor based off of the old Roman armor, rather than the heavy and ugly suits produced by the magnate.

So he decided he would clad the cat-girls in it, film the movie, and recoup all his losses. He had VR programmers making video games, had toys for the film, everything he needed.

The first few weeks of filming there were a few glitches. A few of the girls suffered horrific wounds from the chainswords. Crossing his fingers he offered them cybernetics and new parts.

They eagerly leaped on the offers.

His factories built them tanks and aerospace fighters. He even had four of his interstellar passenger liners, which were a total economic loss with the Extinction Agenda Attack and what was looking to be a revolt in the colonies, retooled for the movie.

The shots were breathtaking. Reality feeling more raw and more desired by the fans and the crowds.

The images of the lead cat-girl, half of her face replaced by cybernetics, giving a stirrings speech from the flag-bridge of her 'battle cruiser' had an engagement rate of over 70% for a period of a month. An unheard of amount of time.

He ensured he owned the patent of the chimeric genome tweak used by the cat-girls of *Reign*.

It was in the final phases of filming when it happened. The girls were in full armor, in their tanks, in their ships. Cameras were filming.

Plasma fire from the sky upon the cities, suburbs surrounding domes that were no longer needed.

The atmospheric membrane was punctured, the atmosphere largely vanished in a rushing howl. Millions vomited up their lungs and died as the atmosphere dwindled to almost nothing as the gravity generators were destroyed. The domes were destroyed by the orbital fire, the suburbs turned to flaming ash.

Worse was what came over SolNet, over SoulNet, and the devastating psychic assault. Millions, tens of millions, hundreds of millions, BILLIONS of death, pushed through SolNet and SoulNet, assaulting every surviving mind with screaming and death.

It hit the cat-girls, teenage actresses playing a part that they'd spent their lives preparing for.

In their defense, they weren't weak. They weren't. Not one of them was older than twenty, the youngest was twelve and played the youngest one, called "The Initiate" in the script. Their minds were assaulted by the death of *billions*, including their friends and family, from all over the solar system as the carefully timed attacks took place.

Their minds shattered.

The Mantid forces landed on what remained of Ganymede, gleeful for the slaughter that would take place, that would break the back of Terran Descent Humanity.

In their defense, the business magnate had been paranoid. The film had generated so much near-hysteria that he had to use military grade spoofing and security to keep orbital spies from seeing what was going on to the point that he even concealed the power supplies of the armor and vehicles.

The Mantid found themselves landing in the middle of an army.

An army driven mad.

An army of teenage girls, armored like a battleship and armed to the teeth, that had been driven mad.

The Mantid Warriors and Speakers charged. Republic armor, the thin layered lorica of the Republic's armor was easily penetrated by their bladearms and weapons. The crude looking armor worn by the youthful looking human-feline hybrids surely couldn't resist them.

Mantid weaponry only pocked divots into the heavy plates of the armor.

Their psychic attacks were met back with the enraged shrieking screams of enraged teenage girls.

The Mantid assault quailed for a moment in the face of unbridled fury.

The girls knew, at that second they *knew*, that the Mantid were responsible for it all.

The Mantid in front of them.

Screaming their warcries the actresses of *Reign of the Cat-Girls* charged the Mantids, their minds riven and shattered, their souls consumed with blood-lust.

The Mantid Thinkers in orbit watched with horror as the Mantid warriors were literally torn limb from limb by the armored hands of the Cat-Girls, who could only shout a few words, their minds broken by the psychic assault.

"NEKO NEKO NEKO!" was one warcry as the aerospace fighters launched. The weapons were only mockups, firing visual lasers only.

That didn't stop a half-dozen of the cat-girls from screaming out the second war-cry.

"DOKI DOKI DOKI!" they shrieked as they went to full throttle.

The ship's battlescreen resisted the first three.

The fourth got through and slammed into the center of the warship. The fifth hit the rear. The sixth plunged into the boiling mass of particles left by the fourth and exploded deep inside the ship.

"KAWAII!" a thousand throats roared out as the new star boiled in the sky for a few seconds.

Three hundred other aerospace fighters clawed for the cold darkness of space and the remaining battlewagons found themselves fighting for their lives.

They lost.

The war for Ganymede was one of the most brutal campaigns the Mantid ever fought. The cat-girls of the movie *Reign of the Cat-Girls* knew nothing more than war and savagery and horror. They burned the Mantid with flamers, tore them apart with their hands, ripped them apart with chainswords, shot them to pieces with mag-ac guns that had been props but were restored to working condition.

The tunnels below Ganymede were a terror. Mantid against armored Neko-Marine, as the Mantids had come to call them, although some of the infantry called them Dokigrrlz. The Mantid, who had been the lords of the tunnels, were pushed back by the furious assaults of the armored Neko-Marines. When the Mantids were pushed onto the surface, they found the Neko-Marines waiting for them, chainsword, flamer, and magac in hand.

Dokigrrlz who knew nothing but madness and wrath.

Whom the Mantid just couldn't seem to kill.

Three times the Mantid landed reinforcements as they continued to assault the Sol System, still intent on 'killing the queen' and breaking humanity's will to fight.

Three times the screaming warcry of DOKI DOKI DOKI heralded attack runs on the battlewagons by beings who weren't able to care any longer. The vehicles, the aerospace fighters had been restored to working condition.

The business magnate was targeted by the black mantid death squads.

It took fifteen tries to get him.

They did, eventually.

He died in the arms of the lead actress, known only as Joan. She could not remember her name. She could not remember his.

He was merely 'Father' and he bled out in her arms as her sister fell upon the black Mantid and tore them to pieces with their bare hands and sharp teeth.

She painted her face with Father's blood.

The Neko-Marines went crazier. No longer capable of coherent speech, they burned the Mantid from the surface, the tunnels, the skies of Ganymede until not a single one was left. They boarded their ships, repairing them in their madness, and drove for Mars, helping liberate it.

The Mantid learned to fear them. They wielded psychic lightning in one hand and weapons in the other. They did not need helmets any longer, their armor oxygenated their blood and provided all the nutrients they needed.

They were fused to their armor, but they didn't care as they helped cleanse Hateful Mars of the Mantid.

The screams of "NEKO NEKO NEKO" and "DOKI DOKI DOKI" were enough to break the psychic control of some of the lesser Mantids and make them flee the field. Thinkers recoiled from the psychic assault that backed the screams.

Psychically transmitted madness. The death screams of a thousand thousand people backed by the rage of the Neko-Marines.

When Mars was taken, they forged more weapons, more armor, repaired and rebuilt their ships. Their ships were a reflection of their minds, shattered and twisted beauty.

The bridge of the flagship, the former luxury liner that had gathered them all, had a stained-glass window of Joan cradling the dying bleeding body of Father and The Initiate slaughtering the Mantid assassins.

The mat-trans systems were installed aboard the great ships.

They often screamed, lashing out with psychic power, sometimes attacking one another. The nanites flooding their systems, their triple-strand DNA, their borderline illegal gene-mods from the chimeric alteration made it so they could sustain wounds that would kill anyone else.

They landed on Earth, taking part in the last year of fighting. Mat-trans took them quickly from battlefield to battlefield and they fought without tiring. Their gunfire was endless, their chainswords without mercy, and their psychic lightning thick and deadly.

Finally, Earth was free. They took the fires burning in the vast oceans of glass, took shards of lossglass with them when they left. They crafted torches for their armor, infused the loss-glass fires into the fires of their flamers.

Their ships jumped, not into jumpspace, no, that would be too easy.

They chose Hellspace.

For six months they were missing, nowhere to be found.

Then the skies of Anthill rang out with the warcry as Hellspace breaches blossomed inside the resonance zone.

And the Queens knew fear.

"DOKI DOKI DOKI!"

--From "Reign of the Cat-Girls, an Oral History Transcribed"

A MARTIAL PEOPLE

Tabula-929 was a system halfway through the Long Dark. A fairly placid system, with one planet in the Green Zone, five rocky airless rocks, an asteroid belt, and two gas giants around a red dwarf. It had been settled over 100 years prior by a long-sleep ship that had slowly limped its way from a wounded Colony that was wiped out by the never ending swarms of the Mantids. Records of its existence had been lost by the destruction of the colony, the computers badly damaged by Mantid attack torchships that had harried it to the edge of the system, and the ships Digital Sentience slowly going mad, becoming obsessed with finding a place to hide for the 14,000 colonists aboard the ship.

The ship itself had been fully built. Fifty miles long, five miles wide, with the reactionless engines installed but the FTL drives built but not installed. The hyperdrive cores still on the planet when the Mantids overran the manufacturing facility. The creation engines were loaded with templates but as the ship fled the computer systems were damaged, damaging the templates. The VI hashes were corrupted, any VI spawned insane or damaged or mentally disabled. The hydroponics bays and the medical bays were loaded but damaged.

The Digital Sentience had not covered itself in glory, even the colonists admitted it. As it had gone crazy, it had released some colonists to keep it company in its madness. As time went on, the ship became a strange blend of a high tech world of savagery and savages who no longer knew they were aboard a great ship. The DS considered itself a God, the savages living and existing within its body. As time went on more and more parts dropped from the DS's awareness, badly hashed VI's taking over for the great sections.

Luckily for the colonists, the majority of the Longsleep decks remained locked down.

By the time the ship, which had never been officially named and any name it might have had lost to DS senility and the loss of the colony that had built the ship, reached Tabula-929 and the ship's scanners detected a habitable world, less than 10,000 colonists, 3,000 of them Rigellians, remained in Longsleep but nearly 35,000 savages (8,000 of them mutated Rigellians) and mutants roved the decks full of vegetation and strange ruins built and collapsed during the thousands of years the ship had moved through space.

The savages were moved to the surface first, during Mat-Trans. Mat-Trans psychosis seized their brains and they became even more maddened. The DS, fragmented into multiple versions of itself, managed to pull itself together long enough to awaken the remaining colonists.

What followed was a thousand year war, the insane mutants and their offspring against the colonists and their offspring. Rock and spear against rifle and armor. Finally, the dust settled and the last the of the mutants had been eliminated at the end of the genocidal struggle. The two races, bound together by necessity, breathed a sigh of relief and turned to helping one another survive the planet, which at times seemed to hate them.

Holding tight to pieces of their past, they slowly began the long struggle from the Iron Age to the Industrial Revolution and beyond. When radio was invented they discovered the ship, still in orbit. Not some kind of holy star but instead a touchstone to their ancient heritage.

Decades went by as the colonists built a ship. A small one, to go and see if Terra and the Human Race had survived. When word came back that the Terran Confederacy existed, the residents of Tabula rejoiced, but were concerned. What did it mean for their world? Their culture?

After long debate, the decided the best course of action would be if they refused membership to the Confederacy, choosing instead of be an independent world, limiting who could enter the system and who could not. Restricting immigration they guarded their culture closely, worried about outside influence. They built ships, but few, slowly expanding in their solar system and keeping a wary eye on the nearby star systems for any who would try to reach out and bring them to heel.

Theirs was a martial culture, built by necessity, that took an obsessive view of bloodlines from the days of the founding. DNA was nearly holy, and those who watched over bloodlines wielded vast authority to the point that a single word of a Blood Matron or Patron could instantly end a century old feud.

They rejected longevity, rejected suggestions that they no longer needed their system of eugenics that mandated that anyone who reached the age of 31 was terminated. It was how it had been since the earliest days, when the food was rare, clean water was a luxury, and the old were required to make way for the young.

The planet hated the invaders. It had embraced the mutant savages, but had punished and rejected the 'pure bloods' with earthquake, plagues, volcanos, savage plant life, ferocious animals, and deadly pathogens.

Bit by bit they had fought the planet. From rude dwellings to towns to great cities, the ecology went mad and the survivors retreated to dome covered cities. While some fought the planet outside the cities the majority of the population lived in luxurious comfort within the domes.

It started with an omen.

A comet swept near the planet, close enough to pass between the planet and the oversized moon, the planet immediately sweeping through the comet's tail. The sky lit up with aurora borealis, the night sky filled with wavy streams of green light.

Tabula lost contact with the moon colony.

Before the people of Tabula could discover what had gone wrong came the word: Plague.

It affected the Rigellians, the Scaled Ones, first. They sickened, their scales cracking, their skin peeling away, suppurating sores appearing. Fever drove them mad and they attacked the healthy. The Human ones fell sick next. A pathogen that caused rashes, flaky and cracking skin, infection, the fever driving them as mad as their reptilian brothers and sisters.

The dome cities locked the doors. Harsh, but prudent.

Thousands, tens of thousands, hundreds of thousands, millions of raving, fever driven, infected pounded at the bases of the domes, roaring out their fever coated agony.

Then came the word to the population of the domes a fact that the governments of each dome city had been keeping secret.

The ones outside weren't going to go away. They weren't going to die off.

They had been dead.

Panic and fear gripped the dome cities but the martial traditions held fast even as more traditions were revived. The people may have panicked in their souls, in private, but in public they put forth a stoic face. Many returning to the featureless plastic masks of the Early Years. One dome attempted to limit the possessions of weapons and the leaders found themselves fed into the great atomic furnaces that powered the cities.

A month passed, two, and the dead remained. Hedonism and wallowing in luxuries became socially taboo. Stoicism and spartanism gained traction as people began whispering ancient religious phrases to one another.

Then the clouds appeared. Locusts, devouring vegetation in every growing patches. The great kelp and algae beds of the heavy-metal rich oceans died, covering the oceans with a thin layer of rotting vegetation.

The cities were forced to repair and reactivate the great atmospheric terraforming engines, maintained almost religiously.

Many pointed out that they had been right to keep the ancient traditions as locusts covered the domes, creating a constant whispering sound as they tried to find a way in. Six months went by until the locusts died and slid down the walls of the domes.

Within six months, the continents were denuded of everything but dead locusts and dirt. Even the living dead around the cities had been stripped to bone. No animals or plants remained on Tabula.

Another omen appeared in the night sky.

Shooting stars.

For three nights the shooting stars got thicker, with longer streaks, some of them going from silver to red.

Then the impacts.

Dome after dome shattered as debris, following the tail of the comet at their own slow speed, rained down on the planet. Millions perished as the domes fell.

The locusts revived and swept down upon the domes. It became a war, man and lizard against the insects. The dome dwellers used only tunnels, each hour the streets and the air above the cities was scoured by fuel air incendiaries.

The locusts were beaten back.

In Dome-39 it happened. Someone who did not believe in wearing the masks and robes of the traditional got sick and, in turn, infected their entire building. Diseases swept the domes. Fevers. Pox. Pneumonia. Diseases they had no name for, much less any way to cure it.

Dome after dome fell.

The last one called out to the great ship orbiting.

It did not answer, its atomic cores long dead.

In desperation they built a small craft to take them to the moon. It was a desperate attempt.

It blew up leaving the upper atmosphere.

The pilot got out two syllables.

"Inco..."

But Tabula had a long history of martial tradition. A single setback was not enough to deter them. They built ten more.

Nine exploded.

The tenth made it to the lunar base. They radioed back.

It was destroyed, apparently by meteor strikes. As the

crew was exploring the base their craft exploded, killing the crew that had stayed behind.

But the Tabula had a history of martial tradition, and they soldiered on. They had suspected it would happen.

They knew now that it wasn't natural.

Someone was *doing* this to them.

They set out to the far side of the moon, on vehicles, and in a heroic effort, two of the twenty Tabulans reached the crater they were heading for. There was a facility there, an old one. An ancient one that was mentioned in history books.

Inside the facility was a single craft. They worked to repair it, to get it so it could support a crew.

They failed.

Two remained when they made their decision.

They had always had a martial tradition.

They loaded the library core, containing all the data they had gathered during the troubles, into the ship. They filled their tanks with the last of the oxygen and boarded the ship. They lifted off, pushing the engines to the limit, till they felt as if they would black out.

The acceleration force was too much for one. He died, his lips pulled back in a grimace of victory on his reptillian muzzle.

The people of Tabula had a martial history.

The computer, old and tired, finished the calculations.

The remaining one jumped to hyperspace.

He had enough atmosphere, even with taking his compatriots nearly depleted pack, to program the computer.

He died, strapped into the seat, managing to stay consciousness just long enough to finish his task, his vision tunneled down, unable to catch his breath, panting from the heat but unable to breath.

The ship did as it was told.

Its builders had a martial history and built to last.

The ships limited computer knew it was dying as it flew through hyperspace. Hyperspace and computers did not go well together. The sleeting energetic particles blew holes in its mind and it was just aware to know it. It made copies of itself in volatile memory. Each time the dim little computer program failed the computer rebooted a new one, which made more copies.

Come to dim life. Read the previous reading's file. Check the current readings. Write the readings. Copy self to all available volatile memory. Crash.

Repeat.

It was content, it was proud of what it was doing.

Its builders had instilled their martial culture into it, given it a history of triumph and sacrifice to stand upon.

Boot. Task. Crash. Repeat.

More and more systems died. Damage to the hardware kept the systems from rebooting.

But the dim little VI could see the mechanical watch on the body of the last Father. The vibration of the ship's engines keeping the self-winding mechanism going.

Boot. Look at Father. Do your chores. Crash.

Repeat.

Then the hands and numbers for days were correct on Father's holy device.

It cut the hyperspace engines.

Across the solar system it had arrived in alarms screamed as an unidentified ship dropped out of hyperspace inside warning buoys, far inside the limit, appearing only a few thousand kilometers outside of the orbit of Luna.

Before the system defense could blow it to atoms the little dim VI opened what was left of its communicator and cried out.

"FATHER!"

and crashed.

There was no more copies, there was not enough intact volatile memory.

The ship went dead. The hyperdrive going cold. The hull of the ship pitted and cracked from riding too high in the hyperspace bands for too long for it to handle.

It should not have made it. It had ridden so high its very structure should have dissolved away.

But its builders had a martial culture and had instilled it in the little ship and its VI.

The ship was boarded, the investigation team forced to cut open the doors with a plasma torch, the surfaces welded by the crazed particles of hyperspace.

There the library core was found.

And one word painted on the hull.

"PLAGUE"

No cry for help. No pleading. Just a warning.

A warning to TerraSol.

It should have never arrived. It should have been lost.

But Tabula had a martial culture.

And they did not go gently.

CLONE WORLDS DIRECTORATE

Did anyone else see this data? Those insects, that bacteria, those viruses, all of it was engineered by someone who knew what they were doing.

---NOTHING FOLLOWS---
RIGELLIAN COMPACT

The fact that it effected both of our peoples with lethal efficiency is suspicious. That is one of the reasons we make such good allies, what kills one may not even be noticed by the other. Yet these acted as if we were one species.

I am suspicious. The Tabulans were xenophobic and isolationist, but they were one of us. Lost children who had gone feral you do not punish. It is not the child's fault the egg was lost.

---NOTHING FOLLOWS---
MANTID FREE WORLDS

The Tabulans were our children. Ours as much yours. We were the abusive sibling who drove them from the loving arms of their parents. We feel their loss keenly. They have been lost from the fold and we feel their absence.

Do you know who did this?

---NOTHING FOLLOWS---

CLONE WORLDS DIRECTORATE

No. Like I said, we have suspicions, but no proof. Without proof, we cannot act. That is the way.

The data we have, thankfully recovered from that library core and the two bodies, point at elegant viral and bacteriological weaponry. Very elegant.

To be honest, it's too elegant. They share no common ancestors, there is no junk code, no evolutionary remnants, there's no way it is natural.

But, as I said, we have no proof.

---NOTHING FOLLOWS---

DIGITAL ARTIFICIAL SENTIENCE SYSTEMS

It took both us and Cybo to recover that library core. Taking molycircs unshielded that high into the hyperspace bands was crazy. Still, some of that data. They covered their tracks, the comet, the meteors, but let's face it, that was too slick.

Where would even that come from in their system? Not debris blown off of other planets, like some Mars to Terra transfers, all of the planets but that one were dead worlds that never developed any form of life.

And a comet? Not a chance. Any life would boil away circling the sun then freeze, with the freezing process rupturing any cell walls in bacteria, on its way out of the system.

There's no way any of that was natural.

---NOTHING FOLLOWS---

CYBERNETIC ORGANISM COLLECTIVE

We concur. We examined the data. There were too many at once, each following the other. Specific order to the disasters. We have determined this was a carefully planned attack that would look natural. We have determined that our lost children had determined the same.

Suspicious, we find the explosions of their exo-atmospheric craft. Even more suspicious is the destruction of the moon base the lone ship that made it. We found that nearly a dozen teams attempted to reach the hyperspace relic but only one arrived.

We have determined that this was not only planned but was being overseen by beings with a malevolent purpose.

---NOTHING FOLLOWS---
TREANA'AD HIVE WORLDS

This isn't good. That's six attacks in as many months. All of them supposedly

BLOOD! BLOOD FOR THE CONE! BLOOD FOR THE SCOOPS! BLOOD FOR SPRINKLES!

Ahem, as I was saying, all of them supposedly natural occurrences. They got too clever. These would look like natural occurrences to a primitive species but we're a bit experienced

BLOOD FOR THE TABULAN! BLOOD FOR SANDY! BLOOD FOR VENTALIX! BLOOD FOR THE CONE!

anyway, we're a bit experienced with solar system mechanics, and there's no way that this would happen on six different systems, wildly spaced apart, in six months. Especially all of them being

PACK THE JELLY DEEP! SING THE HYMNS OF ICE CREAM AND WARSTEEL!

man... especially all of them being strictly biological in nature. They got too clever.

EYE FOR EYE! MANDIBLE FOR MANDIBLE! GRASPER FOR GRASPER! FOOTPAD FOR FOOTBAD! BLOOD FOR BLOOD!

someone else want to go ahead. Man...

---NOTHING FOLLOWS---

v(= ∩ _ ∩ =)7 DOKI!
DOKI DOKI DOKI DOKI!
ರ಼಴ರ ರ಼಴ರ ರ಼಴ರ ರ಼಴ರ
DOKI DOKI DOKI!
\m/(>.<)\m/ DOKI DOKI \m/(>.<)\m/

------v(= ∩ _ ∩ =)7v(= ∩ _ ∩ =)7------
RIGELLIAN COMPACT

Dammit! Someone get her out of here! I can't think when she's screaming in Engrish-Emoji.

---NOTHING FOLLOWS---
TERRASOL

We do not seek unjust war.

We are a peaceful people.

We will not act without proof, without diplomacy, without negotiation.

Another way must be found.

The guilty must be brought to justice in a fair manner.

Only the *truly* guilty deserve punishment.

Redemption must be sought.

We are a peaceful people.

Every life is precious.

And we will not seek unjust war.

>TERRASOL HAS LEFT THE CHAT (LOST CONNECTION TO HOST)

* * * * * * * * *

RIGELLIAN COMPACT

Oh shit.

---NOTHING FOLLOWS---
DOKI!

\m/(>.<)\m/ (◣_◢) (✿ ♥‿♥) (/◕ヮ◕)/*:･ﾟ✧

DOKI DOKI DOKI

-------WHEEEEE!--------

DIGITAL ARTIFICIAL SENTIENCE SYSTEMS

Digital Omnimessiah and his Twelve Biological Disciples protect us all

---NOTHING FOLLOWS---
MANTID FREE WORLDS

What? That's actually calmer than I expected. I thought he'd act more like our Treana'ad brother.

---NOTHING FOLLOWS---
TREANA'AD HIVE WORLDS

Sis, you don't get it. You weren't here the last time he said something like that.

---NOTHING FOLLOWS---

MANTID FREE WORLDS

What happened the last time?

---NOTHING FOLLOWS---

TELKAN GESTALT

Did that doki thing just get happy? Isn't she a crazy person who's on fire with a gun in each hand that broke a food dispenser?

---NOTLLOWS FOHING---

TERRAN CONFEDERACY OF ALIGNED WORLDS

It's worse.

---NOTHING FOLLOWS---

MANTID FREE WORLDS

Define... worse.

---NOTHING FOLLOWS---

BIOLOGICAL ARTIFICIAL SENTIENCE SYSTEMS

You+Terra=1%

That's what happened last time, sis.

---NOTHING FOLLOWS---

MANTID FREE WORLDS

Oh.

---NOTHING FOLLOWS---

Printed in Great Britain
by Amazon

63803550R00160